T0158880

The Youngblood Project

by
Bruce Kost

Trafford rev. 11/11/2019

 www.trafford.com

North America & international
toll-free: 1 888 232 4444 (USA & Canada)
fax: 812 355 4082

The Youngblood Project

A PRESIDENTIAL REPORT
COMPILED BY: Averill Threadmiller

THE YOUNGBLOOD PROJECT

CLASSIFIED

FOR PRESIDENTS EYES ONLY

The Youngblood Project

ORIG: President Averill Threadmiller
IN RE: The Youngblood Project
STATUS: Classified For Presidents' Eyes
Only By Executive Order
ORDER #: 10-35A1
FILE DISPOSITION: NOT TO BE REMOVED FROM
OVAL OFFICE
FILE LOCATION: bottom right hand drawer of
Oval Office Business Desk
DECLASSIFICATION DATE: Jan. 1, 2425

THE WHITE HOUSE

President Averill Threadmiller sat behind his desk in the Oval Office with a classified report in his hands. A report he had compiled concerning a recent operation by the CIA which had gone terribly wrong. The report classified 'For Presidents Eyes Only' was the cumulative evidence submitted by all parties involved and the President outlined the draft detailing the known operation. Only this President knew the full scope of 'The Youngblood Project' and the project name was selected by himself. No one was allowed in the Oval Office while the draft was in the writing and no one knew of its existence. Only himself and the following Chief Commanders would know of its presents and contents.

The narrative, submitted by Lisa Youngblood, was a soul-revealing account concerning her part in the episode with the different views from Mike Tanner, Dion Marshall and Kelly Harry added to allow her story to flow from a beginning to its conclusion. The President sighed as he knew enough couldn't be said for Lisa

Youngblood; the one most wronged and the one who has said the least.

The FBI's investigation into the affair continues with a special emphasis on the association between the late Dr. Hans Schuler and the CIA. President Threadmiller had the unpleasant job of revamping the CIA under the microscope of the House, Senate and the public.

And the episode started from an accident...

JUNE 8TH

The Youngblood Project

FOR REF. SEE   FILE AA84C23W
             BOB CHANDLER @ 504 555-8021

MAIL TO
LOUISIANA DEPARTMENT OF PUBLIC SAFETY AND CORRECTIONS
OFFICE OF MOTOR VEHICLES
P. O. BOX 64886
BATON ROUGE, LA 70896-4886

ACCIDENT REPORT FORM – SR 10

FOR OFFICE USE ONLY

CASE NO 25AW-203

FAILURE TO FILE A REPORTABLE ACCIDENT ON THIS FORM MAY RESULT IN SUSPENSION OF YOUR OPERATOR'S LICENSE.

DATE OF ACCIDENT	DAY OF WEEK	HOUR		STREET LOCATION OF ACCIDENT	TOTAL NUMBER VEHICLES INVOLVED
June 8, 97	Mon	10:00	☒ A.M. ☐ P.M.	St. Peters @ Bourbon St.	2
RURAL LOCATION N/A MILES ☐ NORTH ☐ EAST ☐ SOUTH ☐ WEST				OF (CITY OR TOWN) New Oleans,La.	PARISH Orleans

VEHICLES INVOLVED

YOUR VEHICLE				OTHER VEHICLE (Use additional form if more than two (2) vehicles)			
YEAR 96	MAKE Chevrolet		MODEL Lumina	YEAR 1997	MAKE Toyota		MODEL 4 Runner
TYPE LS	STATE La.	YEAR EXP 1997	LICENSE PLATE NO A321W4	TYPE Jeep	STATE La.	YEAR EXP 1998	LICENSE PLATE NO N85631
VEHICLE IDENTIFICATION NUMBER LSNC52831127635				VEHICLE IDENTIFICATION NUMBER JP672AC51836211			
SOCIAL SECURITY NUMBER				SOCIAL SECURITY NUMBER			
NAME OF OWNER RENTED BY AGENT				NAME OF OWNER STOLEN VEHICLE			
ADDRESS-STREET NO /CITY/STATE/ZIP NAME WITHHELD – C/A TO FILE WITH INSURING AGENCY				ADDRESS-STREET NO /CITY/STATE/ZIP DRIVER VANISHED AFTER ACC.			
OWNER'S DATE OF BIRTH	OWNER/OPERATOR'S LICENSE NO	STATE	SEX ☐ M ☐ F RACE	OWNER'S DATE OF BIRTH	OWNER/OPERATOR'S LICENSE NO	STATE	SEX ☐ M ☐ F RACE
NAME OF DRIVER			IF SAME AS OWNER MARK BOX ☐	NAME OF DRIVER			IF SAME AS OWNER MARK BOX ☐
ADDRESS OF DRIVER-STREET NO /CITY/STATE/ZIP				ADDRESS OF DRIVER-STREET NO /CITY/STATE/ZIP			
DRIVER'S DATE OF BIRTH	DRIVER/OPERATOR'S LICENSE NO	STATE	SEX ☐ M ☐ F RACE	DRIVER'S DATE OF BIRTH	DRIVER/OPERATOR'S LICENSE NO	STATE	SEX ☐ M ☐ F RACE
VEHICLE WAS ☐-LEGALLY PARKED ☐-STOPPED ☒-IN MOTION			ESTIMATED COST OF REPAIRS SEE REVERSE	VEHICLE WAS ☐-LEGALLY PARKED ☐-STOPPED ☒-IN MOTION			ESTIMATED COST OF REPAIRS SEE REVERSE
OWNER OF PROPERTY DAMAGE (OTHER THAN VEHICLE)				ADDRESS OF OWNER WHERE PROPERTY DAMAGE OCCURRED-STREET NO /CITY/STATE/ZIP			

DESCRIPTION OF PROPERTY DAMAGE (OTHER THAN VEHICLE) VEHICLE PENETRATED CATS MEOW	ESTIMATED COST OF REPAIRS SEE REVERSE

INJURED PERSONS (CLAIM FOR PERSONAL INJURY ON REVERSE)

NAME OF INJURED IN YOUR VEHICLE N/A	IF MORE THAN ONE (1) PERSON, LIST ON SEPARATE SHEET	NAME OF INJURED IN OTHER VEHICLE N/A	IF MORE THAN ONE (1) PERSON, LIST ON SEPARATE SHEET
ADDRESS-STREET NO /CITY/STATE/ZIP		ADDRESS-STREET NO /CITY/STATE/ZIP	

AGE	SEX ☐ M ☐ F	RACE	INJURED WAS ☐ DRIVER ☐ PASS. ☐ PED.	AGE	SEX ☐ M ☐ F	RACE	INJURED WAS ☐ DRIVER ☐ PASS. ☐ PED.
DID INJURED PERSON DIE? ☐ YES ☐ NO	WAS INJURED CARRIED AWAY? ☐ YES ☐ NO	WAS THERE VISIBLE SIGNS OF INJURY? ☐ YES ☐ NO		DID INJURED PERSON DIE? ☐ YES ☐ NO	WAS INJURED CARRIED AWAY? ☐ YES ☐ NO	WAS THERE VISIBLE SIGNS OF INJURY? ☐ YES ☐ NO	

INSURANCE AND/OR SECURITY

COMPLETE THE FOLLOWING AS REQUIRED BY THE COMPULSORY MOTOR VEHICLE LIABILITY SECURITY LAW AND SAFETY RESPONSIBILITY LAW (R.S. 32.851). **FAILURE TO TO PROVIDE COMPLETE INSURANCE INFORMATION MAY RESULT IN SUSPENSION OF YOUR DRIVING PRIVILEGES AND/OR REVOCATION OF YOUR REGISTERING PRIVILEGES.**

☐ 1. A LIABILITY POLICY PROVIDING AT LEAST $10,000/$20,000 BODILY INJURY AND $10,000 PROPERTY DAMAGE IN EFFECT ON THE DATE OF THE ACCIDENT.
NAME OF INSURANCE COMPANY (NOT AGENCY) _____
POLICY NO. _____ POLICY PERIOD AT TIME OF ACCIDENT: FROM _____ TO _____
POLICY HOLDER _____
☐ 2. OFFICE OF MOTOR VEHICLE'S SELF-INSURANCE CERTIFICATE NO. _____
☐ 3. MOTOR VEHICLE LIABILITY BOND ISSUED BY _____
    NAME OF SURETY OR INSURANCE COMPANY
POWER OF ATTORNEY NO. _____
☐ 4. $30,000 DEPOSITED WITH STATE TREASURER: CERTIFICATE ATTACHED.
☐ 5. NO LIABILITY INSURANCE IN EFFECT AT THE TIME OF THE ACCIDENT.

SIGNATURE	DATE

DPSMv 3012 (R 8/94)

7

The Youngblood Project

THE YOUNGBLOOD PROJECT

PROPERTY DAMAGES
(IN ORDER TO BE ACCEPTABLE, MUST BE COMPLETED IN ITS ENTIRETY)

I, _____ FORM TO BE FILED BY *CIA* _____ certify that damages to my property

an __ ed to $ _____ as a result of this motor vehicle accident.

I believe I am entitled to recovery of the above amount from _WITNESS STATEMENT ATTACHED_____

_____ driver(s) and from _____AND SUBMITTED TO_____ owner(s) of the

other motor vehicle(s) involved in this accident, and I have not released said party(ies).

SIGNATURE OF OWNER	DATE

INJURIES
(Please complete one section for each party injured)

I, _____ certify that as a result of this

motor vehicle accident my medical expenses are $ _____ .

I believe I am entitled to recovery of the above amount from _____

_____ driver(s) and from _____ owner(s) of the

other motor vehicle(s) involved in this accident, and I have not released said party(ies).

SIGNATURE	DATE

I, _____ certify that as a result of this

motor vehicle accident my medical expenses are $ _____ .

I believe I am entitled to recovery of the above amount from _____

_____ driver(s) and from _____ owner(s) of the

other motor vehicle(s) involved in this accident, and I have not released said party(ies).

SIGNATURE	DATE

I, _____ certify that as a result of this

motor vehicle accident my medical expenses are $ _____ .

I believe I am entitled to recovery of the above amount from _____

_____ driver(s) and from _____ owner(s) of the

other motor vehicle(s) involved in this accident, and I have not released said party(ies).

.URE	DATE

NOTE: USE SEPARATE SHEET FOR ADDITIONAL INJURY CLAIMS.

8

The Youngblood Project
WITNESS STATEMENT

NAME Russel Travers   ADDRESS 1427 Polymnia St.
CITY New Orleans   STATE La.
ZIP 47130   PHONE 504 555-2012

FAMILY None   ADDRESS N/A

EMPLOYER Tidewater Marine, Inc.
PHONE 504 555-1121
ADDRESS 1253 First St.   CITY Harvey
STATE La.   ZIP 70059-0802

STATEMENT;
I, Russel Travers, was walking eastward on
Saint Peters St., on the north side of the
street. Approaching the intersection, I
was passing the business called, 'The Cats
Meow'. Traffic was normal, pedestrians
were moving about and for the early
afternoon, the French Quarter was starting
another business day with a modest amount
of tourists walking the streets. After
crossing the intersection, I proceeded
along St. Peters, heading for the
waterfront. In mid-block, I observed a
Caucasian male sitting in a red Toyota
4Runner land cruiser. I also noticed
numerous cigarette butts on the pavement
near the drivers' door and I concluded
that the driver had been parked there for
almost an hour.
Looking around, the driver saw that I was
interested in either him or the vehicle.
At the time, I thought nothing of it and

continued moving toward the Mississippi
River waterfront. Before I had reached the
next intersection, I heard an accident.
Moving into St. Peters St., I looked back
toward Bourbon St. and saw the red Toyota
land cruiser sitting in the middle of the
intersection. From my position, the
vehicle was vacant and the driver was
quickly leaving the scene. He ran east on
St. Peters St., toward me and then entered
through a private gate located between two
businesses. I never saw the driver again.
The other vehicle involved, a white two-
door Lumina, jumped the curb, sliced
between a parking information sign and a
street-light post, crashed through the
diagonal corner entrance of the Cats Meow
and destroyed a stage where band equipment
had been set up. The car completely
penetrated the Cats Meow.

   For any further required information, I
can be reached at my home phone number, at
my place of employment, at The Culinary
Institute of New Orleans — known as The
Chefs Table or at The Avenue Pub. The
latter two are located on Saint Charles
St. In approximately three weeks from this
date, I will be returning to my job as AB
(Able Body Seaman) with Tidewater Marine,
Inc. I am told that I will be heading for
South America for an unspecified period of
time.

Witt.

Russel Travers

Russel Travers

JUNE 9TH

MAIN TEXT (*THE STORY*)

Sunny warmth and soft breezes caressed the southern city of New Orleans. Tourists ambled along Saint Charles St. window shopping as they also drank in the elegance of ancient mansions that lined the vegetation lush Garden District. Streetcars noisily rolled along the main artery loaded with more tourists heading for downtown and the French Quarter, leisurely sightseeing The Big Easy in romantic style. Delectable aromas wafted from colorful restaurants promoting instant hunger and tantalizing tastebuds, and the exquisite charm of New Orleans was in full bloom.

But the city's charm was lost on two serious CIA agents who were seeking the accident witness and were exasperated at not locating him. Visits to the Chef's Table proved fruitless, phone calls to his residence were unanswered, no one in the Avenue Pub knew of his whereabouts and his employer, Tidewater Marine, assured the agents that the Merchant Mariner was on land and not at sea. Spending the better part of a frustrating day attempting to locate the witness, the agents finally met him in the early evening at The Avenue Pub, a neighborhood bar where many one-time visitors soon became regulars because of the festive atmosphere. From his description given by the officer at the accident scene, the agents spotted Russel Travers immediately upon their third visit to 'The Pub'. Sidestepping through the crowd, fatigue was showing on the agents' faces.

"Mr. Travers, may we speak with you privately?" Tim Handles asked while showing his credentials. Russel, at six-two, towered over the five foot ten inch neatly dressed man with trimmed short brown hair, comforting brown eyes, slender face with high cheek bones who was showing CIA identification. Before Russel could respond, Tim added, "this is my partner, Al Timmer," motioning to a squat portly gentleman who had just arrived next to the slender speaker. Al experienced great difficulty moving through the crowd, in undertones excusing himself for bumping into everyone while trying to follow his quick moving partner. Russel estimated both men to be in their early thirties but the boyish appearance of Al hinted at a younger age. With a rounded scarred face and light complexion topped with red hair, Al's youthful smile promoted complacency in others. But Travers instinctively knew from prior experiences that Al's movements suggested his bulk was more hardened muscle than mere flab and his mannerisms spoke of calculated alertness.

"Yes sir," Russel responded properly even though he had just finished drinking his third Flaming Dr. Pepper. "I'll be back," he said to an old regular, Walter, mimicking Arnold Schwartzenegger.

"Yeah right! Last time you said that, you promptly disappeared for three months to Ecuador! I'll believe it when I see it," Walter bellowed, and then, the tall former Viet Nam Vet preceded the agents through the main doors which faced the sidestreet, Polymnia.

"Is this about the accident yesterday in the French Quarter?" the blond Russel asked as they moved away from the small crowd just outside the doors.

"Yes, it is, and do you know how difficult it was in locating you?" Tim asked.

"Yeah, I can imagine. This is my busy day to get everything done once I'm off the boats. I don't procrastinate. First day on-shore, all I do is move around, stopping at the drug store, post office, shopping, haircut, I'm sure you know the routine. The company knows I'm single and can leave on a moment's notice. They might need me to replace a seaman in another country because of illness or injury. I jump at the opportunity to fill in because the company, in turn, compensates at other times by offering me first chance on boats sailing to foreign countries. It's an unusual life-style but I enjoy it," Russel outlined.

"Well, it's no problem really. Yes, this is about the accident yesterday. You saw the driver of the red 4Runner. We think the driver was hired from another country and flown in for this one job. Depending on who the driver was, that'll tell us what group we're dealing with. We have three books of photographs we'd like you to look at and see if you can pick out the driver," Tim was saying.

"You don't mean 'group of terrorists' do you?" Russel asked.

"Possibly. We won't know who we're up against until we begin identifying who's in the group," Tim explained.

"Why would a group of terrorists be interested in causing an accident?" the well-built Vietnam Vet asked.

"The driver of the other vehicle is a CIA agent who was en route to an assignment when he was hit and severely injured which means someone was tipped to the agent's route and that means we have a mole or a sleeper in our agency. If you can identify the driver, that'll help us pinpoint the group and just maybe, we'll be able to uncover the leak. We're aware that you might not be able to tell us anything at all, but that's a base we need to cover. We're covering all the bases, eliminating the impractical and assessing what remains before we draft a report for the home office. We've established a command post at the Rose Motel over on Airline Highway. That's about fifteen minutes from here. If it's ok with you, we'll take you there, show you our pictures and then, bring you back here," Tim outlined.

"Ooookaaay, but don't be surprised if I can't help you," Russel advised, and they had stopped at the intersection of St. Charles and Polymnia St. to talk.

"Here's our car," Tim said, indicating to a black four door sedan with government plates parked along St. Charles and in a 'no parking' zone. As they were getting into the vehicle, Tim said, "We've interviewed several witnesses and after we have your version, maybe we'll be lucky enough to single out the group and report that to HQ."

To Russel, Tim appeared to be the spokesman as Al had said nothing. Al drove the main roads to Airline Highway and the drive lasted fifteen minutes. Russel knew of the Rose Motel because upon his arrival from California, he stayed at the same motel. Conveniently nearby was the Airline Lounge, an Army/Navy surplus store, a Payless gas station and a Schwegmann Food Mart. Traffic flowed at a normal pace, the day was beautiful and everything seemed normal. As Al pulled into the motel parking lot, Russel knew it was normal for agents to locate and operate from command posts in motels or hotels. Parking the car in front of one of the doors, Tim exited the car first followed by Russel and Al trailed. Knocking once on a door, Tim then entered. Beyond Tim, Russell saw an elderly gentleman seated at a table that had folding legs and on the table top were vials containing colored unknown chemicals. Looking around, Travers saw more vials and more chemicals in beakers that were being heated with monitoring equipment periodically flashing numbers as the monitors continuously tested the chemicals for potency strength. Turning from the miniature laboratory to face the agents, Russel saw them screwing silencers onto their service revolvers while they kept their eyes on him.

"Uh-oh, all of a sudden I get the feeling this isn't about the French Quarter accident, is it?" he asked but it was more of a statement than a question and instantly realizing the serious implications of his situation, Russel shifted his weight to his right foot and with the left, attempted to kick Tim's gun from him. The sudden fluid motion caught Tim completely unprepared. The violent kick shoved the gun into Tim's mouth – knocking out his front teeth as he fell backwards from the blow. Russel's only hope was to shock both agents with sudden kicks and then, vanish out the door. As Tim was falling, out of his peripheral vision, Russel saw that Al had just completed mounting his silencer and was intently watching Russel. Following through his kick and shifting weight to his front foot, Russell spun in a half circle to deliver a roundhouse to the portly gentleman's temple. Al Timmer had anticipated Travers next move and simply raised his free forearm to ward off the blow. The kick stopped at his forearm and Al instantly circled his arm around Russel's leg lifting him off the floor and with his gun in the victim's solarplexes, Al slammed Russel onto the bed beyond the elderly gentleman and the tables of equipment.

"No, Mr. Travers, this isn't about the accident in the French Quarter. Yes, one of our people did have an accident, but because of his own stupidity. On the police report, you indicated no family in the area to contact should the police need to contact you. We needed a guinea pig and with those two words, 'no family', you volunteered. You do have a choice here, you can decline from being the guinea pig and we'll have to kill you because already, you know too much. Or, you can go along with the program and take your chances," Al calmly said with the voice of command and Russel knew that even without the gun, he probably would not be able to overcome the portly agent.

"Sudda-bitch knocked my teef out", Tim shouted coming up next to Al after recovering his gun, spitting blood as he talked and blood had stained his white suit shirt.

Ignoring Tim, Russel said, "kinda like the army, huh?"

"You're going to drink what the good doctor gives you and if you spill it, we'll kill you," Al evenly said.

"I get to kill him," Tim demanded cocking his weapon and aiming at Russel's right eye. Earlier in his life, as a combat green beret and later as a soldier of fortune, Russel had been in extremely tight life-or-death situations but he had always managed to create a way out. This time, the odds were against him and he knew it. There was no way out, except death and that wasn't an option he wished to explore. Stalling for time to discover or promote an escape avenue would be nixed by the angered agents and they weren't ones who could be easily stalled. Still being pressed onto the bed by the portly agent, Russel saw the doctor approaching with a vial containing an orange-colored liquid and the trapped victim realized that his only choice was the final choosing of the lesser of two evils. As the doctor handed him the vial, Russel's perspective was shaken into a surrealistic slow-motion state. Slowly, and with a patronizing smile, the 'good doctor' placed the vial into his hands and he stared momentarily at the orange liquid. Had he known that the CIA doctor had been trained by the most infamous doctor of all time, Dr. Mengele, the agents would have had to kill him because he'd have been too scared to drink the thick substance. Drink or die they said and the words echoed from another time into his brain as he slowly raised the vial to his lips. With guns still trained on him, Russel up ended the vial and let the sweet tasting chemicals slide down his throat, and instantly, the serum began to affect him.

"What's this going to do to me?" he asked as reality began marching from him.

"You'll see. You'll probably want to lie down now. Hee hee hee," the doctor chuckled while removing the vial from Russel's hand. Russel stared at him as he was being assisted. As Travers was losing consciousness, he knew something was desperately wrong with the man in the white smock.

"If I survive, you mean," he barely said as he felt his consciousness slide sideways. Slipping into a light coma, he heard them talking. He heard better in the coma than in normal alertness. He heard the fabric of the doctor's smock rubbing against itself. He heard the low roar of an aircraft at high altitudes. And then, the doctor was saying something.

"The process will take fifteen hours to complete. Until then, he'll be unconscious. The reason prior attempts failed earlier than expected was due to chemical imbalance, thus, killing the guinea pigs. If I've learned accurately from my mistakes, chemical balance will enhance potency strength. Because the serum immediately rendered the subject to a comatose state demonstrates the balanced properties of the reactive chemicals. The serum's full strength will metabolically alter the genetic make-up of the recipient, shifting from one gender to the next. I'm convinced we'll have a successful conclusion on this subject, and now, only time will tell," the doctor said rubbing his hands together and smiling broadly. To date, twenty-three subjects had died under the experimenting hands of Dr. Hans Schuler.

In his younger life, Schuler was Dr. Mengele's protégé, a young genius intern at Auschwitz. The young Hans participated in procedural medicine and was fascinated with bacterial infections. Learning, that after bodily parts were destroyed by deterioration from infections, proportioned reactive chemicals could rejuvenate affected parts faster than the body could repair itself. The same reactive medicine, when applied to a healthy body part, altered the part slightly but the function remained the same. He was allowed to experiment on prisoners, giving them dosages of reactive chemicals in direct proportion to the person's size. When Hans administered a full vial of the chemicals to a prisoner, the metamorphosis ended hideously with an androgynous corpse; equal parts male, equal parts female, and with blue skin tone.

After studying Hans' notes, Dr. Mengele understood how the process was supposed to work and he instructed the young intern that balancing reactive chemicals into a working serum would prove difficult even for an accomplished chemist. Learning the chemical process to reverse a subject's gender would take years to perfect. Dr. Mengele secretly confided to Hans that he wouldn't have the time because Germany was losing the war. Soon, he was going to take Hans home where he should hide his notes, change clothes and, once again, become the young farm boy. Later in life he could continue his experiments – if he found the right people.

When the fall of Auschwitz loomed, Dr. Mengele took Hans to his home, and then, the doctor disappeared. After the war, the Schuler family migrated to the United States and settled in Wisconsin near a German community. In time, Hans entered the University of Wisconsin Med. School where he excelled and topped his class in achievements. Many offers from prestigious hospitals and labs found their way to his mailbox, but because of obscure German war reports referring to him as Mengeles' protege, the CIA recruited him.

Although minor references vaguely linked him to his mentor's experiments, his name never appeared on official documents. In time, Hans realized his new bosses to be as ruthless as the Nazis, only on a smaller scale. He was allowed general liberties in his experimentations, but on this project, he had the green light with unlimited funding, and his failures were appreciated by the alligators in the Louisiana swamps. At the outset, his lab was located near the swamps for easy disposal of the failures, and after keenly observing the failed metabolic metamorphosis of the subject, he knew he was close to perfecting the serum. As his impatience grew beyond tolerances in waiting for the subjects to be transported to the swamp lab, he demanded the lab to be moved into New Orleans, to be closer to his 'subjects.' Failures would be shipped by boat to the nearest swamp.

"And the process still includes the steaming part?" Al asked, wrinkling his nose.

"Yes, the chemical burning process will be present," the old doctor confirmed.

"Completion at 0900 hours tomorrow. We need to check in with Langley and see a dentist," Al said, looking at his watch, and then at his partner.

LANGLEY, CIA HEADQUARTERS

(EARLY EVENING)

CIA Director Will Summers' secretary announced the incoming call, "Al Timmer for you, sir."

"Thank you Marg," Will politely said while looking at his assistant, the lanky Assistant Director of the CIA, Johnathan Walker.

"Al, what have you got?" he asked, and Will rather enjoyed talking to this no-nonsense, succinct type of person. The director, an ex-army intelligence general, always received maximum amounts of information in minimum spans of time from Timmer. Standing six feet, the slightly overweight director ran fingers through his short brown hair while anticipating a positive report from New Orleans.

"The doctor is confident of success. We'll know more in fifteen hours. Checking back with us tomorrow at 0900 hours our time. No problems at the present," Al said.

"Good! Talk to you tomorrow," Will said and both hung up.

Leaning back in his overstuffed armchair, Will stroked his square jaw with thumb and forefinger, savoring the moment. Pondering the report, Will's gray eyes sparkled with delight, a possible future brightening.

"You heard. Think of it, John, an entirely new dimension for the CIA! Once the doctor perfects the serum, our future begins to evolve to its inevitable destiny; the establishment of a CIA nation outside the continental U.S.," Will envisioned.

"That's the doctor you found at that insane asylum?" Johnathan asked as he sat opposite the director.

"Yes, but he's not completely insane. Granted, he's a full bubble off-center, but his chemical engineering theories are on target. I had them assessed before okaying the project. Once the chemicals are balanced, he can chemically alter a person's gender to the opposite. And I can almost guess what you're thinking. What's the big deal of that? That's already happening now, surgically. John, think of it in conjunction with our establishing our nation. If we forced that serum down five senators' throats and changed them into girls, wouldn't that grab national attention? That would be so sensational, the media feeding frenzy would dominate every headline, every talk show, every radio news segment for months! National attention would be so focussed on what happened to the senators, they wouldn't notice us quietly setting up our nation in South America. We'd move in behind our puppets and take over. A little construction here and more someplace else, and before anyone's the wiser, our CIA military is silently growing. Our own budget allocated by ourselves! And all operating outside the United States under our constitution with no limits," Will triumphantly explained.

"You think the United States won't respond to such a move?" John questioned.

"They won't know anything until this office disappears. With media coverage riveting national attention on the senators' gender change, a nuclear bomb detonating would be the only event that *might* distract them. Our military will be operational before we leave. The President'll automatically know we have nuclear weapons. He'll also know we have secret weapons that the U.S. military doesn't.

They'll respond, but not with military force," Will explained.

"I would think it's only a matter of course that the accusing finger points at us," the white-haired southern gentleman observed.

"Yes, I've anticipated that. In fact, congress will immediately conduct an audit of all projects in-progress, on the drawing boards or in past history. There's not one scrap of information, concerning that project, in headquarters. *Everything* surrounding the doctor and his experiments are in the field. All monies allocated for the project is buried in the overseas budget. Nothing available can link us to the doctor, serum, nor the senators. There's only five people who know of the project; you, me, Al Timmer, Tim Handles and the doctor. Of course, the past victims aren't talking, so, we've nothing to worry about," Will said.

"Can we really trust the doctor?" Johnathan asked.

"Once we have a working serum and can reproduce it, the doctor will quietly vanish. It wouldn't be wise keeping an insane Nazi doctor around after he's outlived his usefulness. I needed something that would distract the nation. The distraction needed to be something unique and unusual, something never seen nor heard of before," as Will began to explain, he interlaced his fingers on the back of his head and reminisced of an earlier time. "Three years ago, I stumbled across old war reports which made vague references to a young internist named Hans Schuler. He worked with Dr. Mengele in Auschwitz and after the war, both had disappeared. He resurfaced in a med. school in Wisconsin. After graduating, one of our field offices quietly recruited him because he was a genius chemical engineer. For some reason, he went off the deep end. I found him in an insane asylum in California babbling how man was going to destroy the world through aggression. He reasoned that a female dominated world would survive. His engineering mind detailed the process to alter a person's gender. Because his work kept him quiet, the nurses always gave him paper."

"Of course, the nurses couldn't imagine his genius, and they just threw his papers away. They saw it as gibberish. Another patient used one of his papers and wrote us that aliens were inbound to conquer the earth. The back of a letter was filled with equations.

After we analyzed them, I ordered him smuggled out of the hospital and relocated while we examined him. His engineering mind is intact, and that's all we care about. We located him on the outskirts of New Orleans and are still in the process of erasing his past."

"Once we placed him in a lab, he became the methodical genius. When Hans has balanced the chemicals and provides us with a working serum, our CIA nation will become a reality," Will explained.

Slowly nodding his head in agreement, Johnathan said, "once we have a working serum." The corners of his hazel eyes were lined with worry, worry concerning every aspect of their secret project.

NEW ORLEANS, LA.

After touching bases with Langley, after the dentist visit, Al Timmer bought the doctor's dinner of bratwurst, German potato salad and apple strudel. Upon entering the room, Al observed the tannish steam rising from the reclining subject, the chemical burning would continue through the duration of the metamorphosis, and the process offended him. Making a sour face, he set the dinner down and departed. The doctor laughed at him because Hans considered the agent a weakling in spite of his position. Knowing the agent would not return until the chemical burning had ceased, the elderly doctor had already prepared for a long night. The arduous experiment nights were consumed with observations, recordings, measurements, and, the inevitable waiting.

Alterations within the tannish steam revealing facial features distorting, male definition softening and the overall body mass beginning to diminish. Hans had removed the subject's clothing to scrutinize the minutest detail, of which every change was a significant milestone on the road of chemical alteration.

Hour after hour, the metamorphosis progressed. Body mass was reduced by thirty-one percent, gender reversal was seventy-seven percent complete and the chemical burning continued. At four A.M., three-quarters into the alteration, the critical phase approached.

The last subject died shortly past that phase because the doctor guessed wrong. After analyzing and correcting the problem, the correction inferred the logical next two steps of the project. Excitement thrilled the doctor as the critical phase was successfully passed and the subject was still alive.

As the long hours dragged on, the tannish steam from the chemical burning began to dissipate, pointing to metamorphosis completion. Quickly examining the now, female, with a stethoscope, he heard her heart pound in strong rhythmical patterns and her blood pressure was normal. Sitting down, he recorded the deep blue eyes, long blonde hair, overall body size was five feet, nine inches, facial features contained soft high cheekbones on an angular frame offering the impression of delicacy and the newly altered female was perfectly shaped with symmetry proportions. Dr. Schuler estimated her age to be twenty-one and he envisioned her as the prototype of the perfect German female. His fifteenth hour observations reflected;

'Subject has survived process. Transformation from male to female complete. Mind-set undetermined at this stage. Balanced reactive chemicals functional through final stage. Serum is perfected.'

Rereading the final words, the doctor slowly set aside his notes and while seated, began to savor success with visions of the new CIA nation. Having proven his worth, Dr. Hans Schuler could embark upon any project and with the CIA's blessing. In an ultra-modern lab located in an obscure third-world nation, with unlimited funding and numerous, nameless subjects upon which to test experiments, he could genetically engineer enhanced, cloned secret agents for the CIA. With the serum perfected, the creative possibilities associated with genetics was endless. Excitement filled his pounding heart as his thoughts centered on the new genetic race.

Because he lived and worked in a civilized society, he never had the opportunity to create what the world labeled as immoral, he never had the opportunity to imagine what he could create. He would show everyone that they were wrong. He would show them a superior breed of cloned humans with the capacity of being disease-free, physically superior and always an asset to the human race. As his visions of the cloned-race pushed adrenaline levels soaring to new heights, the genius German doctor, who assisted and participated with the most evil doctor at the roots of the Holocaust, died.

JUNE 10TH

RUSSEL TRAVERS

Seven-thirty A.M. she opened her eyes and the male logical process of Russel Travers assessed that he was still alive. Slowly, he tightened certain muscles, wiggled toes, moved ankles, rolled shoulders and shifted the head from side-to-side, ascertaining bodily functions. Afraid to view his body, not knowing what horrible changes the chemicals effected upon him, while rolling the head, she saw the doctor slumped in a chair with his head back, eyes wide open and mouth agape. Relieved at not seeing the two agents, Russel intended to leave immediately and the doctor was a minor obstacle to overcome.

"Doctor," she said, and instantly Travers knew the voice was wrong. Coughing twice, attempting to clear the throat to regain the bass tonal qualities he was used to hearing, he then noticed her small hands, and her body.

"What??" she questioned aloud in disbelief as she got up. Through her eyes, he saw ample breasts, an hourglass figure and a vacant crotch area, and the logical process of Russel was staggered. "Changed me into a woman!! Why??" she asked aloud, and the vast array of previously unknown feminine emotions slammed headlong into the male mentality of Travers. Anger preceded all others. Anger so intense that she moved to kill the cause. Turning to face the doctor, he suddenly realized the doctor was already dead. Staring at the slumped form and shaking with anger because no answers could be wrung from a corpse and that he was beyond any retaliation, Russel felt like crying. As the powerful feminine feeling struggled to be vented, Russel's mentality was forced to regroup and attempt to exert control over the sea of emotions churning within him. Emotionally, she wanted to scratch out his dead starting eyes, she wanted to rip his throat off his body, and she wanted to kick his testicles up to his neck. Ambivalent feelings imagined a whirlwind of catastrophic havoc befalling the doctor, but he was gone. As she stood facing the still, lifeless form, a tornado of destructive emotions ached to find release. Fury Russel had never experienced, fanned heated desires of vengeance.

Feeling the emotional hot winds of retaliation welling up in her chest, Travers imaginations were cruelly creative, born of the high winds. Emotionally swept along, Russel's mentality was beset on all sides by swirling violent feelings.

Suddenly, a car door roughly slammed. Fear gripped him immobile and the emotional tornado shattered to shivers. Instantly remembering the agents and that they would have a room next door, Russel analyzed every sound she heard. Slowly tip-toeing to the front window, as if bare feet on carpeting would alert the agents to someone moving inside, without touching the curtains, she peered through an opening to see the agents leaving.

They must be going for breakfast – he thought – *I have thirty minutes on the outside to get this girl outta here* – and she watched the agents depart – *I need to focus on survival. Can't let her emotions dominate logic* – he was thinking, as the agents' car left the parking lot and turned onto Airline Hwy – *what hideous project is the CIA working on that they need to change a person's gender? Can't wait here for the answers. Safest place is on the run while I try to figure this out. Gotta go.*

"Well, doctor, it's been unusual and unique, but I should be going shortly," she said to the reclining form, "thank you for making a back-up serum. Think I'll take that with me. And since you're not going to use your ID card, money or notes anymore, I'll take that as well," she said out loud while placing a security strap over the cork vial top, packed it in ice in a water-proof bag, removed the doctor's money and ID from his wallet and located all on a nearby table.

"I need to shower fast and be on my way," she said aloud as she walked into the bathroom and then, she saw her reflection in the mirror. The male mentality behind blue eyes was staring at a stranger.

This is me now – he thought as he studied the reflection and disbelief shoved aside other emotions. The blue-eyed blonde now had no facial hair, only smooth skin on an angular jaw line ending with an attractive chin. His mental facilities were dazed at the vastness of change. Looking at her hands again, he noted all parts were symmetry, right with left. Walking into the shower for a fast rinse-off, Russel was amazed at the accomplishment the serum effected on him. As an amateur chemist, he guessed at the decades it must have taken a professional to perfect a balanced serum that would reverse a person's gender. Strangely, respect for the doctor preceded all other emotions; respect for the untold years required to balance the chemicals, even though this unknown doctor had forever changed Russell's life. And feelings he had never experienced began welling up in her chest – *can't allow emotions to cloud judgment. Too much is at stake. Survival's top priority. Everything else is secondary. Have to figure out why the CIA would alter a person's gender. And what am I – a female with male mentality. What would the difference be between the two? No, move Travers. Work it out later. Priorities first. I have to be gone when those agents return. Can't afford a rematch with 'em – clothes!* – he thought, and he suddenly realized that he had only his former clothing – *improvise* – he rationalized, and following the shower, she folded up the pant legs doubled the belt around herself, tied the shirt tail into a knot and, without socks, slipped the extra-large shoes on, picked up the doctor's notes, ID card, money and the waterproof bag containing the serum and left the motel room. Confident the agents would not return immediately, once outside the room, she saw the Army-Navy surplus store and he decided that was the first stop. Shuffling across Airline Highway, Russel realized the store might not be open as it wasn't eight o'clock yet, but just then, she saw movement within and she breathed a sigh of relief. – *act normal* – he thought, and then, it hit him exactly how **normal** she was. – *just go for it* – he told himself.

"Good morning," she said cheerfully while shuffling in, the over-sized shoes noisily flopping on the wooden floor.

"Well, good morning yourself," an astonished owner said as he surveyed her from head to foot.

"My boyfriend took off with my clothes and all I have are his, and I have his money," she said flashing the owner a devilish grin.

"Well honey, I'll show you where the girls' section is and you help yourself. I'm kinda busy getting ready to open, so you'll have to help yourself. I won't ask you to wait," he understandingly said.

"I've never been in this kind of situation before but, I guess there's a first time for everything," she said still grinning.

"Come on this way, honey. Everything you'll need is in this aisle here," he said and he could hear her big shoes flopping on the floor behind as he led her to the girls' section and then, returned to the counter shaking his head wondering how anyone could treat such a lovely young lady that way.

"Okay, I think I see everything I'll need," she said pleasantly and Russel knew he'd have to figure out the sizes by trial and error. She saw a foot measuring gauge and a tape measure hanging nearby and put both to use. He decided on a pair of Vietnam canvas boots, a camouflaged outfit with an army light-green tank top and green socks. She neatly folded Russel's civilian clothes and wore the camo outfit to the counter.

At the counter, she said, "this'll work for now. Whatta ya think?" and she turned in a circle.

"Honey, even in army clothes, you're a living doll," he said, admiring the beautiful young lady.

"How much do I owe you?" she asked and Russel knew the agents would be returning soon.

"Okay, let's see," he said while calculating the price, "that'll be a hundred and twenty-four dollars even. What's your name, honey?"

Russel grabbed a name, "Lisa," she said while counting out the price and then, he noticed the owner was still looking at her, and she added, "Youngblood".

"I know alotta folk around here, but no Youngbloods," he said while counting the money and then, punched it on the register.

"Well, I have ta go. Can you dump these clothes for me? I probably won't wear 'em again and that louse won't need 'em – he's got mine," she said with a laugh. With a little wave of her hand, she left, walked a short distance to the Schwegmann grocery store and hopped into a cab a lady had just gotten out of.

"Yeah," a tired cabbie merely said as Lisa closed the door and Russel realized the cabbie had the night shift.

"Ah, St. Charles and Polymnia," Lisa said, and he was thinking of returning to his apartment to analyze the situation before initiating a plan of action, but as the cab exited Schwegmann's parking lot, she saw the agents returning.

– *in minutes* – he thought – *they'll find the doctor dead and the subject gone with the serum. It only follows that they'll immediately launch an intensive search to recover what was lost, the apartment is out, they'll go there first, within thirty minutes, they'll have my description from the surplus store and turn it over to local authorities. The train station, bus station, airport and chartered buses will be watched. Can't use my car, so, what's left? Okay, priorities first – they'll be looking for a blonde, a wig will change a lot.*

"Change in plans," she announced to the driver, "let's go to Canal and Crondelet".

"Fine by me. I'm off duty in twenty minutes, and then, it's nighty-night," he responded.

"Long night?" she asked, just to be saying something while he mentally regrouped.

"Typical night driving loud-mouth drunks around. Gets old after awhile," he said, not trying to hide disgust.

"Maybe you could avoid the night partying by switching to the day shift," she suggested.

"Happens next week," he said with a knowing smile and then he concentrated on the traffic, and Lisa withdrew into herself.

It'll be fifteen minutes to Canal and Crondelet – he thought – how would I classify me? Not a hybrid – that's the results from the combining of two. I'm an altered one. I guess I'll have to start at square on and reason through the differences. How different is male mentality from female? I've been around enough girls in my time, never thought I'd actually be one. Ok Travers, since you are one now, you've got to start thinking like one. And how does a female think? With emotions, logic, common sense and rationality, which also could easily pass as male thinking. I never realized the similarities between the opposing mentalities. It's gotta be deeper than that.

"Canal and Crondelet," the driver announced, and the sudden statement momentarily shocked Lisa.

"Oh, thank you. I wasn't paying any attention to where we were," she said and paid the fare. Across the street was Woolworth's where a complete change of clothes and hair color would buy her more time. She bought an over-the-shoulder carpet bag along with new clothes, a short black wig and she kept the army outfit. After paying the cashier, she exited the store at the rear exit which placed her in the French Quarter and on Bourbon St. Russel needed a quiet bar to catch the news and to eat. Three blocks into the Quarter, he found an empty bar where the 'tender was wiping last night's party off the bar top. She ordered a Bloody Mary, buffalo wings and the morning news.

"The wings'll be a few minutes," he said as he switched on the overhead TV, and moved to fix her breakfast. The picture focused on a CNN newscaster saying, "and in southern news, law enforcement agencies have initiated a nationwide manhunt for Lisa Youngblood, pictured here. Youngblood is accused of brutally murdering and robbing a local doctor. The five foot, nine inch blue-eyed blonde who weighs one hundred and fifteen pounds is considered extremely dangerous. In other news... "

She watched the news with indifference while sipping the Bloody Mary and Russel regrouped again knowing that the manhunt had begun. Casually nibbling on the delivered wings, he realized the CIA would slowly and methodically trace her steps to the Quarter in their dragnet-style search. He needed to get her out of the city and fast, but the pressures of recognition wasn't pressing her to act. In the black wig and sunglasses, she didn't resemble her TV photo. Leaving town was the foregone conclusion, *how* she'd leave remained.

As fate would have it, just then, a noisy party paraded, laughing, dancing and singing into the bar. Obviously, it had been an all night party, and from appearances, it would last well into the day. Drinks were ordered for the thirty-plus people who were in various stages of inebriation and a tall slender gentleman paid for everything. Russel noticed the southern elegant gentleman escorted two casually dressed young ladies into the bar, one on each arm. And then, the party spilt over into Lisa's quiet corner.

"Hi ya doin' dawlin'?" one man asked while leaning on the back of a chair to stabilize himself.

"Doing pretty good so far. What's the party about?" she asked.

"Terry Shandoval, da indushtrialisht deshided ta have a party. Shelebrashion, ya know. Har'd da Nashez couple weeks ago ta haul us home ta Baton Wouge. Wanna go?" he barely explained.

"You mean the Natchez, the steam boat paddle wheeler?" she questioned.

"Yup, dat's da one. Wanna go?" he asked again.

"Sure, if it's okay, that is. I mean, I don't know anyone in your group," she said with a helpless look on her face.

"No pwablem. Jush shtopped in here fo' shomethin' ta drink an' den' iss on ta da boat. You can go wit' me," he explained with a lot of hand motions. All the drinks were in to-go cups and Terry, with his two dates, led the party out of the bar with everyone ambling, stumbling or staggering behind him. Finding out his name was Bob, Lisa took an arm over a shoulder and helped him to the boat. Russel knew, once on the boat, most partygoers would pass out from either a lack of sleep or too much alcohol, or both. Approaching the Natchez, Russel heard the vessel's calliope playing with gaiety instilling the several hundred people already onboard with excited merriment. The festive atmosphere elevated as Terry boarded and the paddle wheeler crew made preparations for departure.

"How much did it cost to rent the Natchez?" she asked while the forward elements of their party were boarding the boat.

"Million bucks for two days," Bob said with unusual clarity, and Lisa let out an astonished whistle.

"I guess we don't need tickets," she ventured.

"Dis' ish pwivate, no tickets," he said laughing a little at his date. Propping him up to get a better grip, Lisa maneuvered Bob up the gangway and then, into the lower saloon where, once seated, Bob promptly passed out. As the last member of Terry's party boarded, the Natchez crew began securing the boat for departure. The calliope played as the rendition from a bygone era slowly slipped away from the dock and began its five-hour journey northward. Resting Bob's head on her shoulder and absentmindedly stroking his hair, Russel instinctively knew she'd need weapons because the CIA would throw everyone and everything at their disposal at her attempting to recover the doctor's notes, the serum and her. He mentally sifted through weapons he had used, trying to estimate which would be adequate for her size and frame. Thinking of weapon locations, acquisition, transportation, Russel had to reign his thoughts to a standstill and force himself to go one step at a time. He first needed to ascertain that his escape route had been overlooked by law enforcement personnel. So much had happened in so short a time that the multitude of change pressed upon him to be emotionally sorted out and dealt with. But he shoved the changes aside, deciding that priorities went first. Survival topped the list. Everything else was secondary. Russel wondered how many other people had the doctor experimented on, but from listening to them from his coma, he knew none survived.

Uncertainty clouded his every plan because future moves hinged on the success of her escape and that wouldn't be realized until the boat arrived at Baton Rouge. The waiting and not knowing were the worst parts. Fears materialized and vanished with each passing moment. Deciding that fate was shaping her destiny, Russel chose to simply enjoy the ride. Passing two giant navy freighters that were moored at their lay-berths, Russel reminisced of a happier time; another time where, again, survival was top priority.

He was a Green Beret in Vietnam. Following his father's footsteps, he joined the army and became one of the elite. He excelled among his peers and the brass, some knowing his father, afforded him many opportunities to advance in rank and experience. Russel signed up for and was immediately sent to Southeast Asia. From a base camp in the mountains north of Da Nang, Travers participated in many patrols, spending months living in the bush. Learning of the dangers of warfare in the jungle fulfilled the soldier within. He expressed desires to reenlist and remain in-country with his comrades. The thrill of combat was a drug to him and he refused numerous occasions to leave the bush for rear echelon duty. His field unit had their own forward base camp set up in close proximity to a Vietcong base camp, and they constantly monitored 'Charlies' movements. In time, the Green Beret observation position expanded into a mini-base camp where the primary rule was – absolute silence. Vietcong patrols skirted well past their positions, sandwiching the Green Berets between the patrolling Vietcong and their base camp. The VC's patrolling patterns were also monitored and noted. Green Beret replacements would move into the area knowing ahead of time of 'Charlies' movements and avoid contact as monitoring had top priority as ordered from rear echelon. Replacement would silently move in, hand signals given and those being replaced dropped back several kilometers to the bush base camp, leaving no trace in their passing. From observation notes, the VC never varied from their patrolling patterns around their assigned area.

For Russel, life was at its fullest when death was constantly threatening. He had spent three years in-country and in the bush, and he knew the war was winding down. For Travers, war was a way of life. He enjoyed the thrill and terrors of combat. It was in his veins. He had wondered how he'd ever survive 'back in the world'. From conversations with his commanding officer, Russel had learned of a mercenary group under the command of Colonel Crockett, operating in South America and Africa. Russel intended to continue his military life as a soldier-of-fortune after his tour was completed. With troops being pulled out of Vietnam, for Travers, it was over. Russel expressed his desires to his commander and strings were pulled. One month out of Vietnam, Russel Travers was in a mercenary training camp in the jungles of South America.

The Natchez navigated up the Mississippi for almost five hours while Russel relived a life he could never talk about, a life he couldn't go back to, a life that was now, only a memory. She had propped Bob against a structural beam so she could move around to stretch tight muscles and observe the banks along the river. Any unusual patrolling of police cars would instantly alert him that his escape route had been uncovered.

People laughed and drank, a multitude of spectacular sights lined the banks of the river and the opulent magnificence of the Natchez couldn't dispel the cloud of gloom that hovered over Russel. Men would pass by, warmly smile and silently nod at Lisa and she would return the same, but Russel couldn't fully enjoy the moment. His very existence was held in check by the element of the unknown. Walking to the bow, she scanned both banks for unusual police activity. There was none. Standing on the bow, forward of the boat, she could see a private elaborate dock with numerous gazeboes, a stage on which was an antique piano with an elegantly dressed pianist performing, a complete bar, a large buffet table crammed with exotic food and the dock was resplendent with flowers.

Beyond the dock, manicured hedges and lawns framed a three-story plantation mansion that dominated twenty-five acres and the mansion held a commanding view of the river and its traffic. Ancient architecture and ageless statuary announced the antiquity of a by-gone era and the statuary surrounded the diligently maintained mansion. An elegant beauty on a southern waterway.

"We're almost there!" a woman excitedly said next to Lisa, and then, the woman ran to tell her friends. Lisa looked again at the dock, but this time, she was looking for the law. Natural movement prevailed amongst the dock partiers giving Lisa the impression that her escape was successful. Moving back to the saloon, she gently shook her date.

"Bob, wake up! We're almost there!" she said, excited that the police nor the CIA appeared to have considered the Natchez as a possible means of escape.

"Muff ne on," he tried.

"Yeah, that's what I thought too," she said still trying to raise his level of consciousness. As the boat was docking, Lisa helped Bob to his feet, and this time, she was all but carrying him off the boat. Russel was glad that Lisa was almost the same size as her drunken partner. It was late afternoon and Russel needed to get Lisa away from the party and plan her next move. She saw that Terry had stopped on the dock to talk with several guests and as she approached the host, she said, "think I'll take my date to a motel where he can sleep for awhile. I think he's had too much for one day."

Being the gracious host that he was, Terry motioned for a porter to assist the overburdened lady and said, "put him in one of the limo's and tell the driver to take him wherever the lady directs."

"Yes sir," the porter responded smiling taking the burden off Lisa. And with that, she left the party. Motel 6 was ten minutes away and just before arriving, Lisa saw an Eckard's drug store in a strip mall a block from the motel. Once in the limo, Bob passed out again. Lisa checked his wallet for the last name, intending to register as Mr. and Mrs.

With the limo waiting, her date passed out, Lisa secured a ground floor room. The driver moved Bob onto the double bed, refused a tip, stating they were well paid for running errands by the host and then, departed, returning to the party. Once established, Russel decided Lisa needed a few items from the drug store, and the short walk took ten uneventful minutes. Walking into the women's section, Travers felt as if he entered an alien world. Never had he bought any of the products that lined both sides of the aisle. Before, for his girlfriends, he had purchased gold necklaces, wrist bands or diamonds. For the first time, he was amazed by the multitude of merchandise available for women, and he rationalized to by-pass the frills, going just for the basics; Nair, a razor, hair brush, toothbrush and paste and shampoo.

Returning to the motel room, she set the purchases on the bed and switched on the TV as she walked by on her way to the bathroom. She lifted the toilet seat and was unzipping her pants before Russel realized what she was doing.

"Oh!" she said aloud and then, lowered the seat and sat down. "This is gonna take some getting used to," she told herself. Moving back into the bedroom, she sat on the bed and began to apply the Nair on her legs when she saw a newscaster on the screen with her picture behind him. Increasing the volume, he was saying, "and the manhunt for Lisa Youngblood has expanded to cities north, east and west of New Orleans. The fugitive is believed to have evaded the dragnet set in motion by the sheriff's and police departments. Motive for the brutal murder is believed to be robbery. More on that as we learn it. In other news... " and she lowered the volume.

She needed wheels and with the CIA instigating the manhunt, buying one wasn't an option. She'd have to steal it. But that would have to wait for the following day. Lisa needed a good night's rest, too much had happened too fast in one day. Pulling the knee up, setting the foot on the bed, she wrapped her arms around her leg and laid her head on the knee to reflect on personal problems.

Everyone that sees me, sees the girl – he thought – and inside the male mentality continues to process as if nothing happened. I sound and look like a woman and yet, I still think as a man would. Guess I can't very well ask a woman how she thinks, she'd think I was ripe for the loony bin. Everyone thinks. What in the logical process inherently separates the male from female? Or is there such an element that decides? Aside from the obvious physical differences, both genders share the same psychological qualities, some in more degrees than others. Is the line defining the specific qualities or properties separating male from female so blurred that no one actually knows or would they fear taking a stand attempting to define that line because of brutal criticism from peers? Or, are both genders so closely similar in physiology and psychology that the only differences would be the outward physical? No, that's too simple an answer. A woman is one just because she looks like one, and then, Lisa momentarily drifted asleep but awakened with a start as her foot slipped off the bed. *Oh,* she thought, *I'd better shower and get some sleep. Can't clearly think anymore. Now I've got more questions than answers and no closer to the solution, if there is one.* And with Nair smeared on her arms and the side of her face, she showered, dried off and went to bed.

JUNE 11TH

LISA

Lisa awoke early, dressed and left to repack the serum in fresh ice before leaving Motel 6. Bob hadn't moved since the limo driver put him to bed, and Lisa was grateful he didn't snore. Again walking to the Eckard's strip mall, a Shoney's restaurant was located at the far end where he decided to have breakfast and plan her course of action. Upon entering the restaurant, he noticed that it was crowded in spite of the early hour.

After being seated by the hostess, Lisa said she'd have the breakfast bar. Walking the length of the bar on both sides, Lisa settled for scrambled eggs topped with sautéed mushrooms and cheese, a bran muffin topped with honey, assorted fruit and tea. While walking back to her table, she saw three young men at one booth smiling at her. Acknowledging them, she smiled back and nodded her head once. Sitting down in her booth, she was thinking, *why do I have butterflies in the stomach? Where'd they come from? The only time I had butterflies was when I started... dating,* and the realization that males' romantic desires now centered on her suddenly impacted on her awareness, and she thought, *ok, stop! Just take a few deep breaths. Calm down! Focus on the food. Spread the napkin on your lap. Breathe. Ok, casually eat. Concentrate on the problem. What would the CIA do? No doubt they'll compile a dossier on Travers. They'll be seriously concerned knowing I was a seasoned Green Beret in Vietnam and soldier-of-fortune. They'll know I'm used to guerilla warfare. What tactic would they use? Hit-and-run? Possible, but would they chance hitting the serum or notes? Another plausible possibility. They'd be desperate enough. I'll need weapons. Military weapons.*

Ok, one step at a time. First, I need wheels, she was thinking while eating the scrambled eggs, and an elderly couple behind her were discussing taking the grandchildren to the Louisiana State Fair. Lisa caught the tail end of the conversation and decided to steal the wheels at the fair. The Fair in Baton Rouge was competing with the Jazz Fest already in progress in New Orleans, both vying for the tourist dollar. Satisfying the first problem by knowing where to acquire a vehicle, she continued eating while wondering about the agency. *Why would the CIA be so interested in altering peoples' gender? Doctors are already doing that surgically. I wonder if the doctor's notes'll give me a clue. Maybe, but I doubt it. I'd like to research who that doctor was, but that's a luxury for a later time, if I survive.*

Ok, let's get realistic. Where's a military base? Mmmm, there's the National Guard Armory in Jackson, Mississippi. They'll have what I need. Ok, let's get outta here and head for the fair. After the meal and while paying the cashier, Lisa asked, "how far is it to the fair grounds?"

"Do you have a car?" the cashier asked.

"No, I'll go by cab."

"You'll spend five or six dollars to get there, and take my advice, have the cab drop you off at the main entrance because if you have him drop at the booth entrance, where you pay to go into the fair grounds, you'll have to wait in a five-mile line of cars. That's how long the line is to get into the fair," she explained.

"Thanks! Think I'll walk a little," Lisa said gratefully.

"It'll be about half a mile walk to the pay booths, It's either that or pay twenty bucks for a slow cab ride," the cashier warned.

"I could use the exercise," Lisa confided.

"Couldn't we all, honey," she said quietly, tapping Lisa's hand.

The short cab ride was uneventful and the cabbie wasn't surprised to drop Lisa off at the main gate. Russel wanted opportunity to examine different types of vehicles entering the parking area to select one more suitable for her needs. Slowly walking across the vast parking area, she observed the attendants directing the flow of vehicles into orderly parked lines. Passenger cars would be impractical, motor homes too cumbersome. She needed an off-road vehicle. Several four-by pick-ups entered and parked, but he discarded the idea of using them, too open, easily scrutinized and assessable. A four-by station wagon filed in, but he assessed it too small.

Just then, Lisa saw a four-by van inbound. Walking toward the area the van would park in, she had to dash between the moving line to pass the parked and vacant vehicles. Standing next to an empty pick-up and watching through the windows, she observed the van driver place something above the sunvisor, motion toward the van rear with his thumb while mouthing the words, 'the back's open'. Then turning to walk toward the pay booths, she allowed the van occupants to pass her at a distance as they moved to enter the fair, horseplaying as they went. Russel needed the assurance they'd be inside before she doubled back to steal their van. To the right of the concrete apron before the pay booths, she saw a line of pay phones. Acting like she was calling someone, she watched the trio pay and enter the fair.

Looking toward the van, she saw three more lines of cars had been parked beyond the van and security was moving with the parking attendants. Replacing the phone in its cradle, she walked back to the blue four-by van. Without turning her head, she monitored security's movements, and approaching the van rear, a last look around revealed everything to be normal. Upon entering, she crawled over a custom bed, noticed the custom interior, and above the driver's sunvisor were the ignition keys. A few minutes after leaving the fairgrounds, she entered onto I-10 south, switched to I-12 east and finally, turned north on I-55 to Jackson.

Within one hour, the fugitive exited Louisiana and entered the northern neighboring state with a destination of the Mississippi National Guard Armory.

LANGLEY, CIA HEADQUARTERS

"Progress report," Will calmly asked Johnathan, both knowing what was implied.

"The subject Lisa Youngblood has vanished without a trace. Special agents are monitoring major interstates, bus terminals, airports, train stations and secondary transportation systems. Undercover agents at all locations are stopping and questioning anyone remotely resembling Lisa. Law enforcement agencies nationwide have her picture and vitals, APB's have been issued. Agents are backtracking on the former identity and relatives he – she – might possibly contact are under surveillance. The FBI has been notified of the fugitive's possible interstate flight. Photographs have been distributed nationwide to all news media outlets. It should be only a matter of time before she's picked up," Johnathan reported.

"Time is one luxury not on our side, John. The serum has a potency period of thirty days, and as luck would have it, she's got the doctor's notes, the only working serum in existence and she's the prototype. We need her, the serum back intact and within thirty days. Backtracking on 'his' relatives is useless because they won't recognize 'her' – she won't go there. Everything she does will be creative and or spontaneous. How do we anticipate the unpredictable?" he ponderously asked, and then added, "when her location has been sighted, we want to saturate the area with agents, airborne and on the ground. We need swift capture of her and get the serum under wraps. The longer the serum is in the open, the more chance for project failure, and, you can imagine the consequences should she go public with what she already knows," he calmly stated while staring at his deputy, the rest remained unspoken.

MISSISSIPPI NATIONAL GUARD ARMORY

After locating the vehicle-congested armory compound, Lisa casually drove the two public roads that bordered the fenced base. Undeveloped woods butted against one side and the base rear, the woods then stretched for miles before ending in swamps. Lisa turned off the main drag onto the secondary road which paralleled the base. Leaving the secondary road, Lisa turned into the trees, discovering that the four-wheel drive van easily negotiated the wooded area. Russel decided to enter the base from the wooded area, parking half a mile from the base rear. Lisa changed into her camouflage outfit, moved to an area reasonably close to the base rear, climbed a blue spruce pine tree and scanned the armory roof as a possible entry location. The van owner had a pair of Aerolite binoculars behind the seat, which she found useful. Several three-inch pipes protruded from the flat roof, an exhaust vent measuring two feet by one foot provided ventilation and antennas were scattered across the roof. Inspecting for a ground level break-in, windows were covered over with a steel wire mesh with steel bars protecting the mesh, one door at the front he knew to be heavily constructed to discourage anyone from considering it as a possible illegal entry point and the structure walls were reinforced with steel and concrete. Reexamining the exhaust vent, he knew it'd be a tight squeeze, but it could be done.

To break in from the roof, she would need two lengths of knotted rope, small bolt cutters, bailing wire, pencil and a small notebook, gloves and a flashlight. She descended, returned to the van, changed clothes and drove to town to buy the needed items. Buying a foot-long Po-Boy from Subway before returning to the woods, Russel calculated she'd have three hours 'safe time' before the van was reported stolen. Three hours to tire of the fair, report the van stolen, process paperwork and computer entry. Because the vehicle was in another state, it'd be closer to four hours, but he felt safe limiting her to three. Three hours to find the armory, investigate, buy the necessities and get out of sight.

After buying the items, she returned to the wooded area, changed clothes, nibbled on the seafood sub sandwich, and then, set up a surveillance post to record the guards' watch pattern. During the late afternoon and into the early evening, continuous activity dominated the base; military duce-and-a-halfs were being washed, mechanics worked on various trucks, tires were changed, cargo loaded by forklifts, trucks maneuvering to park for the night and work progressed inside the armory. Soldiers were everywhere. Some in groups taking a cigarette break, drinking coffee, under trucks, in trucks, recording loaded cargo, so many, making a watch unnecessary. Then, he noticed an army Green Beret unit was visiting the guard, and they had brought trucks. Concluding the watch would start near dusk, she left her post and returned to the van to prepare for the night.

With nearly five hours before dark, she delightfully decided to search the van to wile away a few hours. Checking in the built-in cabinets, under the bed, under the seats and every nook and cranny she found, she was dismayed that the owner was neat as a pin. No interesting junk or obscene items were to be found, so, Lisa began preparing her equipment. Cutting the ropes into fifty-foot lengths, she then tied a knot every foot. Next, she set up the notebook on an hourly schedule, to record the guarding pattern. From the van, she found a wool blanket and included it with her equipment. Finally, she relocated the equipment near the observation post to expedite movement to the fence after sundown.

At dusk, Lisa began recording. She noticed the compound contained an excess amount of vehicles, so congested that, trucks were backed up against the armory building attempting to use all available space for parking. The yard activity had ceased for the night, although, soldiers still milled around, some in groups talking, a group played cards near the mechanics' shed, some smoked near trucks, but the subdued activity didn't bother Russel. He knew they were relaxing before retiring for the night. In another hour or so, many would be headed for their racks, the watch then would be different from what she was seeing. He knew it'd be after midnight before she could make her move.

After everyone retired, the watch character displayed itself admirable. Rounds began on the hour, search of the entire compound was remarkable, every vehicle was aggressively searched – inside and underneath. The armory building was closely inspected as were the trucks backed up to it. First round lasted twenty-five minutes, and another round was started on the half-hour. No sooner had the watch returned to the guard shack, he was back out again. But the second round lacked the aggressiveness of the first. Russel reasoned; the compound had already been searched once, no reason to search it again. The second round lasted ten minutes, and the watch returned to the shack. The watches consisted of two-hour shifts. At the beginning of the second hour, the guards were more relaxed, the rounds being ten minutes or less.

When the relieving new watch made the first round, they also aggressively searched the entire compound, in and underneath every truck, paying particular attention to the vehicles around the armory, and the building itself. Each watch appeared determined to find something to acquit themselves honorably before the brass.

As the third watch began, Russel knew in the second hour of

the watch, it would be time to move. A new entry plan formulated; ropes were not necessary to scale the walls, climbing on the trucks provided roof access. After the second round of the first hour, Lisa moved her equipment to the fence behind a truck and observed the guard moving back to the guard shack.

Using the bolt cutters, she cut a hole out of the fence, moved everything inside and, with bailing wire, reattached the cut piece back into place. Peering around the front of a vehicle, she saw no one. Running to a truck backed up to the building, she climbed onto the hood and, carefully, moved to the top of a hard shell bed cover and then, onto the roof. Quietly moving to the side facing the guard shack, nothing indicated she had been discovered. Through the glass doors of the shack, someone was adjusting the volume on a portable stereo unit. Russel knew the wool blanket would muffle noises she had to make. Moving to the vent, she wrapped the blanket around it, laid on her back and with five leg thrusts, she bashed the vent shrouding off its mountings. Quickly moving back to see if the muffled noise alerted anyone, with passing eighteen wheelers inadvertently assisting in drowning out noises, no one noticed. Looking into the hole, an exhaust fan blocked her way, but one kick sent the fan downward. Dropping into the hole, her feet landed on a crate not four feet from the opening. Once inside, to her surprise, the visiting unit brought cargo, obviously storing it in the armory overnight. The crates were stacked almost to the ceiling in the open area of the armory. As her eyes adjusted to the dimness, she looked for abnormalities, for surprises.

Soft red floor lights bathed the armory in surrealism, but in the red and black world, she saw no infrared alarm terminals, no motion detectors, no surprises. On the crates six feet above the floor, he analyzed what appeared before her. The armory was jammed with crated weapons, ammo, empty magazines and different types of explosives. Aisles were intentionally created to facilitate movement to different sections within. Hunched over, she worked toward what apparently was the 'office', a small open area with desk, chair, locker and a coffeepot. Unpacked crates near the office indicated an inventory was in-progress. Hopping down from the stack,

Russel decided not to open crates and look for the appropriate weapons. Opening would waste time and create noise. Looking at the inventory sheet, among the weapons listed were the desired items; LAW's rockets, M-16's, 9mm handguns and bandoliers of ammo for the guns. A quick search located the weapons, she then began relocating the items to the exhaust vent hole.

Atop the stack, near the hole, she pressed the illumination button on her watch, the watch would make his rounds in five minutes. As the soldier walked his casual round, Lisa was quietly placing seventeen LAW's rockets, two M-16's, two 9mm hand guns and four banana clip bandoliers of fully loaded clips of ammo, two for each gun, on the armory roof from inside. The moment he reentered the guard shack, she needed to be throwing the items on the canvas bedcover of a truck. Thirty minutes to move the weapons from the armory to the truck, from the truck to the hole in the fence, from the fence to the woods, and finally, to the van. She couldn't drive the van any closer, for fear of being detected. On the roof watching, the second after he entered the shack, Lisa grabbed guns and tossed them onto the truck canvas. In the process, she learned it required two trucks to support the weapons' weight. Quickly as she could, she relocated the weapons to the trucks. Jumping onto the truck with the hard shell bed cover, then, moving to one canvas truck top, she rapidly retrieved as many weapons as she could carry. Walking fast, Lisa moved to the fence hole and set the items down, inside the compound. The relocation of weapons to the fence hole required five trips. After the last trip, while removing the cut fence piece, Lisa was profusely sweating. Exertion from carrying the pieces, walking fast and constantly looking in all directions was sapping her energy. Checking her watch again, the watch would begin his final round in seven minutes. The relocation took longer than Russel estimated, she lacked his strength. She set the weapons outside the hole and after crawling through, Lisa merely hung the cut piece back into place. Five minutes left. Picking up three rockets, she dashed for the woods. The distance to where she deposited the weapons in the woods, was less than from the armory to the fence. As she was walking into the woods with the last armload, the watch began his final round.

Out-of-sight of the watch, she put the 9mm's in the cargo pockets of her camouflaged pants, slung the bandoliers of ammo on a shoulder, slung the '16's on top of the bandoliers, picked up a rocket and headed for the van. Half way to the van, she set the rocket down, too much weight. Although she needed to leave the area as soon as possible, it was unnecessary to push too hard. In the armory, it was necessary, but, not now. She took her time, spreading the weight over seven trips. Closing the van side door, after the last stolen weapon was finally relocated to the van, sweat soaked her clothes and Lisa was exhausted.

Checking her watch, by the recorded timetable, the guard would have moved back into the shack, presumably assuring her no one outside to hear the van start. Approaching the secondary road, she turned right, heading for the main road. Traveling only fifty feet, she then made a U-turn and headed in the opposite direction. When they discovered the theft, a search of the woods would yield her previous position and exit route. The right turn would throw the pursuers off her track, allowing her time to slip out of the state.

Following the secondary road, his thinking was to turn on a tertiary road paralleling the main drag, thus, bypassing downtown Jackson enroute northward. Suddenly, she crossed over an old railroad bed, the tracks and ties long removed. Russel realized, the abandoned rail line would intersect a great many roads in the state, affording her a traveling mode with the element of surprise; law enforcement would not anticipate discovery of a fugitive moving along an old railroad line. Chances of not being discovered favored her.

Tired and sweaty, Lisa traveled approximately ten miles before deciding to pull off into woods for the remainder of the night. Shifting into four-wheel drive, a left turn into a thick grove of lodge pole pines with oak scrub brushes flourishing at their bases, promised to effectively hide the van from anyone passing by on the railroad bed. In the grove, a generously flowing creek solved another problem; she needed to bathe. She parked the van in the stream, undressed, loaded a 9mm and the '16, opened the van side door, stepped into the rushing water and layed down.

As the cool liquid flowed over her body, while a hand washed water over her breast, it struck Russel odd that this was him now. He never desired nor considered a sex change, being male, more opportunities were available than had he been born female. Tipping her head back, allowing the water to run through her hair, Russel's thoughts drifted back to his early solder-of-fortune days as the flowing stream rushed through her hair and over her body.

His early days presented many a change on a regular basis and sometimes, daily. As a mercenary, covert operations in foreign countries consisted of unusual travel arrangements, spartan life-style, solving impossible problems and creatively accomplishing the objective. Russel exceptionally enjoyed being in Colonel Crockett's unit. Colonel Crockett was proud to be a direct descendent of Davy Crockett and the colonel made sure everyone in the unit knew of his heritage. The man was a natural leader. His excellent leadership abilities encouraged others to act without blatantly ordering the men around. He knew *how* and *when* to be stern and for the most part, his relaxed disposition had a calming effect on the unit. Because of the colonel's inspiration, every soldier determined any performance less than the best was unacceptable. The camaraderie and bonds forged in combat sustained the mercenary unit through numerous hellacious firefights and the insanity of solving problems in combat situations gone wrong. And through it all, they had and depended on each other with Colonel Crockett always encouraging them to work as a unit.

The pleasant reverie faded as Russel knew those days were gone forever. That part of his life was over and couldn't be relived. Deciding to get out of the stream before she turned into a chilled prune, Russel also decided to sleep away from the van for the night even though the van contained the custom bed at the rear. Reaching into the van, she picked up a towel found earlier behind the base. She also found stashed money, military and civilian clothing and toiletries. The van was set up for weekend excursions.

While drying off, he decided to study the doctor notes before going to sleep. Russel realized the chances of actually learning anything from the notebook were incredibly slim as he had had no formal medical training nor would he understand any chemicals the notes might refer to, but it was a long shot. Pulling open a drawer under the bed, she took several blankets and started a pile. On top of the blankets, she laid her blue jeans, cotton blouse, short socks, shoes, flashlight, 9mm, serum, comb and a small pillow. Taking the pile, she walked nude out of the creek, walked approximately fifty feet into the woods and made a bed in the middle of bushy scrub oaks. Returning to the van, she checked the weapons and shut the doors without locking any. If discovered, opening a door would alert her instantly. Walking to the area of her makeshift bed, she scattered dried twigs in likely pathways, thinking if someone tried to sneak up on her, the sound of breaking twigs would awaken her. That task finished, she checked the serum and saw it was floating in icy water. Tomorrow she'd need fresh ice. Dressing as if to leave on a moment's notice, she settled down with the flashlight and the notebook. Pulling the blankets over her head, she read the notebook under the covers.

I was right – he thought as he began reading – *it begins with the chemicals used and the amounts. It's going to take a professional to decipher his notes. Mmmm, occasionally he inserted comments in the margin. At last, now I know the doctor's name, Hans Schuler. Seems he's having difficulty balancing chemicals. Come on, doctor, give me some answers. It seems as he progresses, he gets excited and writes more in the margins. Wait a minute, nine guinea pigs have expired so far? People. This is mad, and the CIA is backing him – or was. Swamp lab? He had the lab in a swamp? Of course, easy disposal of the failures. His comments are so vague, they don't even mention the CIA. Now, nineteen people have died. Come on doctor. Give me something. He's getting excited again, he's writing more. He must be close at this point. He realized he's made a mistake, but the correction has hinted at the next two steps. Twenty-three people have now been killed. The last experiment is about me. He's succeeded. The agency can have their nation now? What? What nation does he mean?* He questioned as he read the final entries. Turning the light off, she threw the covers back while trying to reason through the meaning of the notes. *A CIA nation? The United States would never... no, not the U.S. Oh my God, a third world nation! But how could they use the serum to subvert an entire nation? It took a long time to change me – they couldn't possibly be thinking of doing the same elsewhere. These people are audaciously insane if they think they can pull it off. But then again, the insanity of the act might be the key to their success. Their history would be written in blood. I've got to go public with what I know. Who would suspect that a powerful U.S. agency is going insane?! Can't very well call a press conference... the police, CIA and FBI would love to attend. Why is it some problems merely create more problems? This is getting too complicated. I'd better get some sleep while I can,* and she placed the notebook on top of the waterproof bag and because of physical exhaustion, she dropped off to sleep immediately.

JUNE 12TH

MISSISSIPPI NATIONAL GUARD ARMORY
(ONE AND A HALF HOURS BEFORE DAWN)

"Okay people, listen up," shouted the Green Beret gunnery sergeant to the Green Beret unit temporarily attached to the national guard as they stood at attention in the cool of pre-dawn, "last night some intelligent individual took it upon himself to liberate a number of weapons from the armory. Even though the entry point has been discovered in the base rear fence, Army Intelligence, (he sneered *Intelligence*) in their benevolence, secretly believes that one of us has seventeen LAW's rockets, two M-16's, two 9mm hand guns, and four bandoliers of ammo in their back pocket. Therefore, anyone caught with seventeen LAW's rockets, two M-16's, two 9mm hand guns and four bandoliers of ammo *in* their back pocket *will* immediately be seized and incarcerated under *suspicion* of having broken into the armory. No vehicle will be allowed to leave the compound without first being thoroughly searched, which includes, under the chassis, under the hood, under the seats, in the cab, in the glove compartment, in the cargo area and behind the headlights. Any civilian vehicle wishing to depart the compound will be thoroughly dismantled as part of a routine search. Reassembly will be the owner's problem.

All leaves, passes, vacations and A.W.O.L.'s are canceled at this time. Those wishing to depart the compound may do so - in your underwear, which consists of, one pair of shoes, one pair of socks, one pair of underwear, one set of dogtags, and optional, is one pair of sunglasses and one hat. You will not carry any money, identification, keys nor a wallet. Formation again at 1300 hours. Dismissed."

As the unit broke ranks, three members stared at each other in stunned disbelief.

"How do you like that? We can leave only in our underwear!" stated Dion Marshall, a six foot two big boned muscular black with high cheekbones, full head of short hair and the spec. Three Green Beret specialized in weapons, tactical and forward observer communications.

"They just want to be sure that if you're carrying seventeen LAW's rockets, two M-16's, two 9mm hand guns and four bandoliers of ammo – it'll stand out nicely so they don't have to look so hard to fine 'em," Mike Tanner sarcastically stated. The six-footer with short black hair, hazel eyes set in a playboy's handsome face, wide at the shoulders, narrow at the hips specialized in communications, weapons and explosives.

"Anyone for a morning run?" asked Kelly Harry, a slender six-foot red head whose freckles rivaled his light complexion, specialized in weapons, computers, martial arts and hand-to-hand combat.

"That's about all we'll be able to do – in our underwear," Dion concluded.

"Ten out and ten in?" Mike suggested.

"Sounds like a plan," Dion agreed.

"Okay. Let's change into something comfortable and hit the old track before the sun sees us," Kelly said.

"Yeah, our underwear," laughed Mike.

Three minutes later, having changed into gray running shorts and matching tee shirts that had 'Army' written across the chest area, they were walking through the main gate.

"Bob, check Dion's left sock. I think I see a bulge, It could be a rocket," one guard said to another as the trio was exciting, and the guards visibly searched.

"Ron, is that a bandolier strap hanging out of Harry's left sleeve?" another asked.

"Chet, look at Mike real good. Either that's a '16 in his shorts or he's excited about something," a third guard added. The exasperated looks, the tight smiles, the shaking of the heads of the runners demonstrated mild displeasure towards the guards, but everyone knew they had their job to perform. Once through, running abreast, they rounded the base front, establishing running/breathing rhythms prior to conversations.

"Dion, I'm glad you didn't try to bring any of those weapons through the gate – you'd make me look bad," Mike tossed at him.

"Oh, come on! It doesn't take me to make you look bad! Remember the other night at Gillies when you spilt beer on yourself!?" Dion reminded.

"Hey, that was intentional! Didn't you notice that cute waitress with the tight little body fawning all over me, and did ja notice that I wasn't in the barracks that night!? Ah, just where do you think I was!?" Mike asked, flashing a mischievous smile at his buddy.

"And speaking of other nights – where were you last night when the armory was being liberated of weapons? You weren't thinking of helping your buddies back in Chicago, were you?" Kelly humorously threw at Dion.

"Ah, excuse me, but I'm not the type. I'm the educated type, studies in ancient religions, cultures, Indian tribes, among other things. Last night I was fraternizing with Sonya, in the office," the refined black said.

"You mean the Tahitian with the big chi-chi's?" a surprised Kelly asked.

"Yeah, her. And what was the guy with the two first names doing last night – shaking hands with his best friend under the covers?" Dion challenged.

"Now, that was cold. I was blissfully in la-la-land," Kelly assured.

"Any witnesses?" Mike countered.

"Yes, I was on the space shuttle with twelve other people, but we weren't in space; we were negotiating traffic in downtown Jackson," the redhead said and all started laughing, and just then, they turned onto the old railroad bed.

LANGLEY, CIA HEADQUARTERS

"Will, we might have a slight break in Mississippi," Johnathan said, after walking into the director's office and he emphasized the word 'slight', and then, went on, "the National Guard Armory in Jackson was broken into last night or early this morning by person or persons unknown. The break-in was discovered when armory staff reported for duty three hours ago. Also, a van reported stolen in Baton Rouge was spotted parked in a flowing creek surrounded by dense brush, in the middle of trees and ten miles from the armory. After the APB's were issued, concerning Youngblood, Jackson field agents used heat-seeking indicators on a spotter plane to locate heat sources in unpopulated wilderness areas. They stumbled across residual heat traces where there shouldn't be any. Moving in to the area by ground vehicle, they stopped half a mile away, moving on foot to the location. They sighted a van in a creek. Checking inside through the windows, they saw the stolen armory weapons, but no one was in nor around the van, so, they pulled back to set up an observation post when they reported in. The van belongs to one Mike Tanner, a twenty-three year old Green Beret specialist fourth class whose army unit is temporarily attached to the guard for coordinating field exercises. Tanner reported the van stolen from the state fair in Baton Rouge and last night, he was accounted for as being on the base. Local authorities and the guard have not been notified of the findings, and they await instructions."

The director leaned back in his overstuffed armchair, steepled his fingers together and thought for a few moments before saying, "and no sighting of Youngblood."

"Correct. No sighting."

"What's the inventory of weapons stolen from the guard?" Will asked.

"Seventeen LAW's rockets, two M-16's, two 9mm hand guns and four bandoliers of ammunition, two for each type of weapon," the assistant replied, and then asked, "could this possibly by the work of a militant group?"

"No, a militant group would have gone for the heavier weapons, if they even knew how to break into an armory. What was stolen would hardly equip a militant group of any size. No, this is Lisa, she's arming herself. Tell Al Timmer and Tim Handles that we'll send the cleaners for the motel room. They are to board a private jet and hook up with the agents in Jackson. Give Al the description of the van. Tell the agents in Jackson to stick with the van, back-up is on the way. Have other Jackson agents pick up Al and Tim from the airport," the old general said.

"Are we dealing with a completed woman, a female with male logical process or a hybrid?" Johnathan asked.

"Good question. A completed woman I could rule out immediately because a normal woman couldn't have accomplished what Lisa already has. A hybrid is the combination of two mentalities forming a superior third, and a female with male mentality... good question. The hybrid would have the capabilities to effect the armory break-in, and a female with male mentality... I won't know that answer until I have a dossier of Russel Travers. Put it out that Lisa Youngblood has broken into the armory and is considered beyond lethally dangerous. Have her killed on sight. Let's not take any chances. Even if she didn't, killing her will still give us the answers we need to further the project, and get me a detailed map of Jackson," Will instructed.

"Yes, sir," Johnathan said.

"And have a chopper do a fast fly-by of the van. Have an agent photograph the van with a digital camera. They are not to land. Fly-by, photograph and send the picture here," Will further instructed.

"Understood."

JACKSON, MISSISSIPPI

The trio had been running for almost an hour when they reached the ten-mile limit. Stopping, they moved around, swinging arms, breathing deeply, stretching muscles, rolled shoulders to relax from the tenseness of continuous running before the return run. Their first day stationed with the guard, they had discovered the old railroad bed that was a fifty-mile spur line for a southern meat processing company. The packing company, defunct in the early '50's, merely packed the equipment and left. Southern Pacific Railroad, in turn, dismantled the spur line, picking up the track the wooden ties and abandoned what remained. Contract companies, who constructed the rail bed for Southern Pacific, meticulously packed gravel into leveled and poured dirt, compressing layer upon layer, until the consistency resembled concrete. So much gravel had been used that nothing grew on the old rail line except weeds, which died in the summer heat. Train company experts estimated the beds to last for many decades, and after sixty-odd years, the old spur line was still in excellent condition. Miles of straightaway stretches lay in either direction of the guard base, and the old line bed was favored with many a run by guard personnel. So many that a well-worn ten mile path had been trodden down by hundreds of running feet, in both directions from the base.

A pre-dawn run was the favorite; to run in the cool of early morning and enjoy the breaking of the day. It had been said by many, getting up *after* the sun had, something special was missed.

While bending over with his hands on his knees, Dion was surprised to see something in the bushes off to one side of the rail bed.

"Mike, come over here for a minute, will ya?" Dion said.

"Yeah," was all Mike said from forty-five feet away while drinking in the beauty of the breaking day. The sun not yet up, but on its way.

"What up?" Mike asked, after walking to Dion.

"Isn't that your van sitting in the creek over there?" Dion asked, pointing at the bushes. Mike looked to where Dion was pointing and did a double take.

"What's it…" he started and then, stopped himself, knowing Dion couldn't answer him. Then, he said, "I'll be right back." The facial expression from Dion said 'like I'm going to let you go down there by yourself.' Dion motioned Kelly to follow, and they both trailed after Mike. Cautiously approaching from the passenger rear, Mike silently inspected for external damage. Dion gave Kelly a 'no talking-sight only' gesture before they entered the creek, continuously moving toward the van. Soundlessly, they inspected the interior through windows while walking next to the vehicle. Upon seeing no one within, Mike opened the side door, and all three were dumbfounded, staring at the stolen armory weapons.

"Uh-oh, I don't like the looks of this," Mike said incredulously, looking at Dion.

"I'll admit that this doesn't look good for you, Mike," Kelly chipped in, and both gave him an exasperated look. Just then, Mike and Dion noticed two well-dressed gentlemen approaching from twenty-five feet away, Mike instantly chiding himself for not noticing them sooner.

"Gentlemen, what are you doing near the van?" the taller of the two asked in undertones while showing his CIA credentials.

"This is my van that was stolen yesterday from Baton Rouge," Mike responded also in undertones.

"Then, you'd be Mike Tanner," the tall agent said, and his answer shocked Mike. Stepping off Mike's shocked moment, he added, "yes, we know about the stolen van, the break-in and theft of the weapons. We know you didn't do it, but what we'd like you gentlemen to do, is leave the area immediately and we'll take care of everything," the tall agent said, and Mike saw them as the Mutt and Jeff type. Mike had known married couples where the husband was tall and he had a short, heavyset wife. He had also watched cartoons along the same lines, like the Rocky and Bullwinkle cartoon with the Russian counter-parts, Boris and Natasha. Mike guessed it to be some sort of psychological deficiency: the taller, slender agent lacking the ability to put on weight, and the short, portly agent desiring to be taller and thinner. And here was Mutt and Jeff, standing in the flesh.

Suddenly, before another word was spoken, they all heard a female talking.

"Yes gentlemen, please do leave the area immediately," Lisa said.

The army trio turned to see the female as the agents instantly reacted, attempting to draw their guns. Without any hesitation, Lisa killed both. As the guns report echoed into silence, the trio first looked at the dead agents, then, each other, and finally, at Lisa.

"So, you're the van owner," she stated to Mike, still training her weapon on them.

"Yes, and if you don't mind, why are you doing this?" he asked, a hand pointing at the stolen arsenal.

You don't want to know nor get involved because it could get you killed. Now, if I were you, gentlemen, I'd turn around and run. What you know could get you killed," she warned.

"We'll take our chances. We didn't become Green Berets to play it safe," Mike threw at her while she stood by the van front corner.

"Touche. Yeah, I know you're the van owner. I saw you guys yesterday when you pulled in to visit the Louisiana State Fair. Nothing personal, but I needed your wheels to transport special weapons," she said, uncocking her 9mm and tipping the end toward the van, and then, she put the weapon at the small of her back but stayed near the van front while the trio stood by the side door.

"And I naturally suppose that has something to do with the CIA?" Dion asked.

"It has everything to do with the CIA," Lisa stated.

"And we know you're not fond of 'em," Harry quipped.

"They are desperate for my return on a certain project," Lisa offered without trying to give too much away.

"And you're being a little obstinate against their wishes, Dion said, glancing past Mike to the weapons in the van and then, back to Lisa. Mike said nothing but listened to the calm discussion. No voices were raised and no accusations were thrown nor insinuated. From Mike's position next to the door, he saw a short blonde curl sticking out near the backside of her head and mixed with black hair.

"When you take a stand against that agency, it's be wise to have a little back-up," she easily related and she felt like she was meeting them as an equal.

"Compared to the resources of the CIA, you wouldn't last long in a firefight," Kelly observed.

"When one does not have the position of strength, one does not stand and fight," Lisa corrected, and Russel knew the routine. The followers would question the stranger, giving the leader time to analyze the conversation of points said and things hidden between the lines. From the way they horseplayed going into the fair, it was obvious that the dark-haired gentleman was a leader-type. And here he was saying nothing for the time being, but Travers couldn't waste too much time.

"You're Lisa Youngblood, aren't you?" Mike calmly asked, and his question shocked his partners into silence.

"Yes, I am, Mike," she said, and it was her turn to shock his partners. As Mike's buddies did and said nothing, Lisa relaxed tensions slightly by moving closer, moving next to the passenger door. And in the distance, she heard a chopper approaching.

"The van's registry," Mike simply said to Dion and Kelly, and he added, "what part of the project are you carrying?"

"The serum and the notes. And I'd think it very wise if you left immediately," she urged, and Travers could tell the chopper was moving extremely fast toward them and would probably fly by. He knew someone was in a hurry.

"I know you'll be leaving very soon for parts unknown and we won't stop you. You've stolen my van, broke into our armory, took some of our weapons and generally, made us look bad. The least you can do before leaving is let me see the notes," Mike pleaded.

"You are absolutely asking for trouble on a scale you can't imagine," she cautioned.

"Like I said before, I didn't become a Green Beret just to play it safe," he said, holding his hand out.

"You've been duly warned. If anything happens to you on your way back to the base, on the base or afterward, it's on your head," she said, pulling the black notebook from a side pocket of the waterproof bag and handing it to him. And the noise from the chopper was growing louder. Lisa added, "look three quarters of the way through the book and in the margins."

Mike scanned down five margins until his eyes suddenly stopped, "the agency can have their nation now? What does that mean?" he asked, looking at her.

"That means the CIA is going to establish their own nation outside the continental United States," she was having to raise her voice over the din of the shopper. Through the trees she saw the fast moving bird. It intended to fly-by, but a man was poised just inside the door dressed in a suit, and he was focusing a camera. Dion and Kelly started to look at the chopper, but Lisa grabbed both by their sides and dug her fingernails in. "Don't look!" she screamed, and because of the sudden pain, they focused bulging eyes and grit teeth at her. And the fast flying bird shot by.

"There was a man in the door with a camera," Mike observed.

"Congratulations," she said dryly, "you've just been photographed by the CIA holding the winning death ticket. Your buddies were sufficiently shielded by the scrub brush, but you were in plain view holding the notebook open. I'd say, within fifteen minutes, your picture will be in Langley, they will anticipate the worst and orders will be issued for your death. I have to go, Mike, and you have to decide what you're going to do," she said softly as she gently pulled the book from his hands and replaced it in the side pocket.

"Mike, we can protect you," Dion stated.

"You know we can, Mike," Kelly affirmed, and Lisa walked around the front of the van heading for the driver's seat. Mike quickly analyzed the situation before answering.

"Yes, you could if we were with our own company. Keep in mind that we're in the middle of the guard, and we don't know all of them. It would be too easy for the CIA to slip someone in posing as a guardsman and it'd only take a second with the right weapon to kill me. I trust you and we already know how vigilant the guard is," he said, then looked at the stolen weapons, and he went on, "if I stay, chances are good I'll die because I won't see it coming. If I leave, everyone coming against me means harm. The safest place is on the run. I've got my 'big bullet'. Keep your ears up," Mike said as Lisa slid into the driver's seat and started the engine.

"You won't be missed at the afternoon formation, but you will be in the morning," Dion said as they shook hands.

"Say nothing until then, and remember, we were logged out," Mike advised.

"Don't worry about the log. We'll see to it," Kelly said smugly. Mike closed the side door, opened the passenger door, got in and as Lisa was pulling away, he offered parting wisdom.

"Don't go back by the track, you might run into a bunch of someones you probably wouldn't survive after meeting," and she steered the van onto the track, dropped out of four-wheel-drive and sped away.

"That's a comforting thought. Ok, might as well get started. We don't want to be around when the CIA shows up," Dion said.

"Yeah, right. And we have a long way to go, the hard way. Whose idea was it for this run?" Kelly questioned.

"Yours."

In the van, Mike questioned Lisa.

"How did you come up with the notebook and how were you associated with the CIA?" he asked.

"I worked in the research lab," she lied, "processing the chemicals ascertaining potency strength. The CIA contracted for new chemicals to be shipped into the lab. Each chemical had to be tested and they had to be new. Old chemicals would taint the results. After testing each batch of chemicals, someone would load them into a van and drive off. The amount of chemicals seemed almost insignificant, but I had the lab to myself and the money was good. Occasionally, Dr. Schuler would visit the lab. I think he visited because of me. Anyway, once while he was there, I had an opportunity to study his notebook.

"After examining his notes, from what I can gather, I began piecing together the goal of the project. I discovered he was using healthy people for his experiments. And when the experiment failed, they died. It took a long time to scrape enough information together for the picture to take shape. The portion of the big picture that I could visualize scared me to death. The serum genetically alters individuals' appearance. Somehow, the CIA intends to use it to take over a third world nation, setting themselves up as a CIA nation outside the U.S. And knowing the CIA, they'd have their own military.

"Some of what I'm telling you, I can prove, some – I'm guessing. When you work for the agency, you never know all the ins and outs of a project," she fabricated.

"I'd like to examine the notebook further, if you don't mind. While I'm reading, at the first road you come to, turn left. That'll take us in the back way to the Pilot Truck Stop. We'll fuel up and go from there," he directed.

"What's the distance between here and there?" she asked.

"About eight miles. Why?" Mike wanted to know.

"Because within thirty minutes after that picture was taken, that picture will be broadcast across the U.S. on special news bulletins. Whatever we're going to do, we need to do it fast and leave Jackson immediately, and preferably by the back roads," she stated.

"Agreed. Let me read for a few minutes," he said and Lisa nodded her approval, but Russel's thoughts were many.

How can I be excited and scared at the same time? I've been around men all my life. What is making me so nervous being around Mike? Did he buy my story? It flowed smoothly, I think. Even if he believes my story, what are we doing to do once out of Jackson? We have to go public now more than ever. The notebook and serum is the supporting evidence. I dislike having no game plan, and just knowing, he's going to ask if I have one, he was thinking as she turned left onto a paved two-lane road and Mike kept reading. No traffic hindered her progress and within minutes after leaving the old train bed, she saw the Pilot Truck Stop. Cars, trucks and mobile homes moved about the lot, but Lisa scrutinized the area for police cars. Seeing none, she slowed to enter the lot.

"Access to the gas tanks are on your side," Mike said without looking from the notebook.

"Thank you kind sir, and shall I also check the water and oil for you?' she said sarcastically.

"Oh, God, I'm saddled with a typical woman," Mike groaned as he set the book between the seats.

"Hey, I'm not going out on a limb in accepting that as a compliment, you know," she threw back and when he looked confused she hurriedly added, "right now, I'm accepting all compliments in the attempt to boost moral. With the CIA chasing, it might tend to dampen ones spirit. Compliments help."

"I couldn't know about the dampening part, I've never been chased by the CIA. I'll put the gas in," Mike said as he started to get out.

"There's definitely going to be some exciting times. I just hope you survive, and I need some ice," she said seriously, but as she moved to repack the waterproof bag, Russel's mentality questioned Mike's statements.

How can I be a 'typical woman'? I didn't know there was such a category. I was trying to relate on his level. He must have meant 'a typical liberated woman'. What is 'liberated' anyway? Liberated from an image or role model women were supposedly to adhere to or is it that those females speaking their minds have shed the imaginary shackles created by the many former womanhood generations? When a woman is considered liberated, does that automatically insert her into another category? What I need to do is stop trying to psychoanalyze a label slapped on women and look deeper into why some emotions within are contradicting. I both wanted and didn't want him to come along. I'm actually excited he came and he scares me? Or am I really afraid that the possibility now exists that the man next to me might teach me of the things I don't know about my new self? Is that why I'm so damn nervous? And where are these heat flashes coming from? One minute I feel fine and after he gives me a look, I feel like I could jump into a tub full of ice and melt it all. What am I going to do with this guy? He thinks he's saddled with somebody – it never occurred to me that I might have a partner-in-crime tagging along, and she finished packing the bag, brushed off excess ice, shouldered the bag and stood up. When she turned to the van, Mike stood by the passenger rear corner, leaning against the vehicle, watching her.

"What?" she asked directly.

"What's with all the hand motions, scratching of the head and funny looks?" he wondered.

"I'm working on something. Some aspects won't work and some I can't figure out," she answered.

"In other words, you've not going to tell me what's going on up here?" he said, pointing a finger at his head.

"No!"

"I thought so, and I'm driving," he said.

"Did you pay for the gas?" she seriously asked.

"Yeah, while you were 'working on something'," he said with a smile.

"Well, if you're ready, let's get out of here, and not by the interstate," she stated.

"Don't worry, I know this neck of the woods. I'm familiar with most of the back roads in this area and north," he said and then, walked to the driver's side and hopped in. "Where are we going?" he asked.

"North," she simply said.

"Ah, do we have a game plan or are we winging it?" Mike asked as he wheeled the van onto a secondary artery paralleling the interstate. The sprawling truck stop was north of the city and minutes later, traffic was almost non-existent as they traveled through the dense wooded areas of southern Mississippi.

"Yes, our game plan is survival, it's so simple you might become bored if you don't use the imagination. Whatever it takes to survive, do it," she said, trying to sound confident.

"So basically, you stole the serum and notes and like a common thief, now you're running," he outlines.

"Common thief!" she shouted, "you have no idea what it took to steal those notes nor the serum! Nor do you have any idea how desperate the CIA is to recapture me. If you had half a brain, you'd jump ship at the first opportunity just to get away from me!"

"Lisa," he said after his rearview mirror.

"You insult me as if I were some run-of-the-mill bitch who had nothing better to do than upset the CIA just for entertainment. I've already been scared outta my wits just trying to get away from them and I know the worst is yet to some. What I don't need is some hard-headed army bastard tagging along insulting me!"

"Lisa," he tried again.

"Don't you fully understand what you've done! You've put yourself in their gunsights. Another nice, big target to aim at! I didn't want you along because I don't want to feel responsible when you get your ass shot off! Anybody found with me shares in the winning death ticket, and the CIA doesn't care if you're army or not!" she shouted.

"Lisa," he tried once more.

"WHAT!!" she aggressively shouted, loudly with anger.

"There's a cop behind us and he just turned on his lights for us to stop," Mike calmly stated.

Almost shaking with anger, Lisa looked toward the van rear as if she could see through the curtains, and then, back to Mike she said, "start slowing down and I'll get the welcome wagon ready. When I tell you, take off." Stepping cautiously over the rockets, Lisa moved to the custom bed, picking up a '16 and a full banana clip. Sitting on the bed, she inserted the clip, jacked a round into the chamber, and judging their speed to be under thirty – opened the back door, leveling the weapon at the State Police Cruiser. With the selector switch on automatic, she pulled and held the trigger back. Rounds slammed into the radiator, hood, lights, and when a round hit the passenger front tire, the cruiser skidded off the road, with the officer jumping out diving in the opposite direction of the skid. Raking the length of the cruiser, hitting as much as possible, one round hit the truck area, penetrating the gas tank. The ruptured tank exploded, instantly engulfing the cruiser in flames.

"Go," shouted Lisa, and Mike floored it. Jumping out of the weeds with service revolver in hand, leveling the gun at the van, the state trooper realized the van had moved out of range. Reloading the '16, selector switch on safety, Lisa laid it on the custom bed and moved back into the passenger seat, roughly folding her arms under her ample breasts.

"Nice shooting," Mike complimented.

"Thank you," she unemotionally stated, and then added, "I'm still upset with you. Is it your habit to insult women?" she asked.

"No. Where'd you learn to shoot like that?" he asked, trying to find a way to appease her.

"When I used to shoot turkeys," she firmly expressed, and Mike knew he's better not touch that one. Riding in silence on State Road 25, Lisa's thoughts drifted, *he treats me like I'm a typical woman. I guess I'm acting like one, but unintentionally. What is making me act like a woman? It can't be psychological because that deals with the mental states or processes, and mine are male. Naturally, he's relating with the female he sees, and he knows all females differ slightly concerning attitude, disposition and so on. Where does my male process end and the female begin? No, there can't be a separation because both are combined in one body. So, it boils down to how much influence does the female heart have over the male men-*

tality? He was thinking as Mike turned off the state road and onto a dirt road, moving in an easterly direction in the south-western corner of Winston County. His thoughts drifted again as Mike turned onto County Road 490.

Could it be that the physiology of woman, each and every aspect acting in concert within the complete entity, contributes to the total concept of – what is woman? But woman is only a part of man. Of course, each part is readily identifiable, but man shares many similar qualities as women do; nurturing, sensitivity, child caring, the list comparing the two would read much the same. Only the plumbing is different, but that one singularity can't be the one element that separates man from woman. That's the one visible point which is acknowledged, but is mostly everything else so similar that no one actually knows where the male ends and the female begins? And it vaguely registered on his awareness that County Road 490 turned into State Road 14 at Mashulville, that Mike left Mississippi and entered Alabama on State Road 17. Mike was switching roads often, attempting to avoid any confrontations with law enforcement personnel.

They last rays of light shined over the trees as the miles and hours slipped by. Mike, heading in a north-easterly direction, intended to spend the night in the southern portion of the William B. Bankhead National Forest.

Locating a familiar dirt road entering into the national forest, Mike turned off the dirt road, following hunters' tracks that passed between two cliffs and ended on a ledge whose commanding view overlooked a tree-studded portion of the national park.

"We'll spend the night here and in the morning, we'll stop in Forkville for breakfast," he said as they were getting out of the van. While stretching cramped muscles, Lisa drank in the beauty of the forest. The soft chill of early evening sent shivers through her and she retrieved her long sleeve camouflaged jacket, buttoning it half way from the bottom.

"Sounds good to me," she said indifferently while buttoning her jacket.

"We'll be safe here. Only hunters know of this place. I'm guessing you noticed the road we took into here was almost non-existent because of the overgrowth. You would have to know what you're looking for and exactly where it was to be found or one would drive by it and not notice. It's one of those hidden roads the locals use to enter the forest to enjoy private parties. No tourists would have knowledge of such secluded places," he said as he gathered wood for a campfire. Numerous odd-shaped rocks were arranged in a circle to create a firepit. The pit was fifteen feet from the ledge and from the discoloration of the rocks, Lisa knew many a fire had honoured the pit. Mike crumpled up a piece of paper from the van, laid small twigs against it and then, lit the paper. As the fire grew, he added larger twigs until he was tossing large sticks onto the brightly burning fire. From an area under the cliffs, he returned with two one-foot chopped sections of a tree trunk and Mike set one on each side of the fire. Sitting down on a fallen tree seven feet from the pit, Lisa watched him as he gathered wood to throw on and wood for later. Finally satisfied with the state of the fire, Mike sat down next to Lisa.

"Mike, do you believe in fate?" she quietly asked.

"Unusual question," he said.

"Relevant question. One would say it's a coincidence that I stole your van, met you later and you were... in a way... forced to accompany me. How many times is something coincidental before it's considered more than a mere coincidence? Think about it. You had the exact type of vehicle I needed; you were in the same state and area where I needed to rest and you were, in a way, forced to come with me. The odds are against it as being coincidence. Look at the big picture: the CIA intends to establish itself as a nation, thousands upon thousands of lives would be sacrificed by their emergence or later actions and we're the only ones in the breach to stop them. If they are successful, foreign governments could be toppled, other governments heavily bribed to side with them and those resisting would be assassinated. Where would they stop?"

she asked and while she talked, Mike carefully weighed her words. "That picture reeks of evil darkness. Once they established a toehold, I don't think they would stop nor *could* anyone stop them. I think it would progress from a CIA Nation to a CIA World and living in either sounds bleak," he said and she watched the firelight dance on his face.

"Because so many lives are at stake, I think fate has intervened on the behalf of those who should live, those who have another destiny to fulfil. I think history is going to pivot on us, one way or another," she ventured.

"We're going to keep the notes and serum out of their hands and go public with what we know. That will effectively destroy their plans and protect us in the process," Mike stated and Lisa got up, went to the stack of gathered wood and tossed a few pieces onto the fire.

"Mike, I honestly don't have any game plan on what to do next. Because their plan was so insidious, I had to get away from them. I wanted no part of it. I grabbed what I could and split," she lied. She wanted Mike to trust her. She needed him and at the same moment, she was afraid of him. Mike stood up and walked to her at the woodpile.

"Hey, don't worry about it," he assured her and he gently put his hands on the sides of both her shoulders and squeezed, "we're in this together. We'll work it out. And I'd like to apologize for earlier comments. I was upset because I knew that every aspect of my life was at stake depending upon what I decided next."

"It's ok," she said weakly. His hand gently squeezing her caused a warm, tingling sensation to electrically surge through her entire body. Every nerve, every emotion felt suddenly charged like she was being electrocuted with excitement. Charge upon charge assaulted her emotions, heating and building to a crescendo. As sensations over-charged emotions, a sexual fire swept through her, causing Russel to wonder if Lisa could possibly set the forest on fire by emotion alone. Before he could muster an idea for a response, Mike kissed Lisa.

The fire blasted out of control. Reality tilted sideways, causing

Lisa to put her hands on Mike's hips to steady herself. The fire multiplied on itself, intensifying to a peak and suddenly the peak detonated into ecstatic bliss.

Pulling gently away from her, Mike smiled when he noticed her reddened face.

"Mike," she softly whispered. All she could manage to say was his name before his lips were back on hers. His hands slid up to both sides of her neck, following her skin – they slowly dropped inside her camo jacket, spreading out along the tops of her shoulders – taking tank top straps and jacket out to her arms and down. She felt his hands slide up her bare arms and fondle her breast. When he gently pinched her nipple, Russel was lost in the avalanche of flaming sexual desire, swirling lust and ecstatic bliss. Any imaginary control vanished in the emotional slide into the firey ocean of orgasmic sensation. Somewhere on the firey waves, in a surrealistic world, Russel saw himself standing on the intense sexual swells, and Lisa was walking toward him. Smiling at her, he wrapped his arms around and hugged her tight and then, melted into her. In a sexually gratifying valley between peaks, Russel was inseparably fused with the new feminine entity, and she alone... rode the waves.

Waking up under the stars, she found herself in his arms, in a bed of blankets, pillows and guns, and nude. Lisa didn't remember undressing nor being undressed, knew nothing concerning the bed and she wasn't about to ask.

"Wow," she softly said as she looked lovingly into Mike's sparkling hazel eyes.

"I was thinking the same thing, 'wow'. If anyone would've showed up, I'd have killed 'em," he whispered while gently stroking the side of her face.

"You better have. Because if someone would have interrupted us, I'd have become one unmanageable bitch," she warned.

"Uh-oh, I hear a word to the wise," Mike perceived.

"No, you'd never have to worry about that. We might get upset with each other, but it'd never come to that. Oh, I'm not explaining it right," she said, burying her head on his chest.

"I think you did," he stated as he rolled her gently onto her back.

"We should probably get some sleep," she suggested.

"Yeah, right," he said, but started feverishly kissing her.

After nearly two hours of intimate play and lovemaking and Lisa having fallen asleep, Mike quietly left her side, moved to the van driver's seat and reached in the door pouch for his 'big bullet'. The gigantic bullet, when power was applied, parted at the pentad-curved summit, imitating a small satellite dish. It was the Green Berets' miniature satellite link-up transceiver, which boasted of reaching earth's four corners. Placing the 'bullet' on the roof, he plugged the adapter into the empty cigarette slot, inserted the earpiece and seconds later, the unfolded summit linked with an orbiting satellite.

"Dion, you got your ears on?" he asked, quietly speaking into a mini-microphone while sitting in the van.

"Yeah, I hear you man," came Dion's clear voice ten seconds later. "Hey, where're you at Mike?"

"We're south of the Tennessee border and tomorrow we'll be moving northward. Lisa's asleep now and I don't want her to know we've talked. I'm not exactly sure how she'll take it. Ok, here's what happened after I left you guys…" Mike replayed the day's events, concluding with the seduction of Lisa.

"Oh… gee… that didn't take you long," Dion said dryly.

"She's unique, Dion. She's different from any girl I've known before," Mike related.

"Buddy, every law enforcement agency is after you two, you've got the best of women and she's carrying a classified secret that needs to be make public! I envy you! Need any help?" he asked.

"I feel we'll need it before this is over, but I don't know where. She's not told me where we're going – all I know is that it's somewhere north," Mike said.

"There's alotta north from where you're at now, buddy. Let us know when and where and we'll be there," Dion assured.

"Yeah, just keep your ears on – don't know when I'll be able to contact you next."

"No problems. Guess you know I expect to be called on the carpet tomorrow for your actions today," Dion advised.

"If Stranton asks, tell him everything. He's a fair commander. Tell him what we suspect and that we have no solid proof, except a couple of dead bodies," Mike instructed, and then went on," I'd better get back before she wakes up and misses me."

"We wouldn't want that, would we?!" Dion snickered.

"See you soon," he said.

"Yeah, see ya," Dion repeated.

Mike unplugged the power source and the mini-satellite dish folded back into a bullet. Without unplugging the peripherals, he laid the transceiver in the door pouch, laying the microphone/ear piece wired on top. Sliding out, he quietly closed the door, noiselessly tiptoed to the open-air bed and slowly crawled under the covers without disturbing his partner-in-crime as she drifted in dreams.

JUNE 13TH

MISSISSIPPI NATIONAL GUARD ARMORY

After the state cruiser was destroyed, police tracked the owner, learning he to be a Green Beret stationed at the National Guard. Contacting the base commander, Major General Hammond, the chief requested the whereabouts of Mike Tanner. Explaining the situation, the chief desired feedback ASAP. The call came in the wee hours in the morning, and feeling it prudent not to wake the brigadier general over a trivial matter of locating personnel, the commander immediately ordered the base searched for Tanner. Learning from the watch that Tanner was AWOL, the commander also learned Tanner did not return from a morning run, from which, his partners did. After reporting his findings to the police chief, Hammond prepared a report for the Green Beret unit's commanding officer for review first thing in the morning. Breakfast was at zero five hundred hours, at zero five thirty hours, spec.'s three Dion Marshall and Kelly Harry were standing at attention before their well-seasoned commanding officer as he sat behind his office desk.

"Good morning, gentlemen," the brigadier general calmly stated, and went on, "a report has come across my desk that I feel needs straightening out immediately. Yesterday, a woman named Lisa Youngblood shot up and destroyed a police cruiser about fifty miles from here. Normally, we're not concerned nor interested about civilians who shoot at the police, but this one was shooting from the back of Mike Tanner's van while the van was in motion, and all of a sudden, we can't find Mr. Tanner. Now, you three went out on a morning run yesterday and returned without Mr. Tanner. Did you... lose Mr. Tanner... somewhere? Mr. Marshall, you stand at ease, tell me everything you know, and... don't leave anything out," he calmly ordered.

Dion recounted the events, adding his own impressions and ended by saying, "after Mike and Lisa left, we started back through the woods. A few minutes later, numerous cars sped into the area. Well-dressed men got out of the cars and began searching the area. We're assuming it was CIA. Again sir, we lack the physical proof. Mike called last night after Lisa had gone to sleep. He's doing so without her knowledge. He's not sure of her reaction. They're moving northward and as yet, she's not imparted a destination, just the direction."

"Very good," Stranton said, "keep a lid on it and when Mike calls again, I want to be informed immediately. I don't care what time of day or morning it is, I want to know. Dismissed."

As the soldiers marched out of the office, Stranton leaned back in the large, black leather, over-stuffed office chair and said, "something is definitely wrong with that picture. I don't blame Tanner in the least for his actions. Damn, I wish it were me next to her," he was saying to Hammond, who was sitting on a couch to one side of the desk. "But those two are in for it. Knowing the CIA, they'll stop at nothing trying to get the serum back under wraps. You'll be surprised how much that agency throws away in the attempt. The agency has an incredible arsenal at their disposal. Lisa didn't steal enough weapons to stand against them," the brigadier's demeanor soured recalling the stolen inventory.

"True," said Hammond, "but they have the element of surprise.

How many battles have been lost because of that one element? I have almost no information on Youngblood, but from what I know and have just heard, I'd say her training would closely rival Tanner's. They're a loose canon with the element of surprise," and hearing that, the brigadier brightened.

"Think I'll call a war buddy in Washington and find out how things are jumping at the CIA. Major, you can sit still, this isn't private and if things start to jump off, you're going to," the brigadier advised. He dialed the White House and was connected with the Army Joint Chief-of-Staff Bill Hansen.

"Bill, Tom Stranton, how are you doing?" he asked.

"Tom, haven't seen you since the Gulf War, in fact the only times I have seen you, there's a war going on. What's up?" the voice over the phone asked.

"Well, Bill, I hope you're sitting down 'cause the fighting's about to start," Stranton advised.

"Ok Tom, let me have it," the Joint Chief said, and the brigadier general recounted everything for the five-star Washington general, including his orders to the enlisted men, and at the end of his narrative, the Washington general said, "that explains why the CIA is getting jumpy. Some at the House are noticing it, but the President hasn't as yet. If things continue to escalate, you can be sure he'll not only notice, but he'll demand answers. Tom, I'm not going to say anything to the Chief yet. Let's allow events to run their course. You've got he green light on what you need to do, and Tom, keep me posted. Thanks very much for this call, bye," the chief said.

To the major, Stranton said, "there's nothing to equal getting the green light from the White House."

WILLIAM B. BANKHEAD NATIONAL FOREST

MIKE AND LISA

Scented breezes swirled wispy clouds in the midnight sky. Moonlit rays softly illuminated earthen paths on which the young blonde danced. Tulips sang the midnight song of fragrant butterflies, of blazing fireflies and of harmonious red robins. A manicured forest observed a delicate radiant dancer twirl in emotions of love on earthen paths softly illuminated by moonlit rays. Roses respond to her love, giving their precious perfume to the wind, to encourage the tiny dancer. Gracefully flowing to unheard music, young fawns witnessed her beauty, shining above the soft moonlight. A slender girl danced amidst the fragrant butterflies, past the tulip's chorus, past the red robins' song, leaving no trace on earthen paths softly illuminated by moonlit rays. Transparent clothes slowly floated away from her thin waist as she played. Thick carpets of green grass rushed by as she danced through meandering meadows, to meet her love, to spin magic anew.

⊕

Lisa awoke quietly to forest sounds, slowly observing everything around them without moving. She was on her back with Mike
partially on top of her. The black of night was past, several hours
away was dawn. One hand lay on a gun, of which, she guessed,
Mike placed by her side. His breathing caressed her shoulder and
as she tenderly touched his lips with her thumb, his eyes slowly
opened.

"I had an incredibly beautiful dream," she softly whispered.

"I'm still having mine," he whispered back. Rolling onto his
back, he pulled her on top of him, enjoying the warmth of her skin
on his. Slowly caressing her back and posterior, Mike took his time
waking up.

While lying of top of Mike with her eyes closed, Lisa's thoughts
reflected on the night before. *Russel's mental process feared to let
go of his identity and that maintained the conflicting duality of personage within one body; the feminine entity struggled for its own
rightful existence while Russel's mental process was afraid to release control of all he once was and had known. Within the element
of fear, the uncertainty, the terrors of the unknown forced Russel to
attempt to control the feminine person because she was now the
visible part of his new remodeled self. He was afraid of becoming
part of that new self in fear of losing 'his' identity. But that fear
blinded him to the fact that his identity in his former personage
was already gone. The physical part of him was sacrificed and the
mental part feared total loss should it lose control of the new self.*

*Somehow, Mike erased that fear, thus paving the way for the
male mentality to completely accept the remodeled self as his new
identity. Because Mike forced the compromise between the dual
entities, fear was set aside and acceptance took its place.*

And now, we're blended as one.

"It's a beautiful morning," she softly exclaimed, and she realized, last night's dream was the first since she evolved into a new
self. Russel dreamt on a regular basis, sometimes normal dreams,
some unusual and a few, extremely weird. But he dreamt. No dreams
occurred after the metamorphosis until Russel's mentality surren-
dered control and accepted the new entity as the visible part of

him, allowing the feminine side her own existence as an individual. Lisa reasoned, a peaceful balance was achieved from the dilemma of male logic attempting to control or restrain the vast array of feminine emotions.

"Let's not waste it by getting up," Mike whispered in her ear, and then, started kissing her neck.

"Oh no you don't! If you start that again, we'll be here all day," she said, and then, she took his face in both her hands to tenderly kiss him 'good morning,' simultaneously feeling her body responding. "Ah, let's get up," she suggested, throwing the covers back, grabbing her clothes and starting to pull them on. Mike merely leaned on an elbow, watched her ample breasts sway slightly, his gaze swept over the curves of her hips, shapely legs, and, her protruding posterior thoroughly excited him. Dressing and watching him watching her, she tenderly said, "you hard-headed army bustard."

"Uh-huh," he said with a large smile.

"Better get up and get dressed – we're leaving, unless you intend to go naked," she said, trying not to smile as she pulled on her camo tank top.

"I guess you're right," he said, after Lisa had finished dressing. Throwing off the covers, Mike slowly pulled his underwear on. Retrieving her weapon, she, in turn, watched him. With nipples hardening, breathing deepening, her body was responding to his well-trimmed physique and endowment.

"You bastard!" she said, turning to check her bag and the van. The serum was floating in icy water, the van; untouched.

"We're in an isolated location. This place is miles from the main entrance. There's hundreds of dirt trails leading to secret camp sites that the locals use to avoid contact with tourists because the locals enjoy their privacy," he explained.

"So, this is part of our old stomping grounds?" she asked.

"Ah, I've been here on different occasions – partying, but I wouldn't consider it 'old stomping grounds.' I was raised in central Tennessee and naturally, friends show friends hidden entrances to private sites to avoid the deluge of tourists, so we can enjoy our party without strangers asking stupid questions like 'got an extra beer, man,'" he further explained.

"So then, you'd know a good place in Forkville where we could have breakfast, or did you want to try my seafood Po-Boy? I'm sure it's still good," she wondered out loud.

"Yeah, I'm sure it's good enough for the animals, but not this animal," he said, pointing at himself as Lisa folded the blankets. Deciding to further dress, Mike pulled blue jeans and a subdued-blue paisley-print short sleeve button-down shirt. Having clothes stored in the van meant he'd carry minimum amounts into the barracks. The lesser amount in the barracks reduced the possibilities of getting gigged during inspections. Standing in the open side doors, Mike had completed dressing when Lisa returned with the folded blankets.

"Awww, and I was just getting used to seeing you parade around in your underwear! You do look delicious in blue jeans and button-down shirt, but wouldn't you like to run around more in your underwear?" she jested with a devilish grin.

"The owners of Marie's Diner are rednecks who wouldn't be amused with someone showing up in their underwear, and we don't want to attract attention to ourselves," he stated.

"Killjoy," she said with an askance look, placing the blankets on the custom bed as Mike tossed out her Po-Boy, then closed the side doors. Mike wheeled the van from the ledge, retracing their steps along the dirt road until it intersected with another. Turning onto the second dirt road, it ended at State Road 195. Passing through the southwestern portion of the national forest, SR195 would take them directly into the corporate township of Forkville. Upon leaving the ledge, Lisa tucked her blonde hair under the black wig and put her shades on, attempting to disguise herself.

Enroute to the township, beyond every curve in the road, Lisa imagined potential threats looming just out of sight. Numerous possibilities ending with their capture assaulted her nerves as they approached each curve. She expected a massive police roadblock around the next bend in the road with back-up suddenly appearing behind the fugitives. Dark thoughts conjured images of menacing, bulky, heavily armed troopers lurking the shadows of trees, anxiously waiting for them to round a curve. She anticipated involvement in a shootout with fifty angry state police who lusted for their death, to avenge their fellow officer. Fears whispered defeat. Nerves expected disaster. Breathing deeply, Lisa forced herself to calm down and deal with events as they occurred.

The sun was shining as Mike pulled into the parking lot of Marie's Diner, both relieved over the uneventful trip. Casually looking for official type vehicles, the fugitives scanned the lot before parking next to another van, effectively hiding their van from passing law enforcement personnel.

"There's no clean official police cars present. This looks good from the outside," Mike said, as they exited the van and began walking toward the front doors.

"Let's have a fast meal and then, get outta here," Lisa said quietly, out the side of her mouth as they walked in the diner doors. Taking her bag, Lisa figured she could obtain ice without too much trouble or attention. Once inside, a quick survey of the patrons indicated that those present appeared to be nothing more than locals. After being seated near the front windows and isolated from other customers, she ordered a western omelet with a small bowl of fruit. Mike ordered scrambled eggs with ham, grits, hash browns, bacon, toast with grape jelly and a short stack of pancakes. Mike noticed Lisa wanted to say something, but her teeth were locked together while she glared at him.

"Ah, you're not hungry enough for the other half of the menu, darling?" she asked with heavy acid on the fringes of her voice.

"Well, I figure it this way; this is probably our theoretical last meal and I'll need all of my strength if I'm going to be running around with you not knowing when we'll eat next," he said, and both stopped talking when the waitress brought coffee.

When the waitress set the last cup down, Lisa asked, "Do you have ice I could buy to keep my medicine refrigerated? We have four hours of traveling before reaching our destination and I have to keep it cool until then."

"Oh sure honey, jist go b'hin' the counta' an' hep ya'self," the waitress drawled.

"Thank you, I will," Lisa said genuinely appreciative, and then, she turned to Mike after the lady left. "That's a quality I like in you; the unmistakable air of confidence."

"That 'air of confidence' is being promoted by hunger. I haven't eaten since yesterday morning," he pointed out.

"Don't talk to me about hunger. Remember, I offered you my Po-Boy. And now if you'll excuse me, I need some ice," she said, quickly grabbing her bag and sliding from the booth. A smirk crept across his face when he realized that she had gotten the last word in. He watched her move around the counter and his thoughts centered on her.

Almost a typical woman, he thought, *having to get the last word in and yet, so different from any I've known. She tracks right with my conversation and adds to it periodically. This is one intelligent girl. Stealing anything from the CIA is an accomplishment. There's more to it than what she's saying, but I can't push for it. It'll have to come out on its own. I wonder what the serum looks like and what it actually does. Patience is the best approach; just let it come out at its own time. Don't think I could force anything out of her and it'd be embarrassing finding out the hard way that she could kick my ass. What a girl, and what a mystery! Not too many girls I know can shoot a '16 accurately and none of them could break into an armory. Am I excited about her because of the thrill of the danger involved? Or is it because she's so different? Think I'll start probing gently. Here she comes, and the food too!*

As Lisa was sitting down, the meal arrived. Not wasting time, Mike attacked the scrambled eggs first, eating ferociously. While Mike wolfed down his meal, Lisa intentionally ate delicately, a few locals grinned when they noticed. The morning meal passed uneventful and Mike was finishing his coffee when he saw two state troopers pulling into the lot. The troopers backed into parking spaces in front of the diner, two burley officers got out and walked in for breakfast. Sitting also by the front windows, they were seated three booths from the fugitives, and the cops were between the outlaws and the door.

"See, I told you we should have a quick meal and then, split. But noooo, Mister Growing Army Man has to have his last meal as if he'd never eat again," she quietly chided.

"You just sit there, finish your coffee and I'll pay for the meal. When I motion, you simply get up, join me and we'll leave. Put your shades on, act natural and everything'll be fine," Mike quietly instructed, and then, slid out and walked to the register.

"How's da meal?" the cashier asked.

"Hit the spot with no problems," he responded, and after paying, he motioned to Lisa.

"Ya'all have a nice day now, ya hear," she said.

"I hope so," he answered wistfully. Watching her walk toward him, a trooper said something which he couldn't hear.

"Pretty young lady, if you had blonde hair – you'd look exactly like a fugitive named Lisa Youngblood," he said while studying her profile, and Lisa knew she didn't have much time.

"Well gentlemen," she started, her left hand going toward the wig while in her right hand, she concealed the 9mm between the bag and her hip. Pulling the wig off, dropping it on the table, she then shook her blonde hair out. Instantly the troopers went for their guns, but Lisa merely moved hers from concealment, aimed it, cocked it and said, "good guess, you're right".

"Gentlemen, put your hands on the table," Mike ordered, walking up from behind them. Lisa removed the trooper's service revolver nearest her, placed it in her jeans and Mike handed her the second one from the other trooper. "Gentlemen, let's take a walk out front," Mike ordered, and walked backward before the cops out the front doors. With the troopers between, Lisa scanned the diner, noticing the frozen patrons hadn't moved but merely watched. Looking again toward the police, Lisa saw Mike give her a shooting and a phone indication, and she emptied the revolver into the pay phone. Setting the empty revolver on the cigarette dispenser, she glanced around before leaving.

"Gentlemen, step to the front of your cars," Mike was ordering as Lisa emerged, and she said, "Mike, get the van."

"I don't want to kill you, but I will if I have to," she said walking toward them and stopped next to the driver's door, standing between their cars. Switching the 9mm to her left hand, she pulled the second revolver, smashed the driver's window, shot the police band radio to junk and then, shot one tire. She then, broke the passenger window on the second trooper's car and repeated the action.

"You know, sooner or later, we'll get you," one officer threatened.

"You don't want to try it. No one is going to stop me from doing what I have to," she said as the van backed up to her and stopped. Opening the back door, Lisa climbed onto the bed, dropped the handgun, picked up the '16 and told Mike to leave. From the corner of her eye, Lisa saw the patrons moving toward the rear of the diner. Moving the selector switch to full automatic, the moment Mike exited the parking lot onto the state road, both troopers dashed for their cars, going for their rifles. She squeezed the trigger, bullets instantly slammed into the nearest squad car, the officer dove over the hood of the far car for additional cover. While racking the trunk area, attempting to destroy the radio transmitter, a tracer round penetrated the gas tank. A deafening explosion violently ripped apart the back portion of the squad car, spilling gas under the second car and onto the front of the diner. The troopers abandoned their plan and dashed away from both cars as the second car exploded, flames engulfing both cars, the intense heat setting the diner on fire.

Ejecting the spent banana clip, Lisa inserted a fresh clip, jacked a round into the chamber, switched the selector to safety and laid the '16 on the bed. Moving to the passenger seat, she felt elated and depressed at the same time.

"That'll be a memorable breakfast," she said dryly, "first time I've ever burnt a diner after eating".

"If it's memorable times you're looking for – you could always join the army! They'd be very forgiving if you returned the weapons and apologized! They're good about that, and they're not really looking for you! He excitedly said.

"Join the army?! Why would I want to do something crazy like that?" she asked, the oddness of the statement almost shocked her.

"Why would you want to do something crazy like that?" he

repeated, and went on, "if you're worried about doing crazy things, maybe you should reflect on your recent activities. Already, you've angered the CIA, pissed off the national guard, upset the state police, secured your own special place on the FBI's most wanted list, and, you're worried about doing something crazy??!! I think you need to put recent events into perspective a little, dear."

"Ah, excuse me, dear, but I'm basically misunderstood by most law enforcement agencies, but that can be easily explained once I have opportunity to calmly discuss things with the proper authorities, and preferably not the CIA. What's crazy, is someone volunteering to jump into the fire with me, and we both are crazy if we stay on this road too much longer. It's a safe bet their angry buddies are on the move toward us," she advised.

"Already working on it. There's a dirt road off this state road which'll cut through the northern portion of the national forest, placing us between Mount Hope and Landersville where we'll pick up 101 north. Then, we'll be an hour south of the Tennessee border," he said, and Lisa noticed Mike failed to address the issue why he was with her. She let the moment pass.

"It's another safe bet the CIA will have Interstate 40 saturated with agents, on the ground and in the air. I suggest we cut across the countryside to avoid the major arteries," she ventured, and went on, "if this isn't part of your old stomping grounds, how is it you seem to know all the dirt roads and where they go?"

"When you're a youngster driving without a license in an unlicensed vehicle with no insurance trying to move around without attracting attention from local police, you stick to dirt roads and creeks. You'd be amazed how far you can travel without using the interstate or main streets. Dirt roads are the least traveled with no traffic lights or cops to stop you, and the scenery is always on the plus side," he explained, and then asked, "exactly where are we going?"

"North," Lisa simply said.

"North is a direction, not a destination," he countered.

"North," was all she offered.

"The North Pole is north," he tried again.

"Then, I won't have to worry about obtaining ice, would I?" she tossed back. Mike smiled and shook his head at his beautiful partner.

CIA HEADQUARTERS, LANGLEY

"Will," Johnathan said to his boss over the intercom, "we have a sighting of Youngblood".

"Where is she?" the director asked.

"Thirty minutes ago, Tanner and Youngblood were in Forkville, Alabama. They destroyed two state police cars, which, when they exploded, ignited a diner where the fugitives had breakfast. The van was last seen heading north on State Road 93," the assistant said.

"Excellent! Flood the area an hour north of Forkville with agents and have Interstate 40 patrolled, east and west from the location north of Forkville. Tell Al Timmer and his partner to board a gunship and be ready to move further north. I sincerely don't believe the fugitives would use the interstate to reach their destination, but there's a slim outside chance they would. With Tanner next to Lisa, our problems have doubled. Tell the gunship pilots, once they have sighted the van, kill both fugitives immediately," Will ordered.

"But they could hit the serum as well," Johnathan observed.

"A fifty-fifty possibility. If they do, then we'll capture the doctor's notes and Lisa. The good doctor was noted for meticulously documenting his procedures and we can gather the additional info from Lisa's corpse. Impress upon the pilots to kill first, ask questions later," Will firmly instructed.

"Yes sir," Johnathan said.

MIKE AND LISA

NORTHERN ALABAMA

Mike had turned onto a dirt road from 93 and skirted the northwestern portion of the national forest attempting to evade the southbound troopers who were aggressively hunting them. The dirt access road, used mostly by forest maintenance crews, was vacant of any traffic. Fears rested on a large margin of safety as most policing agencies rarely traveled the access roads and were only seen when called in.

The flatlands of Alabama was giving way to the rolling rugged hills of southern Tennessee and the fugitives observed the lush verdant undeveloped backwoods of Alabama's northern neighbor. Jagged rock formations jutted from tree studded hills and the timeless beauty of the wooded expanse wasn't lost on Lisa in her flight from certain violent death at the hands of the ruthless and relentless professionally trained killers of the CIA. Lisa felt nature's subtle siren which promised to reveal the mysteries of its lush green meadows almost hidden just past majestic stands of singing pines whose branches motioned for her to stroll amongst the towering evergreens. The exquisite natural beauty of the tree-shrouded secluded areas backed by vertical cliff faces summoned for her curiosity to investigate the seductively shaded ponds where shared love would magically create love anew.

And the memories of Russel came flooding back into her. In times past, when on missions in South America as a soldier-of-fortune, he had viewed many countries whose vegetation was staggeringly breathtaking and he had paused momentarily to appreciate nature's beauty. Once he had felt that he could easily make a home away from the chaos of life, lose himself in the jungle of South America and he'd be perfectly happy. No bosses over him, no one to kill, no special time to be anywhere and no one dictating how he should live his life. Russel had seen nature's splendor on grand scales, but now, nature itself was calling out to Lisa. She could *hear* it. She felt the tenderly woven net nature had cast to ensnare her heart to remain forever within the beauty of its wooded countryside. Shaking her had, Lisa had to break the spell nature had spun especially for her.

"Pilot to co-pilot, are you ok over there?" Mike asked when she shook her head.

"Oh, I was just… it's ah… " she started slowly, and then, "my mind was someplace else for a moment, alright! Don't go getting excited over nothing, will ya! And if I want to trip out for a minute, it's my trip, ya know!" suddenly she verbally jumped at him.

"Aahh, short and sassy, just how I like 'em! Then, I know everything's doin' just fine. You haven't said anything for awhile and I was afraid you were getting melancholy on me over there. Welcome back – hope you had a nice trip," he said with a chuckle.

"Are you like this after every big meal or did the army subject you to some weird psycho training?" she earnestly asked.

"What?!"

"Never mind. You just stay over there and don't get funny," she stated.

"That was a curve ball, wasn't it?" he asked, smirking.

"Don't ever interrupt me again when I'm on a trip or I'll throw you a curve you won't recover from," she threatened.

"Put out your 'gone fishing' sign next time and I won't," he said, and they traded pert smiles.

⊕

The dirt road wound through the dense forest, crossing several creeks, then, exiting the forest, the fugitives wormed their way to State Road 101. They switched from one type of road to another, turning off dirt onto asphalt, off the paved asphalt onto gravel, and then, back to dirt as Mike drove the back roads attempting to by-pass the main thoroughfares.

Both agreed using main arteries increased chances of early capture while traveling back road afforded safer movement as the CIA lacked the manpower to investigate the lesser used roads. If the outlaws encountered lone roaming police patrols, the element of surprise favored the fugitives. Should the agency have one opportunity to focus their resources on the fleeing pair, their flight would rapidly end. Traveling the back roads eased tensions noticeably. Lisa didn't imagine massive road blocks around the next bend nor was her nerves stretched taunt; she relaxed some on the back roads.

As promised, Mike entered the highly maintained 101 between Mount Hope and Landersville, and immediately headed north.

"Both of us needs to be acutely aware of everything that passes us, either on the ground or in the air," Mike stressed.

"Yes sir," Lisa said, saluting him.

"Are you getting cute with me?" he asked.

"Can't because I'm already cute," she said, shrugging her shoulders and laughing at the dual meaning.

"Just keep your eyes open, ok?!" he exasperatingly said.

"No problem," she stated with a big grin. Picking up the binoculars, she scanned the roadway forward. Traffic seemed normal, oncoming vehicles contained average people in average cars pursuing private lives. The sparse combination of trucks and cars allowed the outlaws time to investigate each oncoming vehicle. When the first vehicle approached from the rear, Lisa moved to the custom bed, retrieved the loaded '16 and returned to her passenger seat, prepared. Using average speeds, the occupants overtook and passed the van without incident. Breathing relief as they passed, Mike scanned to the rear while Lisa watched forward.

"You know, they have no sightings of us in this area. So, it doesn't follow that without a sighting, the area would be saturated with agents," Lisa offered.

"Agreed. But nonetheless, keep watching. Now is not the time to get complacent," he warned, and just then, a single engine aircraft passed overhead, following the road northward.

"Uh-oh, if that plane was part of the police patrolling the roads, they'd have visible police markings under the wings. That one has nothing, no markings of any type anywhere," Lisa stated while observing the plane through the binoculars.

"Could be some of your buddies on a chance encounter, what do you think?" he asked.

"Nothing with the CIA is by chance. They react systematically based on logic. They would know how little I removed from the armory and how would they reason... they would know I won't stand and fight. They would enjoy us wasting our limited supply. Not knowing where they are is unsettling, but, I've got a feeling they're around us," she said, rubbing her arms as if cold.

"I haven't seen anything suspicious. In fact, since that aircraft passed, I haven't seen any traffic either. Nothing, coming or going. All of a sudden, I don't like this road," he stated.

"I've got a bad feeling, like we're walking into a trap. Now would be a good time to find a dirt road or a creek to fol... aaaahhhh," was all she said when Mike suddenly turned right, drove down a sloping embankment, crashed through an old wooden gate and proceeded into an overgrown pasture.

"You hard-headed dial-a-brain!! The next time you execute a radical column right, I'd appreciate, at the very least, a one second notice of your intentions!! I almost pissed all over myself, you hear me soldier!!!" she was screaming, baring her teeth and glaring at him.

'If you scream any louder, you're going to decalcify my spine using my ear, and I'd be surprised if half the county doesn't hear you. It'd probably be an excellent idea if you sat down and fastened your seat belt, it's going to get rough," he calmly said to a furious pretty lady with a beet-red face, and he knew she wanted to strangle him.

"Rough is what it'd be if you weren't driving just now!!" she hollered as she sat down and roughly grabbed the seat belt, and added, "when we get out of this trap, I'm driving".

"I don't know if I trust you yet," he said, and she gave him a dirty look.

⊕

The warm afternoon sun saw them cutting across country, following cow trails over hills, driving on dirt roads and in creeks. After three hours, they were north of Town Creek. Prior to reentering the pavement of 101 north, they changed drivers, Mike trying to appease Lisa by allowing her to drive. Continuing northward, the lush vegetation blanketed the rolling hills of the upper state, but the green beauty could hide death, again concealing potential danger around each curve.

"Are you still upset with me for following your wishes so fast?" he asked soothingly.

"Yes! You could have told me what you intended to do. You almost threw me out your window," she stated aggressively while occasionally glancing at rear traffic, and then, she accelerated.

"You see something?" he seriously questioned.

"Maybe. I saw four cars together about a mile back. It's hard to tell because of the hills," she answered.

"Lots of traffic backs up because of the inability to pass on the hills," he offered.

"Maybe. It was just the way they were moving, fast and together. No, it's another bad feeling," she said. Cresting the next hill, she saw an unused staging area once employed by the highway department for storing materials and equipment used in repairing state roads. An entrance road branched off from the pavement in the valley between two hills, an exit road reentered the asphalt at the top of a hill, affording a driver clear view in both directions before pulling onto the state road. The entrance construction road angled upward, ending on a leveled plateau with a small mountain of gravel at the rear end.

Quickly formulating a plan, one second before its execution, Lisa shouted loudly, "hang on," simultaneously turning onto the rough construction road, heading for the gravel hill, the hill large enough to hide the van. Mike had one hand on the roof, the other, trying to hang onto the door while he bounced around. Turning and sliding to a stop, she said, "we're here!"

"Whatta ya mean 'we're here'! Why are we here? I'd appreciate knowing your plans ahead of time to voice approval or dissension accordingly! And just what are we dong?" he demanded.

"I gave you a one second notice as to my intentions, which is a lot more than you gave me," she started, getting out, she ran to open the side doors. Mike got out to face her.

"What happened? Didn't you have your seat belt fastened? Oh, never mind, here, hold out your arms. I've got something for you. You see, if those are the bad guys, here, hold this rocket, well, we'll take 'em by surprise, here, we'll put this one next to the other rocket. But, if it's not the CIA, here's another rocket, then, we'll just repack the van and be on our way, here, you take four and I'll take two. Set 'em next to the pile while I get the binoculars. Isn't payback a bitch sometimes," she jumbled together, leaving Mike confused and mentally trying to catch up. Retrieving the Aerolite binoculars from the van, Lisa returned to Mike at the base of the gravel pile to observe the approaching suspicious vehicles. As the short parade of official-looking cars crested a far hill and began a downward descent, Lisa saw three vehicles with CIA agents and one state police car, second from the end.

"It's them," she said, scanning the parade through the binoculars, and added, "we don't want to kill the troopers – just the CIA".

"How do you propose to not kill the troopers?" he asked.

"We'll give them five seconds to clear the vehicle before destroying it," she answered, and just then, both heard a familiar noise.

"Choppers!" he stated.

"Follow the old rule; divide and conquer," Lisa offered.

"Agreed, and I can't believe how generous you are! Giving those guys five whole seconds," he sarcastically stated as the parade began cresting the hill, all four moving into the kill zone. Pulling a canister to its full length, Mike prepared two rockets for firing with Lisa following suit.

"I'll take the first out, you hit the second. Next, I'll hit the third, you – the fourth. Then, the choppers'll be here," she numbered.

"Agreed. Don't think about the choppers until it's time, it'll distract you," he advised. As the CIA moved downhill, the fugitives shouldered the rockets, aimed, and Mike said, "fire". "Whoosh". "Whoosh". Two rockets leaped into the air, a smoking trail marked their path. The first rockets impacted, a roaring detonation blew the official cars into flaming scrap metal. "Whoosh!" "Whoosh!" The second set was airborne. The last two cars locked brakes and were sliding toward the flaming wreckage when two more rockets leaped from canisters. The troopers reacted instantly, bailing out and rolling, getting away from their car. The remaining agents lacked the troopers' response timing; they died when the last rockets impacted, rendering the four cars to burning scrap metal.

The serene country atmosphere was instantly transformed into a scene of flaming chaos, death and destruction as burning wrecks blocked the roadway. Suddenly, two UH-1, 'Huey' gunships gained altitude from behind the tree-covered hills and menacingly turned toward the fugitives, firing mini-guns as they banked in the turn. Without a word or thinking, Mike and Lisa instantly prepared the last two rockets, aimed and fired at the gunships. Hundreds of rounds swept toward the exposed pair, chewing up the ground as death clawed closer.

Death poured through the six-barreled mini-gun, the guns were rapidly raining steel at maximum velocity. For Lisa, time dragged in slow motion as she saw the ground being chewed up in a path heading toward their position, the deadly rain destroying everything it touched. Flight time for the rockets to impact on targets was two or three seconds, but an eternity passed as she visibly saw the dark rain being spit from flashing barrels. Her eyes followed the dark death as it chewed the ground, destruction's path was turning toward her. The hypnotic effect of earth being rapidly chewed up by an invisible monster not five yards from her held her immobile.

Suddenly, two roaring explosions ended the steel rain, shocked her back into real time and violently ripped apart both choppers. Flaming debris fell from the sky, adding chaos to the carnage already burning on the roadway. Viewing the flaming wreckage, the fugitives heard a third chopper, but couldn't locate its position. Intentionally, the pilot was using the trees for cover, trying to remain safe in a dangerous situation. Viewing through the binoculars, Lisa saw the local news chopper behind the trees.

"It's a local news chopper. It has no externally mounted weapons. Let's go," she directed, picking up two of the spent canisters and placing them in the van.

"The news chopper must have heard the call and followed the gunships, obviously hoping for footage for tonight's telecast. This'll work to our advantage. When we finally go public with the truth, it'll be like a nuclear bomb going off," Mike said.

The blonde outlaw knew the chopper would over-fly the burning carnage to film footage for the evening report and then, they'd see the surviving troopers who would flag them down to again pursue the fleeing fugitives. Lisa knew that, not too far down the road, she'd have to deal with the chopper. After reloading the van, Lisa drove from the staging area. Just before entering 101 from the staging area, both fugitives silently reviewed the flaming battle zone, realizing it easily could have been them on the receiving end.

Continuing north, both were silently wrapped in thought. Lisa knew their position would have been reported, they needed to exit 101 ASAP and find another route. While contemplating their next course of action, Lisa rounded a bend and the massive complex of Wheeler Dam lay before them.

"Take the binoculars and check out the activity on the dam. If you see anything funny, we'll find another route. We can't afford getting trapped on the dam," she instructed. Observing the full length of the mammoth complex, Mike saw large numbers of tourists with children sightseeing the different areas of the ultra-modern facility. Traffic flowed as it slowly moved across the dam, nothing seemed out of the ordinary, but Lisa knew the CIA to be extremely tricky. They'd stoop to anything in accomplishing their goals, even placing children in danger if it meant success. With guns at the ready, they proceeded to cross.

Youngsters played under adult supervision, elderly couples looked and pointed, young lovers sat in the shade of stone gazeboes built especially for tourists while at the dam and middle-aged men explained some function of the dam to their wives as the blue van slowly rolled across. The attendants and guides paid no attention to the van, everyone was too busy with their partners or charges to notice an average van. Nearing the far end of the dam, both fugitives heard the rotors of the chopper approaching. Rolling even with the security guards' station, looking in the windows, both saw the guards communicating with someone on a radio. Assuming the guards were in contact with the chopper, Mike pointed the '16 at dam security while Lisa covered them with her 9mm. Looking up from the radio, the guards stared at the grim faces of two armed outlaws as they rolled past the checkpoint. Quickly moving to the rear, Mike opened the door and pointed the '16 at the emerging guards to dissuade any attempt at stopping the van. Recognizing Tanner, the guards realized they'd have no chance against an alert, armed and dangerous Green Beret.

Upon leaving the dam complex, traffic picked up speed immediately. Away from the cleared area of Wheeler Dam, the heavy vegetation and forest grew unchecked, providing ample coverage for the fugitives to hide. The news chopper necessarily needed to be directly overhead to keep the van in sight. Mike and Lisa knew they had to down the chopper, but the feelings were different. It wasn't the CIA shooting at them. It wasn't an armed police chopper. It was an unarmed civilian chopper, loaded with civilians. "When are we going to shoot it down?" Mike asked. No excitement filled his voice, he didn't seem to be thrilled knowing what had to happen and actually, he was slightly depressed knowing they had to down the civilians. Lisa was driving long stretches under tree limbs which had grown across the road, making the road invisible from the air. In between the long stretches, open areas appeared where the chopper caught view of the van before it again disappeared under the tree cover. After the third time running through an open area, Lisa stopped at the next open space, got out, ran around to the side door, grabbed a rocket and moved forward to the open area, but stayed under the trees.

"Here's where we'll get 'em," she stated.

"I'll do it," Mike offered.

"No you won't either. We just want to down the chopper, not kill everyone onboard," she firmly said, and Mike knew no argument would change her mind. Hearing the bird cautiously approaching the open area, Lisa moved forward of her cover, activating the rocket as she stepped. Looking up, she saw the rotor blades spinning over the trees. The pilot was hesitating before moving into the treeless area. Not having time on their side, Lisa launched the rocket into the outermost edge of the turning blades. One second later, an explosion damaged the blades which would force the light chopper to land. The experienced pilot turned the chopper one hundred and eighty degrees which provided a slight lift only for a few moments, but that short time afforded him opportunity to pick his crash site.

Running along the treeline and onto a rocky outcrop, Lisa watched the landing. Looking across a deep gorge, she saw another clearing where the pilot elected to land. The experienced pilot demonstrated his skills in bringing the disabled craft to a hard landing, harming no one in the process. Lisa saw the occupants hurriedly disembarking the damaged bird at a quarter mile distance.

"We have to go, Lisa. Even though they're down, those troopers are using their radios," Mike softly said as he gently took the spent canister from her.

"Yeah," she whispered, and after a few moments, she turned to follow Mike. She should have been elated that no one was injured, but Lisa was depressed. Not wanting Mike to know how she felt, she perked up. Mike slid behind the wheel and they continued on 101 for another five miles before leaving the road south of Elgin. Traveling across the countryside, they crossed into Tennessee using cow trails, dirt roads and creeks until they were south of Loretto, Tenn.

The small town of Loretto was located on State Road 43 and both fugitives decided Mike would walk the short distance into town, buy take-out dinners while Lisa waited nearby in the van. Afterward, they'd move north of town and into the hills where they might spend the night. Without any trouble, Mike found a fast food stand, bought two dinners to go and returned. They ate a relaxed meal and then, pushed on to find someplace for the night.

The day had waned with both fugitives tiring from the emotional strain of constantly pushing forward, constantly unaware of the dangers lurking behind every bush around every curve in the road. Darkness offered no promise of solitude from the relentless hunt by the aggressive agency that pressured them to continuously move to avoid capture. Lisa knew Mike was unaware of the agency's ability to not only inflict direct pressure on an individual, but also apply indirect pressure, forcing one to act when physical presence was absent. Knowing the agency was responsible for past actions and future attacks, pressed one mentally to maintain the one step ahead advantage or else, failure meant death. She knew the federal agency was adamant concerning recovery of the serum and her, and now, desperation for recovery at any cost was becoming obvious. Lisa feared for Mike's life as he was inexperienced with their ruthlessness and deception. Having had no dealings with the CIA on any level, he was learning of their treachery from experiences on-the-job.

She wondered if this similar reason produced the depression within; her having to shoot down someone she respected, and now, someone she loved might be killed because of her actions. Lisa didn't want the responsibility deciding who lived and who died, forcing some to die so that others could live.

Those types of decisions shouldn't have been thrust upon her simply because of a kidnapping for an unthinkable experiment by a mad doctor. Lisa concluded the agency's lunacy exceeded that of the doctor's but, what astonished her more, it was a United States Federal Agency which was going crazy. The situation wasn't happening in some third word country, it was in progress in the most advanced country in the world. The situation was bizarre by anyone's standards, and to make matters worse, it promised to get crazier before it was over. For her, it had an insane beginning, forcing her to go along with insanity as if it were a normal route, just to get by to maintain her own sanity. Lisa reminded herself that she was normal, the agency was crazy. Then, she remembered how 'normal' she really was. Shaking her head in her hand, Lisa knew only to keep going.

"Pilot to co-pilot, how're you doing over there?" Mike asked with a smile, and Lisa started laughing and crying.

"I'm going nuts over here, but I'm trying to do it quietly so as not to disturb those seriously questioning or assessing their own stability," she barely got out between fits of laughter.

"Now I respect you for that. That's thoroughly considerate of you to quietly go nuts and have presence of mind not to bother anyone in the process. I'm humbled by your consideration of other people's feelings and I feel ashamed to ask if you would take time from your profound thinking to perform a menial daily task with me," he said, the solemnness of the proposal stilled Lisa momentarily.

"And what would this daily task be, sir?" she properly asked.

"Would you… bathe with me… in yonder creek?" Mike proposed.

Lisa howled with laughter, held her sides and barely said, "yes," between the tears of euphoric happiness and tears of dismal depression. Mike, kind enough to say nothing more, allowed Lisa time to vent her emotions. Realizing she had endured tremendous amounts of harassment, the levels of which he could only guess, but would never ask, the question would force her to relive painful experiences. Knowing no way existed to relieve her pain, he sought to soften the experiences through love. Mike was in love with this girl, he wanted to do everything perfectly right by her. He already fantasized waking up to her every morning as her husband, their beautiful children surrounding them. She was the perfect lady, bold, daring and dangerous. Mike was excited about Lisa and he carefully avoided offending her.

Mentally strong with towering confidence, to offend her, one only needed to ask the wrong question. Asking about her participation within the agency pushed her off button.

He could question the agency's motives, practices, operations, anything associated with the department, but the subject of her involvement was taboo, if he wished to remain her lover. Not asking would be smart and wise, and he knew it.

He had left the state road, followed a dirt lane heading toward a tree-shrouded mountain, scouting for a night camp. From the lane, he saw trees congested in two separate lines which seemed to stretch for miles, he knew a creek ran between the trees. Turning toward the mountain, he followed hunters' tracks across a field to a stand of trees. The tire tracks led to an old campsite nestled among numerous trees naturally and spaciously set apart from each other. In stories he'd read, the old campsite setting was referred to as 'hobo jungle'.

Mike realized he could not express his feelings, now was inappropriate. Lisa, already, subtly objected to his accompanying her, assuming his death would result from his inexperience with the agency. He acknowledged his lack of experience with the agency, but, he had received elite training from America's best to challenge any contender, and he hungered to prove himself. Regardless that it was the CIA, he was a Green Beret, his training ranked him superior, and he ached to prove it.

Mike never expected the relationship to grow so fast, but then, he never dreamt of meeting a woman such as Lisa. Her abilities, determination and aggressiveness to accomplish a singular goal set her apart from all other women. To him, Lisa was the epitome of womanhood – all the desired qualities selected from many women formed into one individual, and she was his lover. He knew not to say anything concerning his feelings toward her, his proclaimed love might distract her at a crucial moment, the hesitation then promoting her death.

"M' lady," he said after parking near the flowing stream and upon opening her door.

"You're too kind sir. I'm afraid you're going to spoil me," she said, responding to his chivalry.

"Ah, me heart doth d'sire to spoil such a lovely young lass all t' days of her exquisite life. I be yore slave 'till eternity deem it proper to separate so powerful a love no two people on earth should share. A love known only to t' immortal gods and they be jealous o' two mortals sharin' a combined heart o' pure and innocent love, an innocent love so sweet to rival t' nectar made by eternal bees," the shining knight said while taking Lisa's hand, leading her to the stream and beginning to undress her at the water's edge. And he went on, "m' lady, common sense doth fail me in t' light of thy shining youthful beauty, but boldness replaces all seeing time besets us while we steal precious moments f' ourselves. And now," he said removing her top, "I display to t' envy of all nature, t' wonderful creation of Zeus, but I fear, he hath wrought a wonder to stand by his side as his queen. With boldness only doth this dastardly fellow dare to place defiled hands on t' pureness of a queen to cleanse away t' day's filth," he elegantly stated, his hands and spread fingers intentionally dragging over her hardening nipples.

"If the gallant knight should stop, the queen would have him flogged with a cat-o'-nine-tails or her fury might include the Catherine Wheel, such as her sadistic pleasure would dictate," Lisa breathed heavily as her emotions followed his hands.

"Stop! I say thee nay! Ever would my hands, and yes! Even my mouth, would compliment thy beauty, thy charm, in a feeble attempt to satisfy m' lady forever and ever again," he recited as he led her into the water after each had undressed the other. Lisa was experiencing light orgasms anticipating Mike's advances, and he went on, "m' lady, reline thyself here and allow they knight to wash away t' day's toil and troubles," he said, helping her to lay down and, with his hand, he pushed water over the length of her leg, starting at her feet, he pushed and caressed toward her inner thigh. "M' lady - , " he started.

"Mike, shut up and kiss me, you bastard!" she said with a husky voice, and she grabbed him.

⊕

Their lovemaking started in the creek, moved to the custom bed and finally, Mike threw blankets outside, making a bed under the stars for the night. He intentionally prolonged their sexual activity to wear Lisa out, intending later to call Dion without her knowledge.

An hour and a half later, by her deep slow breathing, Mike knew she was sound asleep. Retrieving both handguns, he placed both under the pillows as he silently stole around. Leaving her under the covers, the Green Beret stealthily moved to and entered the van, plugged in the bullet and softly said, "Dion, can you hear me?"

"Yeah man, I'm right here, Fill me in and don't leave out the juicy parts," he said, and Mike could tell Dion had been awakened to take the call.

"Ok, here's what happened today… " and he replayed the day's events supplemented by his own impressions, ending with their frolicking in the creek and van.

"You can't possibly guess how much I'd give to be in your boots right now, Mike! You've got to be the luckiest bastard in the world! You know, Stranton called an old war buddy in the White House and some of them on the hill are noticing funny activity happening at the CIA. People are noticing the results of your actions, you and your lady's that is," Dion informed.

"The White House??" Mike incredulously said.

"Yeah man, you and your lady are rocking the power boat. The Chief hasn't noticed yet, but it won't be long before he starts asking questions. With you two downing that news chopper, you could safely bet your family jewels he'll find out now," Dion related.

"Yeah man, it's just that I was too busy trying to stay alive to give it any thought," Mike slowly said as the import of Dion's words sank in, and then he said, "I'd better get back to her".

"Yeah, give her a big and long kiss you know where from me," Dion suggested.

"Ok, see ya," Mike answered, and the last words he heard from Dion were 'lucky bastard' as he pulled the earpiece. Tucking the bullet in the door pouch, he reflected on the events associated to his actions. The seriousness of the situation, of all parties now involved and those becoming so, began impacting on his awareness. Moving from the van and returning to the outside bed, sleep eluded him for hours. Finally, he dozed off.

CIA HEADQUARTERS, LANGLEY

A stone-faced assistant walked into his boss' office with devastating news.

"What is it, John?" Will asked, looking up from paperwork.

"Something we never anticipated. The aerial and ground force, which was to kill Tanner and Youngblood, were both wiped out to a man without inflicting any harm on the fugitives, and they're still at large," Johnathan ominously stated.

"Damn!" Will angrily stated, slamming his fist on the desk.

"And there's more. A local television news chopper was following the gunships attempting to get footage on a story for the evening news when the fugitives destroyed both units. The news chopper was later shot down, injuring no one onboard."

"A strategy move. Wipe out both strike forces and leave the news to report it," Will analyzed.

"The state troopers accompanying the agents were not killed in the attack. It seems the fugitives allowed them seconds to abandon their vehicle before destroying it," John reported.

"So, they're partial to state troopers. Ok, have the back up force in Florence, Alabama start moving north and get on State Road 43 to search. Order a spy plane to use heat-seeking equipment to search unoccupied areas. Have State Road 101 searched. I don't think they'll stay on it, but that's a base we need to cover. Have half the units on Interstate 40 begin converging and searching Wayne, Lawrence and Giles counties in Tennessee. We need to start pressing those two to continuously move. Flush them from hiding places, keep them moving, wear them out, and in the process – nail 'em. I'm moving up to the area to personally direct the capture. With them downing the news chopper, it'll be in the papers and on the evening news. We need to effect capture immediately. Johnathan, if you want something done right, do it yourself. I'll be directing the operations from there and we'll be talking every day," the director said while gathering papers together he planned to take with him.

"Sir, do you think it wise, going there yourself?" John asked.

"The impact of my personal presence will spur everyone into action. You'll be surprised how fast we'll catch those two once I'm on the scene. We need to bring this fiasco to an end before anyone finds out what we're up to," Will stated.

"Should we send agents to the area north of Wheeler Dam?" John questioned.

"No, the news chopper was downed there and the fugitives would have left the road north of that. Look at the map, John, and pick a place where you'd think they'd go – I'd be doing the same thing. Use logic to extrapolate an approximation. That's the best either of us could do since we have no idea where she's going, except that she is moving northward. Send another memo to Nashville and Memphis concerning the fugitives' possible activities in their area, and if you'll excuse me, I've got to be running," Will said as he picked up an attache case and left.

THE WHITE HOUSE

President Threadmiller had watched the news reports on television and something bothered him about the accounts. In the Oval Office, he questioned his staff about the reports.

"Marsha, contact Channel 12 in Alabama and ask how the two choppers were shot down by the fugitives. Their news report neglected to specify exactly how they were downed. Something about that case isn't fitting together right. At the last press conference, questions were asked if we knew anything about the Youngblood problem. Find out what you can. If the press corp. asked once, then, they'll be asking again. I don't like being caught off guard. Get Barney to work on it also", the President directed her. Marsha Benning, chief-of-staff, was formerly an investigative reporter who still maintained contacts within news media offices and those knowing her jumped at the chance to assist her simply because she was next to the 'man' in Washington.

"Yes sir, and you have a meeting with the Security Council in five minutes and after that, Speaker Hall wants to discuss the new Gun Bill with you," Marsha said.

"All I get is five minutes for coffee," he noticed.

"It'll work if you only have half a cup, sir, that way you actually cut your caffeine intake by half and you'll be able to sleep tonight," Marsha advised.

"Add caffeine to the list, Marsha," the President said.

"List, sir?" she asked.

"Yes, everyone is concerned about my calorie intake, cholesterol level, sodium build-up and carbohydrates. Add caffeine to the list, ok?" he said.

"Yes sir," she acknowledged.

CIA FIELD OFFICE, FLORENCE, ALABAMA

EARLY EVENING

Director Will Summers moved into the CIA Florence Office to personally direct the on-going operation. Agents searching the southern Tennessee area secured information concerning Mike Tanner's appearance at a fast food store, and that, he was walking. Search areas were established, search teams dispatched. After sunset, teams with heat sensor indicators were dispatched to search areas where heat sources should be non-existent. Rolling hills sprinkled with farms and one minor subdivision lay to the north of Loretto. The aggressive search was pressed into the wee hours of the morning with the upper echelon hoping to catch the outlaws sleeping.

At two-thirty am on the 14th, a three-man team located residual heat traces near a stream where no residence existed. Leaving their cars a mile from the suspected site, the agents quietly moved into the area using hand signals to minimize noise.

As the trio neared a mountain with a stream at its base, they observed a van within a stand of trees and, apparently, the fugitives were bedded down for the night outside the vehicle. Using hand signals, they backed away from the area to verbally discuss the situation.

"Why don't we just kill 'em and be done with it?" one asked.

"If we take them alive, it'll look a lot better for us than having several bodies, unless you'd rather stay in Florence, Alabama," the leader said, emphasizing the state name, and then added, "if we take 'em alive, we'll have a chance of relocating our jobs to Washington, D.C., because the director himself is overseeing this operation which indicates its importance. Those two are sound asleep, why kill when we don't have to?" he asked his subordinates.

"Ok, let's do it," the third man said.

"Use hand signals and take 'em quietly," the leader said, and the government team moved out.

JUNE 14TH

MIKE AND LISA

(EARLY MORNING, 3:30AM)

She saw them coming in her dream. Three hooded Ninjas, skillfully crawling on the ground, hiding behind trees, silently jumping over minor boulders and noiselessly sidestepping twigs as they approached the slumbering lovers. They materialized out of a night mist which covered the ground, and their appearance didn't strike her as odd. Mike slept on his back, unaware of the trio, and Lisa was on her side – watching them. Slowly, her hand pulled the 9mm from under the pillow and held it under the covers.

She knew they came to kill or capture, but what baffled her, they knew she was watching their every move, and yet, they continued the approach. Lisa could only see their eyes through the slits in the hoods, the black Ninja outfit covered the entire body. She felt an aura of evil about them. Two swords were strapped to their backs, the handles protruding above and to either side of their heads, she knew those swords to be incredibly sharp. Throwing knives were in their belts, knives in the boots, and when they were twenty feet from the outlaws, Lisa quickly pushed herself up, threw the covers back, leveled the weapon and rapidly fired three shots. At the first report, Mike's eyes popped open to see Lisa firing at a target beyond him with her eyes closed and nude. After the third round, he turned to see the target. Three figures were slumped to the ground, and the sight shocked him. Looking at Lisa, she was blinking her eyes and looking around, that told him, she killed in her sleep.

"You awake now?" he asked.

"Yeah," she answered in a small voice.

"I'll check it out," he said, pulling a gun from under the pillow. All three agents were dead, Mike returned to Lisa. Still on her knees, Mike knelt in front of her, hugged her and said, "they're dead. You killed them in your sleep, honey."

"They appeared as Ninjas in my dream and I knew I had to kill them before they got us," she tried to explain.

The warmth of her body was exciting him to arousal, and Mike knew they had to leave immediately because the agents would have called in before moving in themselves. Letting his hand slide down her back to caress her butt, he said, "we have to leave right now, baby. The cavalry won't be far behind and they're already moving," squeezing her posterior, he kissed her.

"Ok," she said weakly.

"Dress quickly, and let's move," he ordered helping her up, and as he grabbed his clothes, they heard a chopper approaching in the distance. Mike scooped up the blankets, threw them in the back door while Lisa finished dressing and moved to the van.

"They're coming," he shouted at her from the driver's side and both fugitives jumped in the van at the same moment. Starting the van, driving across the creek and up the mountainside. Mike inwardly chided himself for not being the one to kill the approaching agents. He was the Green Beret who was trained for such occasions and it should have been him protecting her. He felt belittled because she diverted the attack, neutralizing the agents. He chided himself again for not being tuned into the fight, but then, it was

Lisa's fight from the beginning. Lisa. When he first left his buddies, he knew he had to run to stay alive. He knew he had to trust a nationally known fugitive just to stay alive, but he never expected to fall in love with her.

Cresting the tree-studded mountain summit, both fugitives saw the low flying chopper using a searchlight to sweep the stand of trees they had slept in. Stopping the van in a clearing from which he could see down the mountainside, Mike saw the spotlight sweep over the three prone figures near the tree stand. Then, the chopper began to move forward, continuing the search. He knew what they were doing. He would have done the same. Relentlessly pressing the quarry into motion, attempting a capture through attrition. He also knew that behind the chopper would be more agents to maintain pressure. He knew it. He practiced the same tactic while on maneuvers, and he knew how to avoid the pressure, break contact and drop from sight. If the pursuing element had nothing to focus on, they couldn't apply pressure. And drop from sight – he would. Then, he would savor stolen moments with Lisa. Everything about her appealed to him; her attitude, her unpretentious intelligence, her humor, her mannerisms, her drop-dead gorgeous body –

"Stop!" Lisa ordered, and instantly, Mike's foot slammed the brakes on. Stunned immobile, Mike was wondering if Lisa read his mind and had ordered his train of thought halted. With no explanation, Lisa bolted from the van and ran to the rear. Looking through the trees, she evaluated the chances of hitting the chopper. Watching the spotlight swing back and forth on the mountainside, she estimated the chances would be slim. If she attempted to, the telltale smoke trail from the rocket would pinpoint their location. Running back to the van and jumping in, she told Mike to leave. She explained as he was leaving what she hoped to accomplish. Luckily for the fugitives, the density of the leaves hid the brake lights.

Driving over the crest of the mountaintop using no headlights, Mike hastened to put distance between them and the pursuers. While the chopper searched for them, he dared not use the headlights. For the first time since owning the van, Mike was glad the van was painted blue. With no interior lights on, Mike used his night vision and the moonlight to drive by on the hunters' trail. The trail was made by hunters coming and going. The dirt tire tracks was easy to follow and sometimes, draining water from a storm had cut one side deeper than the other. In some places, the going was slow and they could still hear the chopper looking for them.

Following the downhill grade, Mike broke the silence, "Lisa, how do you know to shoot rockets, load and operate '16's and 9mm's?" he asked.

"I read the instructions. Isn't that why the military put the instructions on the boxes?" she innocently responded.

"Damn considerate of the military, isn't it?!" he stated.

"The military has instructors to teach the new recruits how to operate the different types of weapons, but criminals like me need to read the instructions," she offered as they had descended from the mountain and were nearing the range base. Nearing the mountain base, they entered onto a long unused gravel road. Tall weeds grew on the unused road but no trees. Driving through the tall weeds, Mike got the impression that someone was allowing nature to take over the road but only so far. As they continued on, Lisa saw a minor road suddenly appear, parallel the gravel road and disappear as fast as it appeared.

Driving on, weeds and now minor trees grew more abundantly in the road forcing Mike to dodge the short trees. After veering around three substantial pines, Mike had to stop as the lay of the land fell into a gorge. Sliding to a stop, both got out to inspect the forward area.

"There used to be a bridge here," Mike said looking at the remnants of a two hundred and fifty-foot wooden bridge that had become dilapidated over time, portions had rotted and fallen into a generously flowing wide stream. "We'll have to find another way," he added.

"Wait a minute! Half a mile back there was a side road paralleling this one. It wasn't much but if someone wanted to preserve this area from the public but still have access, logically, they wouldn't repair the old bridge allowing ruin to set in which would in turn lead others to think that the road is no longer passable because the bridge is out. If that was the case, then the responsible people would have another way in. Let's backtrack on the side road to see where it leads us," she reasoned.

"Sounds logical! Let's find out," Mike agreed, both returning to the van and backtracked. Half a mile away, Mike saw what Lisa was referring to. "That would hardly pass for a road, dear. That's what most would call 'hunters' tracks'," he stressed.

"Well dear! Let's see where the 'hunters' tracks' lead us and just maybe, they'll lead us to a main road while it's still dark," she shot back.

"The things I have to put up with," he groaned.

"I'll drive if it's too much for you," she quipped.

"Oh no you don't! I still remember the last time you drove – damn near drove me crazy!" he stated.

"At least, it'd have been a short drive," Lisa said grinning, Mike giving her an askance look with a tight smile, and he turned easterly onto the hunters' tracks. The tracks angled downward into the gorge, passing under the old bridge while not surprising either fugitive that no debris blocked the road and a mile past the bridge, the road disappeared into the stream. Looking across the stream, both could barely see the light tan hunters' tracks on the opposite bank. Assuming the 'road' cut straight across, Lisa jumped out, started crossing the stream to ascertain water depth, Mike following in the van. The water was a foot and a half deep the entire width which afforded easy passage. Lisa surmised that whoever wanted to preserve the wilderness area had also found or built the crossing. The opposite tracks ended on another heavily used gravel road, and traveling at high speeds, the fleeing fugitives discussed the possibilities of being discovered within the next hour on the road as opposed to 4-wheeling off-road. Both agreed progress was a definite plus on the roads, Lisa pointed out that once sighted on the roads, the CIA would move in quickly after their recent losses. Mike stated that the infrequency of their appearances on the different roadways kept the policing agencies guessing and off-balance. And they continued arguing while speeding down the road.

The sun had risen and the weather report promised a mild day with no rain in the forecast. The gravel road intersected with paved State Road 242, which would pass through Gaitherville.

"Would you like to have breakfast in Gaitherville?" Lisa delicately asked.

"You've got to be kidding!! Every coffee shop, diner, donut shop or restaurant in the state probably will have cops lurking about in massive numbers since you burnt the diner in Forkville. I wouldn't be surprised if every place that serves breakfast in Tennessee is under surveillance, waiting for us to show. Either we skip the breakfast idea and wait for lunch or stop at some hole-in-the-wall where we can see clear through to the back from the front," Mike suggested.

"Hey, I was only thinking of Mister Growing Army Man who hasn't eaten since yesterday morning. If you don't feel like stopping somewhere, fine. We could always patronize a drive-thru. That way we don't have to get out of the vehicle and you'd feel all kinds of safe," she said sarcastically.

"Do you usually get sarcastic when you're hungry?" he seriously asked.

"Who me? I was offering alternative suggestions. For instance, if you want, the next cornfield you see, we could stop and graze a little. That way, we wouldn't have to stop in town at all, and you still get a nutritious meal! Mmmoooo," she said with heavier sarcasm, and then, started laughing while Mike just shook his head, smirking.

CIA FIELD OFFICE, FLORENCE, ALABAMA

"Director Summers, incoming reports," the Florence Police radio dispatcher stated, and went on, "three field agents are reported killed. The chopper is continuing the search.

"What area are they searching?" the director quietly asked, reflecting sorrow upon hearing the loss.

"They are in the wilderness between Loretto and Westpoint. A follow-up team located the remains radioed to them by the chopper," the dispatcher said.

After studying the map, the director said, "I'm moving up to Lawrenceburg. That pair is still moving northward, presumably to Interstate 40, which will lead to Nashville or Memphis. Two major cities and where would they go?" he spoke the question out loud to no one, and went on, "my money would be on Nashville. Either way, they must be stopped. Contact the agents moving southward from I-40 and have them meet me at the Lawrenceburg Police Department for a briefing. Order them to change into police uniforms.

I'll secure police cars upon arrival for an operation to apprehend the fugitives. Order two Cobra gunships to land at the police station or nearby somewhere. I'll call Langley from there," he instructed and then, left.

THE WHITE HOUSE OVAL OFFICE MEETING

"Ok ladies and gentlemen, what do we have today?" the President asked, addressing his staff.

"The NRA wants to meet with you when you can set aside thirty minutes," Chief-of-Staff Marsha Benning started, "The security council needs your signature on the revised pollution bill. You're having lunch with Senator Armbruster. Ambassador Jennings has returned from Peru and wishes fifteen minutes to brief you on conditions there which he feels might affect our industrial relations and the staff has conflicting reports on the Youngblood incident."

"Nobody gets thirty minutes of my time. I don't even get thirty minutes of my time. Cut the NRA's time to fifteen minutes and schedule the rest accordingly. Now, let's hear what you have on the Youngblood incident, Barney," the President said while sitting down, speaking to a resourceful computer wiz who had the unusual ability to ferret out facts on any given subject.

"The police in northern Alabama said they only lost one police cruiser which was destroyed. The two troopers bailed out moments before the car was blown up," Barney stated.

"Blown up with what?" the President asked.

"With LAW's rockets, which also destroyed the helicopters," Barney said.

"Wasn't Youngblood the one who - ," the President began, trying to remember a report he had heard.

"Who broke into the National Guard armory in Jackson, Mississippi – yes sir, and the report I've compiled gets worse as it progresses," Barney finished and advised.

"Wait a minute. The police say they only lost a car and no personnel. Did anyone actually die in the... incident, or is this some smoke screen?" the Chief asked.

"Yes sir, there were personnel that died, but they weren't police, they were CIA," Barney said.

"Uh-oh, ok Barney, start and don't stop until the report has been delivered. Already, I don't like what I've heard."

"Yes sir," the wiz told of known facts of the doctor's murder, van theft, and break-in and the association concerning Mike Tanner.

"Barney, you know as much as computers tell you. The computers aren't stating why a trained Green Beret, with no past record, would side with a known fugitive. Computers aren't revealing why the CIA is attempting to avenge themselves over a simple murder. With the CIA, some incidents are never as simple as they let on, but keep digging," he said to Barney, and to Marsha, the President instructed, "tell Director Summers, I want a meeting today or tomorrow, as my schedule allows and I want to discuss the Youngblood incident. Have Barney inform him of what we have and I expect him to fill in the blanks. Ok, let's break. Who am I seeing next?"

"The Security Council just needs a signature. I figured we'd have an easy morning today," Marsha said.

"When you throw the CIA ingredient into the mix, complications abound and nothing comes out easy," the Chief said.

"It's not going to be that bad, sir," Marsha said, and the President merely looked at her.

"I hope so."

⊕

Two CIA agents had been listening to the Oval Office meeting on their closed-band radio receivers. Earlier in the week when Marsha was at the White House, they had quietly entered her apartment and placed a 'bug' inside five of her favorite pieces of jewelry, jewelry that she wore while working. Today, she was wearing a cameo brooch and the agents were listening. They had listened to the meeting after the press conference and heard the instructions issued to Barney.

Rick Fender, a neatly trimmed dishwater-blond junior agent, analyzed the problem and concluded by saying, "the project will be exposed now that the press corp is asking questions".

His partner, Brad Jeffers, a neatly trimmed dark-haired agent, disagreed, "not exactly. If the director can capture the fugitives, the rest can be explained away."

"We should inform the President of the entire project and seek immunity from prosecution," the taller blond agent said.

"And when the director, in fact captures Tanner and Youngblood, what will be your answer then?" Brad asked.

"Too many people have already died for this project. No more," Rick insisted.

"People like you frighten at the first sign of trouble. Don't say anything until we hear from the director. This is why you've been yanked out of the field and put into a cushy job, because you frighten too easily," Brad sneered.

"You have your agenda and I have mine. I'm going to inform the President because of the death toll of this project. This project will kill no one else," Rick promised.

"No, that's not what's going to happen," Brad sternly stated, and when Rick saw the hatred in Brad's eyes, both went for their guns simultaneously. Firing at each other at point-blank range, both were determined to stop the other. After eleven rounds were exchanged, both agents slumped dead to the floor.

LAWRENCEBURG POLICE DEPARTMENT

"Ok everyone," Police Captain Buford Randolph was instructing his department concerning the movements and possible avenues of travel through his county, "the fugitives' last known position was in Loretto. Chances are great those two aren't suffering from senility which would cause them to continue traveling on Highway 43, however, just in case we could be mistaken, one squad car will proceed south on 43 to confirm our suspicions. More than likely, they've cut across country to intersect with another main road. The mountainous terrain will force them, sooner or later, to use main thoroughfares, which when they do, we'll be waiting. You'll find, when you pick up your assignment sheets, that everyone not in the search patterns, will be designated an intersection to watch. If you should sight the fugitives, do not, and I'm going to repeat myself, Do Not under any circumstances engage the fugitives. From all indications, they are heavily armed and not the least bit afraid to use lethal force on you people. They've done it before and they'll probably do it again. I don't want you people getting killed because of something I didn't say. We need to locate them, call in and everybody rolls on the call.

Needless to say, when we locate the fugitives, if they bless our county with their presence, we'll probably have one helluva fight on our hands. Don't anybody think you can take 'em out by yourselves. You've seen the reports, don't chance it. The unit that sights the van, alert central and shadow at a distance, being careful not to get too close. Again people, these two are beyond being lethally dangerous, they've already killed quite a few people and it won't bother 'em to add additional notches. Now, there's... " the police captain suddenly stopped as he caught sight of Director Summers walking in with fifteen agents behind dressed in police uniforms.

"Police Captain Buford Randolph," the director started, "I'd like to requisition a number of cars from your motor pool, if I could. There's two fugitives moving, I believe, through this area and we'd like to apprehend them, any assistance from you would be appreciated. Naturally, once we've captured them, you may take the credit, if you wish."

"Well, of course, Director Summers, if that what brings you to our fair county, you may have whatever vehicles you need," Buford said over-graciously, and then, "I'd like to talk with you privately while Bobby here," he indicated to a staff member, "will assign cars to your people. This way, sir," Buford showed Summers into his office, and the director remained quiet, allowing the captain time to have his say.

"Ok, here's how I see it. You've lost a bunch of your people trying to nail those two criminals, and in the process, you've noticed how the fugitives allowed troopers to escape because, for some reason, the fugitives aren't holding grudges against policemen, only against the CIA. And now you come in here all dressed up like policemen thinking to confuse those outlaws long enough to capture 'em without getting yourself or too many of your people killed. What gets me about some of you Washington bureaucrats is that some of you let on that these country bumpkins can't get the job done properly, so you exalt yourself by coming down here to take over. Mister, I've got some pretty good men out there that could easily capture your fugitives while you lounged in your air-conditioned offices.

"Which brings me to an all-important question: why are you in the field instead of letting local law enforcement agencies catch that pair?" Buford sincerely asked the point-blank question.

"Captain, from time to time, I supervise field operations that are in-progress. It just happens that this one coincides with capturing two known fugitives," Will diplomatically stated.

"Bullshit! You obviously take us to be nothing more than idiots. You're after Lisa Youngblood because of a reported murder in New Orleans, the break-in of the guard armory, the shooting down of three choppers, the destruction of seven cars and burning a diner. Not to mention the number of your people killed. Mike Tanner is a Green Beret, army. The CIA is attacking the army who is protecting a known fugitive. A very interesting picture which leaves me asking one question: what do they have that the CIA is willing to throw away so much in the attempt to recover?" Buford asked.

"It's classified," the director simply said.

"Well, of course it is! It's either 'classified' or it's secret because of 'national security!' Those are the two catch-all phrases you use when you don't want to answer a question," Buford answered sarcastically, and then added, "you can have as many cars as you need, but you're taking the lead and we'll back you up. If those two decide to launch any rockets, you'll deal with 'em."

"I wouldn't have it any other way, sir," Will said respectfully.

"Let's see if the troops are ready," Buford said, eyeing his new partner with mistrust. Walking out of the office, Buford saw an agent give the director a slight nod. Buford then issued final instruction, "everyone in my group, the CIA is going to take the lead and we'll back 'em up. Juan and Patty will follow Bobby and Carrol west on 64 toward Waynesboro. Juan and Patty will fork off south on Natchez Trace Parkway to Woodlawn, and then, to 242 heading north to Westpoint. If no sighting, continue north to 64 and link-up with an intersection unit.

Bobby and Carrol will go to Waynesboro and take 13 south to

Collinwood. Then, get on Natchez Trace Parkway heading north, picking up 241 heading southeast back to 64.

Tom, take Ben with you up 43 and get over to Barnesville, and then, south on 99 to Waynesboro. The rest of us are going up 242 to Henryville, we'll split three directions from there. We're crisscrossing, doubling back and retracing our search area. I don't think the fugitives are still in the county, but if they are, we want them. Remember, do not engage them. Call in, report their position and everyone rolls on the call," Buford was saying, but the noise from landing choppers drowned him out.

"I'll be in one of the Cobra's directing from the air," Summers said.

The enlarged contingent of law enforcement officers excitedly moved toward their vehicles, each wondering if they'd be lucky to spot the fleeing pair, and their hopes soared for a capture. Approximately fifty vehicles departed the station with two choppers lifting off as the last car pulled out. In its essence – the plan was simple: scour all the county roads for the fugitives.

Three hours into the search, three quarters of all county roads had been scoured with no reports of the fleeing duo. The police radio continuously reported status results transmitted by various units as assigned areas were thoroughly searched. As the crisscrossing units continued their normal speed search, the main body was approaching Henryville, and as various units completed their assigned sectors, they fell in line with the main body.

The day was bright and sunny with a warm breeze blowing puffy white clouds across a blue sky. Before the main body neared the desired city, their numbers swelled and stretched over a mile long. Everyone knew that if they spotted the fugitives, the fugitives didn't stand a chance with so many officers in pursuit, and their hopes soared with the clouds.

MIKE AND LISA

The fleeing pair chanced a quick meal at a fast food drive-thru. Lisa wanted a light meal, Mike ordered three burgers, large fries, two apple turnovers and a coke to go. Lisa drove while Mike wolfed down everything. They finally decided to travel cross-country, eliminating the possibility of contact with the law. Lisa proved herself in four-wheeling across cow pastures, along deer trails, creeks, overcoming every obstacle that threatened to impede their progress. Lisa felt at ease driving across country enjoying the lush verdant scenery that lacked human population, thus increasing its beauty.

The hours slipped by as the fugitives slowly made their way northward, the hard way. Mike had said he knew better roads not too far to the north of their position, and once on those roads, the traveling would be faster with no police contacts. Lisa surmised that he was obliquely referring to his old stomping grounds. She wanted a faster route, but at the same time, she wanted to avoid entanglements with the law. Somehow, when Mike talked of better northern roads, he also instilled a confidence by the way he said it. She needed him in many ways, and in ways she'd never say aloud. Deeply, she appreciated his aggressive and selfish nature, it thoughtlessly satisfied its own desire while solving a number of her problems. Problems she now knew she couldn't have solved on her own. Mike was the perfectly right man at exactly the right place at precisely the right time. Had it been anyone else, more harm than good would have occurred. Was it destiny?, she wondered while driving. Was life predestined or did happenstance inadvertently shape destiny?! Was it chance, that the right man happened along who owned the required vehicle for the situation?! If the entire incident was predestined, it seemed incalculable that destiny would result from happenstance occurrences. Or was destiny merely a word conveniently used in answering the question – why.

"Co-pilot to pilot, how are we doing over there?" he asked.

"Hey, I'm working on something," she shot back, and then, with a devilish grin, looking at Mike, she said. "I've got a better idea – since I'm busy driving, and we don't seem to be killing anyone at the moment, I want you to figure out something for me. That way I can devote my full attention to driving."

"Ok, I'll bite. What is it?" he gingerly ventured, and he knew he was being baited.

"How does chance accidents or happenstance incidents influence predestiny? How do accidental incidents result in destiny? Can I have an answer in fifteen minutes, essay or otherwise? Thank you," she said smugly.

"Are you serious, or is this a curve ball?" he seriously asked.

"I'm serious. That's what I was thinking about when you so rudely interrupted me. For instance, if the conclusion of an event is termed 'destiny', the actions preceding it are accidental in essence, then how are the accidents relative to destiny? One might say that the conclusion would have happened anyway, regardless of the events leading to it. If the end of a matter is considered destiny, is one progression of events irrelevant to the end, because if it didn't happen one way, it would have occurred another, with either set of events resulting at the predestined end?" she sincerely asked.

"A penny for your thoughts is serious underpayment," he said dryly, and he added, "if I ever interrupt your train of thought again, please, slap me back to my senses. I'll consider it a backhanded compliment."

"No, think about it! If the end is considered destiny, and the events prior are accidental, how would you term the relationship if you knew the events prior to the end could be modified into another set with the same end?" she earnestly asked.

"I've just given it all the consideration it's due," he sarcastically said, Lisa looked at him and stuck out her tongue.

"Was that destiny, or an emotional event?" Mike asked.

"That's a response, smart-ass!" she jabbed, realizing Mike didn't want to be drawn into an intellectual discussion.

Approaching an asphalt road, Mike said, "we're coming up on 240, just outside of Henryville. We need to go north and just outside of the city, we'll swing west to an area I know will safely move us further on our way."

Looking both ways before pulling onto the road, Lisa asked, "see any bad guys anywhere?"

Quickly scanning both directions, noticing everything seemed normal, Mike said, "no, the coast is clear". Moving onto the roadway and accelerating to cruising speeds, Lisa was quick to notice approaching traffic on the divided highway and vehicles overtaking from the rear were suspected of containing CIA people. Her eyes darted from one vehicle to the next, scrutinizing the occupants for possible danger. Her fears expected a car to approach from the rear, fully loaded with heavily armed CIA men and they'd be grinning as they pulled alongside the van. No threat materialized enroute the five miles to Henryville. Knowing two main roads were to intersect inside the city limits, the fugitives viewed normal traffic flowing and nothing appeared as odd.

"Maybe everybody thinks we're someplace else," Lisa speculated.

"Yeah, maybe, but I wouldn't bet on it. Another minute here and we'll get a look down road 242 to see if anything is jumping," he said, and as they drove through the intersection, where 242 dead-ended into 240, both outlaws looked down 242 and saw a mile long line of police cars moving in their direction, and red and blue lights started flashing along the line.

"Uh-oh, there they all are! Well, at least we don't have to worry about *where* they are, now we know. All-of-a-sudden, I feel a lot better knowing where they are," Lisa said as she accelerated the van.

HUEY COBRA GUNSHIP

"Hendricks, this is Cobra One. Have the fugitives sighted at the intersection of State Roads 240 and 242," Summers announced to his agent leading the line of police cars that stretched a mile behind him.

"What's the plan?" Hendricks asked.

"Allow them to leave town and we'll close in for the kill. No sense in getting anyone killed in the city," Summers outlined.

"Roger that."

MIKE AND LISA

"Ah, excuse me, but I don't share in the same sense of security knowing there's a mile long line of police cars coming after me. Maybe, I mean, obviously, I was brought up differently than you which would put things into opposing perspective and, and, I hate changing subjects so fast, and I don't mean to nag or be a back seat driver - " he was saying.

"Will you please – get to the point, or is there a point to your babbling!!" she screamed.

"There a cop behind the sign near the red light you're about to run, dear," he calmly said.

"Well, pardon me, dear, but I'm in a hurry and I'm running that light safely, if it's any consolation. And that cop'll just hafta understand," she said sharply.

"Obviously, he didn't take his understanding pills today because here he comes," Mike observed.

"Well, don't just sit there with your teeth in your head, get back there and shoot his engine out. Or did you want to change horses in the middle of the stream and me do it? And try not to kill the cop in the process, we don't have any grudges against cops today," she loudly said.

"After I shoot his engine out, you won't be able to convince him of that," he said while moving to the rear, and muttering to himself, he said, "only one stop light in the whole town and she runs it. Naturally, and as a matter of course, there's a cop waiting for some sucker to do something wrong."

"You're muttering! Are you going to mutter when you get old?" she asked.

"Being around you I won't have to worry about getting old," he retorted. While negotiating through traffic, in the rearview outside mirror, she saw red lights come on. She then, heard Mike open the back door, followed by the roar of an automatic '16. Checking the passenger outside mirror, she saw the police cruiser veer off the road, smash through a fruit stand sending people running in all directions before finally plunging into a ditch.

"Good shooting," she complimented.

"One down and the rest are beginning to slide around the corner back there and the worse news is, there's two fully armed Cobras hanging in the distance. It's a safe bet they're waiting until we're out of town before taking us out," he guessed.

"Staying in town would be suicide, and running isn't much better, but it's the only avenue available," she verbally analyzed.

"Agreed. See? Our communication is getting better," he said, and Lisa just gave him an exasperated look. Both looked forward and half a mile beyond city limits was the Henryville Bridge, an old steel structure that spanned six hundred feet across a deep rocky gorge with a wide generously flowing stream that noisily splashed over rocks. Seeing the rusting bridge, a plan immediately clicked into Lisa's mind. Instantly, she checked the road layout beyond the bridge and the distance between the van and the police. The road past the bridge turned left and angled slightly upward, a viewing area peeled off before the road turned right and disappeared over a hill. Accelerating more, she raced across the bridge and using the inside lane to keep momentum up, she slid around the curve riding the brakes to negotiate the turn and maintain high speed.

"Andretti would be proud to be married to you, or you could drive for him maybe! That was beautiful, hair raising, but beautiful nonetheless!" Mike said sarcastically.

"I've got a plan!" she excitedly said.

"Is getting killed part of the plan? Please, keep in mind that this is not a Formula One Car, it's just a humble van, dear," Mike pleaded.

"Not with that custom bed, it's not so humble, buster," she said as she slid into the viewing area. Jumping out, she shouted, "grab two rockets, hurry," and then, Mike stepped through the van, picking up the rockets as Lisa opened the side door, grabbing one rocket and activating it on the run. Stopping near the edge of the viewing area, she aimed it at the steel support footer across the gorge and fired. The rocket's three second noisy flight exploded at the base of the steel leg, shattering the steel foot and concrete reinforced base support. The entire leg dropped two feet until the unaffected leg portion landed on the concrete base.

Mike launched his rocket to detonate five feet above the base area and the bridge groaned under the offset weight.

"Fall you bastard," she shouted, and then, Lisa grabbed the last rocket and launched it at the leg on their side of the gorge. The violent explosion so weakened the bridge that it slowly began to irreversibly fall, steel supports loudly groaning as they buckled, wooden planks noisily splintering apart as collapse was inevitable. Not waiting to see the end, both fugitives quickly picked up the empty canisters and ran for the van. As they were leaving, the thunder of concrete, twisting steel girders and splintering timbers resounded with a deafening roar as the bridge crashed into the deep gorge.

Gathering like angered bees, the police swarmed at the yawning chasm where the old bridge had proudly stood for a century, and the police saw the blue van roof disappear over a hill. Just then, both Cobras flew low over the destroyed bridge and everyone knew the burden of stopping the two dangerous outlaws rode on their stubby wings.

"Don't worry, Agent One," the director was saying to his lead agent, "we're going to fight fire with fire. We'll get 'em," and both choppers took up the chase.

Again, Mike and Lisa were passing under tree cover and running through open areas in their continuing flight. Periodically, Lisa stopped, turned off the motor to ascertain the attacking birds' position before moving. They were playing cat and mouse and suddenly, the cat was tiring of the game. Rockets started impacting in the covered areas, areas in which the pilots couldn't see the road. In the areas where small clumps of trees blocked viewing the road, the pilots fired a healthy burst from the mini-guns.

"We're gonna have to contend with the Cobras before leaving the tree cover," Mike announced as she angled the outside mirror skyward.

"No kidding!! I thought I'd have to tell you that!! You're getting better!!" she threw at him.

"I thought you were sarcastic only when you were hungry. What's happening to you?" he asked as a rocket exploded seventy-five yards to their rear and both ducked.

"Conditions are warranting that we do something, and preferably quick," she stated.

"Pull the van off the road about seventy yards and let's watch a few of their passes. They don't know where we are yet, so we can use that to our advantage," he instructed. Turning a right angle away from the road, Lisa stopped almost a hundred yards away. Both got out and worked their way back to the road to watch the Cobras. From behind a full-grown tree that grew hard against a boulder, Mike watched the Cobras work.

"Notice how the one Cobra covers the attacking bird. If I were to launch a rocket at the attacking Cobra, the one covering would see the smoke trail and instantly attack the obvious area with mini-guns and rockets. The Cobra making the firing runs is the sacrificial bird. The sacrificial bird is here to be sacrificed in order to kill us," he analyzed.

"That's a cold move. Whoever ordered that maneuver has ice

instead of a heart," Lisa said.

"Yeah, they're out to get us at any cost. We can't sit and wait. Time is on their side," Mike said.

"We gonna down both of 'em?" She asked.

"Not necessary. Notice the crisp moves the covering chopper makes as he follows the other's flight path. Watch when the attacking bird is near the end of his run, right now. Did you see how both were facing away from us for fifteen seconds. The covering pilot correctly followed through after the first made his pass. The attacking pilot, after the pass, should have banked hard left, taking him away from our suspected area. Instead, he just pulled up with a soft left bank turn. The pilots in the sacrificial bird are inexperienced and that's why they are leading the attack. They're here just to draw us out and set us up for the kill. The covering pilots are combat veterans. They've done this sort of thing before. If we just knock down the experienced ones, the other bird will attack wildly, hoping for a lucky hit. Stay put and I'll get a rocket to hit Mr. Experience up there," he said and dashed for the van before she could respond. Retrieving a rocket from the van, Mike knew where the birds were from the impacting rockets and mini-gun fire. Arriving back at the boulder next to Lisa, Mike was winded and sweating. "Let's move parallel with them and move further away from the van," he instructed.

"Why?" she asked as they started running.

"Because we don't want us between them and the van. When we knock down one, the other will shoot in our direction and beyond. We don't want the van in a straight line with them and us. We desperately need the van, and especially, right now," he explained.

"They're turning back this direction," Lisa observed.

"It's ok. There must be an open road area devoid of cover. They didn't see us pass through, so they know we're here somewhere. Their firing pattern will be wider to encompass more of the off-road areas. We need to find something substantial to hide behind. A fallen tree won't work. Follow me quickly, there's a tree with a thick trunk just ahead," he shouted as the Cobras' mini-guns were chewing a wide swath parallel to the road, working toward the fugitives and swinging left and right resembling a drunkard's path. Mike and Lisa had just jumped behind the large old tree when he saw incoming rockets.

"DOWN!" he shouted, and he pushed her down and covered her. The roaring explosion shook the ground from fifteen yards away blowing dirt, dust, small rocks and tree bits into the air which then, rained down upon the fugitives.

"He's starting to get serious!" Lisa yelled over the din of the choppers, mini-gun firing and exploding rockets.

"He's still shooting blindly. When I tell you to run, run back to the boulder with the tree growing next to it," Mike instructed, and he was watching the covering chopper as it hovered in position, acting as rear guard for the attacking bird. As the attacking chopper passed his hiding place, Mike began counting the seconds. With the hovering Cobra still turning to protect the stern of the passing bird, Mike knew he'd have only nine seconds before the Cobra broke hover and moved. Activating the rocket by extending the canister to its full length, Mike sighted in the Cobra. He couldn't fire while the Cobra's nose was aimed at them because the pilot would instantly fire the nose-mounted mini-guns. With a clear avenue of fire, Mike watched the nose turn to follow the stern of the attacking chopper. When the Cobra showed its broadside, Mike squeezed the trigger.

As the rocket was enroute, Mike noticed that horror registered on the rear crewman's turned face. Seeing the inbound rocket, the crewman realized his imminent death with only a moment's warning. The rocket impacted at midship, instantly killing both flight personnel. The deafening explosion brought the CIA Director and his dreams of a CIA Nation, complete with military, to a burning ruin. Watching the flaming wreckage fall from the blue sky, Mike knew the agency dispatched their best against him, and it wasn't good enough.

"RUN!" he shouted over the tumult. Lisa scrambled to her feet and dashed back toward their first position. Hot on her heels. Mike saw mini-gun fire chewing through the dense foliage and arcing toward them. Mike could envision the bird turning in the air while firing his mini-gun as the maximum setting of five thousand rounds a second, desperately attempting to destroy the entire area and everything in it. He leaped into the air, grabbed Lisa and both landed behind the boulder as rounds cut the tree in half, ricocheted off the boulder and continued in arcing away from them.

"LET'S GO! HEAD FOR THE VAN!" he shouted again and both raced away from the boulder as the tree was falling, rockets detonating thirty yards from them and the mini-guns were cutting the forest down, down to ground level. Mike knew the potential of mini-guns at maximum settings; a selected forest area would be reduced to mulch in a few minutes. Breathing hard when they reached the van, Lisa started laughing while grabbing Mike. Releasing the insanity of the moment through laughter, both laughed and hugged each other while tears rolled down her face.

"It's ok, honey," he said while stroking her cheek, pushing hair back and kissing her.

"Yeah, I'm so glad you're ok," she said between kisses.

"We'd better get out of here 'cause that pilot's gonna rip this place apart," he suggested, kissing her tear-stained lips.

"Yeah," was all she could say as she caressed the side of his face.

"I'll drive 'cause I know where another dirt road is that'll take us away from the inexperienced nut in the air," he said as his eyes held hers.

"Ok, let's go," she whispered.

Rolling further into the woods, Mike angled the van to the left and headed down a gentle slope. As they eased down the tree-studded hill, the sharp clap of impacting rockets softened with distance and then, ended. At the base of the hill, Mike turned onto an unmaintained dirt access road which followed beneath power lines, taking them away from Henryville. He drove the dirt road until it intersected with a gravel road. He then left the dirt and followed the gravel.

Kicking up a dust rooster tail, they traveled for miles before turning right onto a farm's dirt access road. The road lay between miles and miles of plowed and planted fields. Even though early in the season, Lisa saw tender green shoots poking through the furrowed brown dirt. Looking in all directions, the miles of fields gave the impression that it was one huge farm. Mike had traveled fifteen minutes on the dirt access road and when Lisa was about to question him concerning the farm size, he turned left into a flowing creek. Saving the question for later, she allowed him time and space to concentrate on negotiating the creek.

Glancing to her right, in the distance, she saw four rocky 'fingers' protruding from a mountain range. Each rocky 'finger' extended nearly a mile from the range with tree-filled valleys and no attempt was make to reclaim the land for cultivation. Just visible over the embankment of the creek to one side, she saw cultivated pastureland, to the other was forest. As Mike continued driving in the flowing water, they were moving deeper into the trees. Far in the distance, Lisa saw a main paved thoroughfare with traffic moving along.

But with Mike driving the van on farmland, Lisa felt secure as their direction promised to lead deeper into the forest. All of a sudden, it struck Lisa odd concerning the relative smoothness of the creek.

"Am I imagining things or is this creek unusually leveled and free of obstructions?" she asked.

"You're right, and that's because it's part of a road system," he answered.

"Road system?! Why would a farmer concern himself with clearing a creek when he only needs to use the land paralleling the creek? Most farmers use that land for implement movement to different pastures or as access roads. Usually, land near creeks is not cultivated because of threatened washouts from storms and they could also be used as dump areas," she presented.

"You'll see," he said as he exited the creek onto a well-traveled dirt road that angled upward. The sudden appearance of the road surprised Lisa because it seemed to originate from the creek.

"Where'd this road come from?" she asked, awestruck.

"You'll see," he answered again.

"I wish you'd stop saying that and answer the question," she pouted and then, she saw the trees from the inside. The normal full-grown trees were dwarfed by gigantic trees intentionally planted in two rows; one row on each side of the road they were on. They were traveling under a double canopy of trees and then, she looked down from the sight of the trees to see an old town.

"It's a hollow!!" she excitedly said.

"You pronounce it as a visitor would," he said, smiling as he enjoyed her amazement and fascination. By the way she tried to take everything in at once, he knew she has only heard the word 'hollow' but never had opportunity to see artists' conceptions of how one would possible appear.

"How do you pronounce it?" she asked, still looking around.

"Holler," he said.

"Wow!" was all she said, and just then, a vehicle rounded a building, turned and entered the road heading into 'town'. Lisa knew if any policeman in the world had seen that vehicle on public highways, they'd immediately seize it, impound it and haul it off to be crushed out of existence. It consisted of a frame, power train and wheels. One-inch oak planks were fastened to the frame, the driver had a rigid chair bolted to the planks, the shotgun rider had an easy chair that reclined. Behind them, a couch was fastened down with another couch near the rear. The 'car' was packed with eight people and everyone was holding onto their hats. They waved at Mike as they rolled by, and at first, Lisa stared and then, started laughing.

Lisa saw no streetlights, signs, crosswalks nor markings of any kind, and everyone merely moved aside as the vehicle approached. Mike slowly rolled along what appeared to be the main street, allowing Lisa opportunity to look at both sides of the street. The buildings, devoid of paint, seemed as if they were transplanted from the early 1800's. The exterior of every building lacked the luster of fresh paint, the dull gray appearance promoting an image of shabbiness. Peering inside one structure, the lively interior was brightly painted with a rainbow of colors.

A boardwalk extended from the first building and continued down the long street, fronting shops as well as homes. No neon signs advertised a business was in operation nor was any painted sign visible anywhere. The smooth dirt street wound around the massive trees and ended under the boardwalk, no grass or weeks grew in the roadway. It was the neatest dirt road she'd ever seen.

Barefoot kids ran and played it the street, young lovers strolled along the boardwalk, old folks sat on the porches in rocking chairs and waved as Mike rolled along. Lisa returned the gestures. A knot of little boys and girls, with bare dusty feet, ran by the van, waving at Lisa and it was obvious, the bib overalls and dresses they wore – was all they had on. Several old men were walking the boardwalk when the knot of kids ran screaming by, followed by a pack of barking dogs and it appeared the old men never noticed either. It seemed to Lisa that the street was used more by pedestrians, animals and wagons than by autos, or renditions of automobiles.

Mike slowly rolled to the left side of the street and stopped under an overhead cover.

"Gas station," Mike said, and she saw two antique pumps whose red exterior paint was a memory a hundred years ago and their operational status was questionable. The pumps were under an overhead cover that appeared solid but needed paint or minor repairs when the pump's red exterior became a memory.

"I need ice," Lisa said with an urgency.

"You'll find some inside, this is more of a general store than a full fledged gas station," he said.

"I don't know if I'd call it either. Is it safe to go in there by myself?" she asked.

"Honey, you're safe anywhere in the holler. I'll gas the van," he said.

"If you say so, and ok," she stated. Getting out, she then moved to the front door. While Mike drank in her sensuous walking movements, his left hand was on the bullet. When Lisa entered the store, he plugged in the power source while setting the bullet on the van roof. He knew where an ice machine was and approximately how long she would take. Since no urgency pressed them, she would empty the bag, diligently pack it with fresh ice before she was ready for departure, and that time span allowed him opportunity to get a message to Dion.

"Dion, can you hear me?" he asked after quickly setting up.

"Yeah Mike, hear you fine. Give it to me, buddy", Dion said.

"I've got a few minutes – Lisa's getting ice. Listen up..." and Mike replayed the day's events, concluding with his present location," we're in my old stomping grounds – you know where – and we're still moving north. In three or four hours, we'll be in Kentucky."

"Do you have the full kit with the bullet?" Marshall asked.

"You mean the remote mike and ear piece? Yeah, I've got that. Why do you ask?" Mike questioned. "It might come in handy if you need to get away from the van and still be in touch. Hear this, both the Senate and House members stopped discussions on legislation and bills to take a short vacation, and the majority has left town," Dion related.

"Then, they've noticed how nervous or crazy the CIA is getting and decided to leave town until things settle down," Mike guessed.

"That's how we're seein' it," Dion admitted.

"Then, the Chief'll be asking questions pretty quick," Mike ventured.

"Things'll be coming to a head before too much longer, I suppose," Dion guessed.

"I'd better go for now. Call you after she goes to sleep," Mike said.

"I'm jealous," Dion swooned.

"Bye," Mike said, signing off and had just enough time to remove the bullet from the roof before an old timer walked up to the driver's side window.

"Wull, if 'in ain' Mike Tannah! Whur yo' bin got to boh? H'ain't see'd yo', mus' a-be goin' ohn two y'ars now," the old guy said.

"Howdy Jess. How've you been?" he asked, instantly recognizing the old man.

"Betta 'dan a setta wit' a burd in 'ees jows. Whur yo' bin?" Jess asked again.

"Oh, I joined the army and have been moving around with them for the last couple of years," he answered, and then asked, "how's

Emma?"

"Same's ev'a. Whot's dis trubba you's an' dis gurlie in?" Jess asked.

"You mean, that girl?" Mike asked, pointing at Lisa as she emerged from the general store.

"Dat's hur," he affirmed.

"Jess, it's a complex situation and it's not over yet," Mike said, trying to avoid a lengthy discussion.

"Ah figgerd it'd a-bin somethin' estinooatin", Jess said as Mike was getting out of the van.

"We stopped in for gas and ice, and we'll probably have to take off pretty quick because trouble isn't too far behind," Mike said.

"Is yo' t'inkin' dem rev'noors kno'd 'bout dis place?" the old guy asked.

"I don't know, but if they ask the sheriff, he'll have to show 'em or he'll get into trouble," Mike answered.

"Hi! I've replenished the ice, and I'm ready to leave any time you are," Lisa said after walking up to the two men.

"Lisa, this is Jess Hawkins. Jess, Lisa Youngblood," Mike said.

"Hidee Leza," Jess said, tipping his hat.

"Hi Jess," she responded.

"If 'in y'ont, ah'll gas da van fo' ya w'iles ua sho'd t' li'l ladah 'roun'," Jess offered.

"That's be sweet of you, Jess," Lisa remarked.

"Remember Jess, I've got two tanks on here," Mike cautioned.

"Ah's a-born at nite, but not las' nite, Mika," Jess chided and Lisa stifled laughter as Mike gently steered her onto the boardwalk.

"Obviously, you've noticed the lack of paint on the buildings…" Mike started.

"Among other things, like the thickness of the roofs, the lack of any signs, street, neon or otherwise, no telephone poles or aerial wires, no streetlights and for all the trees – the street is relatively clear of limbs…" she started.

"Ok, I get the picture, we'll take it one thing at a time," he said, and she was grinning ear-to-ear.

"During the fall, when all leaves have fallen off the trees, people passing on the interstate notice the dense wooden area and no more. If the holler folk were to paint the buildings, passing motorists might see the paint through the trees, become curious and stop to investigate. As it is, the buildings' dull gray exterior blends in with the trees, and the motorists never think something might be here. It's the old adage, 'out of sight – out of mind'. Even with no leaves on the trees, the roofs blend in under the double canopy of tree limbs, and the roof layers consist of fallen limbs. The holler was long ago designed to be invisible from the interstate and the air. Planes flying overhead must be cautious of the rocky fingers and hills beyond. While flying, they're concerned with things that directly affect flight. This town is so close to the fingers, they're more interested in flying into the valleys between the fingers and then, gaining altitude to hop over the mountain range. We've seen lots of planes flying toward the fingers, but they're not looking for us, only for the sport of catching a thermal updraft to hop the mountains," he explained.

"What about the middle of winter, wouldn't passing motorists see a flicker of light through the trees?" she asked as they were approaching an intersection.

"No. Long ago, a wall of evergreen trees were planted the length of the holler, between the houses and the interstate. So, from the roadway, all you would see is trees, evergreens and snow. From any angle, no lights'll shine through," he replied.

"Hidee Mika, h'ain't see'd yo' in 'wile. Whur yo' bin?" the owner of a corner vegetable stand asked as the fugitives stopped by while they talked.

"Hi Lizzy, joined the army. How's business?"

"H'ain't chan'. Ya kno'd whin yo' po'ed oht to' crik t' 'hole holler kno'd in 'bout minute, if 'in ya ketchin' mah drif'", the stout Lizzy said. Mike had been holding Lisa's hand as they walked, but when they stopped in front of the stand to speak to the owner, Mike slid his arm around her waist.

"Mmmm, these vegetables look delicious, and did Lizzy mean that one of your holler gals might show up?" Lisa lightheartedly asked.

"Possible."

"Did one of 'em catch you on Sadie Hawkins Day?" she asked – trying not to laugh.

"Sweetheart, you've been reading way too much of Al Capp! You've go too reach out to reality," he threw at her and Lisa burst into fits of laughter. As they left the vegetable stand and stepped into the street, three elderly men approached from across the intersection. Before the two groups met, a ten year old boy wearing bib overalls, ragged at the cuffs and proudly sporting a tattered straw hat, obviously inherited from his father, ran up to Lisa and asked, "st'open?" (phonetic pronunciation long o)

Feeling like an alien uttered something to her, she said, "yeah honey, right," and the happy youngster giggled and ran off.

"Wh... what did he just ask me that I said yes to?" she stammered to Mike.

"He asked 'is the store open?' He knows it's open, he just wanted to say something to you," he clarified.

"He crammed an entire sentence into one word?" she asked, still stunned.

"Actually, he combined two words and inferred the rest. You'll get used to it," Mike said.

"Thanks for the vote of confidence, and given enough time..." she was saying when the old men interrupted her.

"Hidee Mika. Yo' bin gon' 'wile. Whut brangs ya here?" the old timer asked.

"Hi Crandall. First, I'd like you to meet Lisa Youngblood. Lisa, this is Crandall Jenkins," Mike said.

"Liza, we'in's hear'd bout ya. Soory ta say, it weren't nuttin' good," Crandall admitted.

"Crandall, the bad guys are feeding lies to the news people and they are reporting it nationwide. We've got something they desperately want and they'll do anything to get it back, and no, I didn't kill that doctor in New Orleans," she said.

"I know Lisa is telling you the truth," Mike affirmed to the three men, "because I've seen what she's got and if she was lying,

I wouldn't be here with her. The problem is, the CIA wants me killed because I know what she's carrying."

"C-ah-A?" another of the men questioned.

"Rev'noors, Timmah," Crandall said and Timmy Jenkins' eyes lit up.

"Is yo' figgern dey's still b'hin ya?" Timmy asked.

"We had a little trouble with them over near Henryville, but they couldn't have followed us, not with the route I took," Mike said.

"We'in's gonna chick ohn it an' fine out. Com' ohn bohs," Crandall directed and all three men walked a little faster toward the general store.

"Let's head back to the van for now. Crandall will start making calls to the holler people who live in town and work in key positions. He'll touch bases with them to learn what the law's doing," Mike stated.

"Key positions?" she questioned.

"Yeah, like supermarket owner, the sheriff, a real estate office, newspaper editor and so on. People in the right place who do different things for the holler without arousing anyone else's suspicions," he explained, and while he talked, hollerfolk nonchalantly started showing up. Acting as if they were going to the general store, once they saw Mike and Lisa, they had to stop and talk.

"How's da' armah, Mika?" a young boy asked.

"It's ok, but you rarely have chance to go home when you want. It's a full time job that keeps you busy," he answered.

"Is ya'll stayin' hyar fo' a'wile, Mika?" a teenage girl asked.

"I don't know, Tess, I guess that depends on what Crandall finds out," Mike said, and he was looking at Lisa when it struck him as a good idea.

"I don't know either, Mike," she said, considering it a possibility and then asked, "would the CIA know of this place?"

"T' onla outsid'as dat bin hyar wus t' rev'noors back in t' thurdies," Crandall stated, answering Lisa's question after he exited the general store. And he went on, "ovah at Henervull, t' 'hol police deepartment is hotter den a otomic reac'shun. Did yo' chillurn blo'd up t' Henrvull Bridge?" Crandall asked.

"Yes sir, we did," Lisa began, "we had to stop the bad guys that were chasing us. That was the only way we could think of on the spur-of-the-moment. Crandall, I stole a classified secret from the CIA which describes an illegal project they're working on. After we go public with it, either we kill the agents or the President will execute 'em. Either way, their future is extremely dark at this point," she explained.

"Pappy," Timmy said, coming up behind his father after leaving the store, "dem rev'noors is searchin' t' wuuds ovah nee'a Henervull fo' Mika and Leza. Deys dearchin' nort' o' whur t' bridge usta bin. Ah's calt all t' folks 'long t' way hyar an' dey's not seen no blue van. Dey kno'd it bin Mika an' t' holler'll prete'k 'em."

"Whul, Mika, yo' an' chile cun stay at Homer Barnes place, if 'in y'ont. He's a working' t' still, ya kno' whur, Mika," Crandall offered.

"Sounds good to me," Mike said looking at Lisa for her answer.

"Sounds good to me too," she said.

"Ok, we'll stash the van in his shed and Crandall, pass the word around about us," Mike directed.

"Mika's bin gone too long," Crandall was saying to his son, Timmy, "hee's t'inkin' we don' unnerstan' t' sitcheeashun."

"Tis a sad day in t' holler whin t' chillurn t'ink dey kno'd mo'e den t' elderfolk," Timmy said.

"Let's head on down to Homer Barnes' place, honey," Mike said to Lisa, and to Jess, he said, "thanks for gassing the van, Jess."

"No trubba, Mika. See's ya 'round," the old timer answered as Mike and Lisa hopped into the van. As Mike was pulling away from the store, Lisa noticed that everyone was smiling, and she couldn't help but smile back. Mike slowly rolled along, giving Lisa opportunity to look in every direction. She noticed the boardwalk surrounding the business district, and beyond that, dirt streets met front yards. The grass in the yards appeared to be eaten than cut, and a well-worn path meandered through yards that were devoid of fences. The only fences she saw, kept livestock penned up. The homes were well spaced and the lack of paint presented a shabby picture, but she knew appearance were deceiving. People waved at each other across yards, children played while moving down a street and dogs tagged along. The hollerfolk were routinely pursing everyday life while enjoying their continuing privacy from world scrutiny.

In the van, while Lisa looked in all directions, she said, "I have every intention of taking a bath a Homer Barnes' home. I know I've already had a dirt shower, but somehow I don't *feel* clean," she stressed to Mike, and he just smiled.

I'll set up the bath 'cause we both need one. I'd take you to a place in the stream where we used to bathe but all the young boys know of it and they'd be in the bushes watching," he said.

"I hear the voice of experience talking," she said with a knowing smile.

"That's just part of holler life, honey. Where that wagon is pulling out from is where we're we turn to head for the Barnes place." It was a stripped car frame with wheels. Two-inch thick planks were bolted to the frame, front to back, one bench seat was forward and the remainder of the level wagon was used for hauling odds and ends. Lazily moving along, the young couple driving appeared in no hurry while three kids played in the back. As the horse-drawn wagon cleared the intersection, Mike turned right, backtracking on the wagon tracks.

"Homer Barnes won't mind if we stay at his place. I've done it many times before, but what would really tighten his jib is if we left his place a mess," Mike said.

"Don't tell me he's a neat freak," Lisa challenged.

"No honey, he's not that bad. To Homer, everything has its place and where he put it, that's where he wants it," Mike specified.

"Well, I hope he excuses me for moving his coffee pot, and I hope he doesn't get his dander up because I ate off his fork," Lisa pouted.

'Dander? Where'd that come from?" he asked bewildered.

"From the same place as 'jib'," Lisa stated, and Mike laughed at her, shaking his head.

"Here's his place now," he said, pointing at a large cabin with a wrap-around porch.

"Ni-i-ice," she said, admiring the finish work on the log siding. The cabin was set back from the road about twenty-five feet and neatly trimmed scrubs lined the front. On the porch were four rockers and a hanging swing. The single-story cabin had a fireplace centered in the dwelling which threw heat in all directions. Pulling in the rock drive near one end of the porch, Mike explained part of Homer's life.

"Homer learned how to make 'shine from his father and as a young boy, Homer used to run 'shine'. Homer's grandfather built the still back in the late 1700's. Makin' moonshine runs in family. And now, he's teaching his nephews how to make good 'shine'," Mike said as they were getting out of the van.

"The 1700's? Mike, you're talking about the time we were established as a nation!" Lisa said in disbelief.

"Honey, you know when refugees come here from other countries, not all of them come of their own accord. Some are sent. Meaning, some countries dump their criminals on our shores. It's not a new practice. Not too long after the Mayflower landed the pilgrims on Plymouth Rock, England decided to empty their prisons on our new shores. The ships which followed the Mayflower's course encountered severe weather and were blown off course by five hundred nautical miles. They landed on what now is known as Cape Hatteras, North Carolina. Homer Barnes' great-grandfather was on one of those ships. Homer Barnes is a hundred and thirty-five years old. His father was a hundred and forty-seven years old when he died and the records before that are sketchy. We know his great-grandfather, Hezekiah Barnes, was a prisoner from England," Mike explained and seeing Lisa near shock, he helped her into the cabin.

"What accounts for their longevity? Is it genetics?" she asked while absorbing a holler revelation.

"Back then, I can't answer for. Now, I know that all the food they eat is naturally grown. There's no additives nor chemicals introduced into the soil to enhance production or quality. Hollerfolk actively participate in soil preparation prior to planting, during planting and at harvest time. Everyone has a healthy attitude and they eat healthy food. You'll find quite a few people well over a hundred years old. Crandall is a hundred and twenty-five. His son, Timmy, is a hundred and nine. That's the way it is here," he was saying.

"Wow! There's so much to learn about this place! Let's take a bath and then, a walk around," she suggested.

"Sounds like a plan," Mike agreed.

MISSISSIPPI NATIONAL GUARD ARMORY

"Sir! Specialist third class Dion Marshall requesting to speak with the brigadier general, Sir!" Dion properly announced while standing at rigid attention in front of the brigadier's desk.

Looking up over his reading glasses while still holding several reports he had been absorbing, the Green Beret brigadier general said, "granted". Laying the reports down, taking off his glasses while not taking his eyes off the soldier, the general proceeded, "and what would the nature of our discussion be?" he questioned.

"A three-day leave, Sir!" Dion announced.

"In the middle of a coordinating exercise with the guard and with a man down, you want a three-day leave?!" the general asked, standing up and slowly walking around his desk while Dion stood rigidly in place.

"Yes sir!" he said with eyes still focused on the same spot on the wall he had been staring at since arriving at the general's desk.

"And would this leave have anything to do with Mike Tanner," the brigadier questioned and his voice lowered, heavy with analysis rather than for privacy.

"Roughly, yes sir!" Dion properly responded, still staring straight forward.

"And would you know *where* Mr. Tanner is?" the general asked, folding his arms across his chest.

"Roughly, yes sir! Precisely, no sir!" Dion said.

"And with every law enforcement agency unable to locate him and Lisa, you're telling me that you have an idea where he might be?" the officer asked, leaning against his desk and arms still across his chest.

"Yes sir!" Dion aggressively stated.

"And if you, somehow, located him, would it benefit me?" the general asked, closely watching the soldier.

"Absolutely, Sir!" Dion stated.

"Granted," the brigadier said and Dion stepped back one step from the desk, crisply saluted and after receiving the general's relaxed acknowledgement salute, dropped his left foot back, smartly pivoted one hundred and eighty degrees and rigidly walked out the office door.

MIKE AND LISA

"I've noticed there's no tree limbs in the street," Lisa was saying after they had their bath and was walking hand-in-hand with Mike as they meandered around the holler.

"The street department trims lower limbs which provides clearance for road traffic, clears the streets after storms, maintains the creek beds and clears the road system to the north," he answered as they were heading toward the general store.

"Mike, does this place have a name?" she asked.

"Yes, it's called Cliffty Creek. When the area was first settled, it was referred to as the cliffs an' creek place. In time, it was called Cliffty Creek. It's sometimes unusual how things are named. For instance, long ago, the butterfly was actually called, the flutter by, because it looked like it fluttered when it flew. Someone, probably a kid, transposed several letters and accidentally called it a 'butterfly', and the name caught on," he explained as a small group of barefoot kids quietly ran up behind him.

"Mika," they all sang out as one, and startled Mike.

"Gee, I thought you were a Green Beret. Aren't you supposed to hear people running up behind you?!" Lisa questioned with a big grin.

"Hi kids," he said with a smirk, and to Lisa, he said, "Lisa, this is Billie Joe, Bobbie Jean, Jo Jack, Timmy, Randy and Tom. Kids, this is Lisa."

"Hidee Leza," they said, and then, they took off running.

"You watched 'em grow up?" she asked as they continued walking.

"Yes, since they were babies," he answered.

"And I noticed they didn't scare you a bit. While we were talking, you tilted your head in their direction slightly," she said smugly.

"You're perceptive and correct. It doesn't hurt anyone to play into their game occasionally. They got a kick out of it and are none the wiser, and it keeps me on my toes," he said as they stepped onto the boardwalk. After they had taken a half dozen steps past the corner market, both heard a female voice.

"Hidee Mika, yo' lookin' a-mite skinneh that. Don' dey feeds ya well in da armah? Ah's got two baked poss'ms in t' ovin, if 'in you' hoongry," the lovely voice said behind them. Turning, both fugitives saw a sensuous black-haired young lady scantily dressed in a breathtakingly short ragged skirt which was one thread from being illegal. Her black polka dot top sleeves had fallen off her shoulders and she seemed not to notice. The skimpy tight-fitting top was low cut, revealing ample breasts, shamelessly displaying her stock for those wishing to take inventory.

"Mary Beth, hello," Mike said as the fugitives turned to address the newcomer. "Mary Beth, this is Lisa Youngblood. Lisa, Mary Beth Howard," He said, being the gentlemen.

"Chahmed," Mary Beth said, ice frosting her tone.

"Mike would love to have both poss'ms and more because he's going to need all of his strength," Lisa said, staring evenly at Mary Beth and Lisa could feel her fingernails growing into claws. A sudden emotional whirlwind dropped on Mike and he knew he had to separate the girls gracefully.

"Ah… Mary Beth, we have to go to the general store to meet Crandall. He's calling town about us. We might have to leave presently and suddenly. I'll have to take a rain check on the poss'ms," he tried.

"If 'in ya don' mine, ah's'll go w'ich ya," she offered.

"Mary Beth," Mike began, "I don't mean to offend you," and Lisa, standing just back of Mike's shoulder, was mouthing the words to Mary Beth, 'yes, he does', "but Lisa and I need to speak privately with Crandall concerning what's happening in Henryville. Depending on what's going on there will dictate what we do here," he said firmly.

"Mika, ah unnerstands'. Ah'll see's ya 'roun'. Plees' t' huv' met ya' Leza," she said, and then, walked back to the corner market.

"Why do I get the feeling she'd have been more pleased to have had a loaded double-barreled shotgun in her hands upon meeting me?" she asked.

"Boy, did I ever have to get you two separated, if I didn't, she'd have created a scene that'd been the talk-of-the-town," Mike said while rubbing his forehead.

"Miss Shapely Legs there looks as if she just stepped out from an Al Capp comic strip. How long has she been chasing you?" Lisa asked.

"Nosey!" he said firmly and Lisa burst out laughing.

Mike took Lisa into the general store to meet with Crandall and his sons who had been discreetly seeking information from outside sources. Using the telephone, Crandall called holler members in the nearby city of Pine Bluff and the neighboring town of Henryville. Mike had seen the holler routine before; when a threat looms, calls are made, every holler citizen is aware of the problem, the situation is assessed from gathered information and a solution is agreed upon. In times past, every external problem promising to expose the holler to the world had been delicately handled and successfully concluded. Walking into the store, Mike knew the ruling fathers would be at the store rear, some sitting at a round table, others sitting on a bench and leaning against the wall.

"Hi Crandall. Any word back from Henryville?" Mike asked as he joined the assembled elders.

"Yassuh, ol' Gus ovah at t' police stashun is saying' t' C-Ah-A is runnin' 'ron' like a bunch'a chickins wit' dey's haids cut off. Mika, ohn dat helecopta ya' shot down was da C-Ah-A Direktur. Ya kil't 'em, an' now, don' noboda kno'd whut to do. Dey's a regroupin' rite now an' doin' t' oth'a stuff, ya kno', pickin' up t' peeces. We'ins figgered ya'll have a few days breathin' spell, three at t' mos'," Crandall related.

"That explains why the one chopper had the experienced pilot and the other didn't, they didn't want to waste a good pilot knowing he was going to get shot down. Isn't it unusual how fast the tables can turn on you," Mike ventured.

"Wit' all t' cunfushun' gion' ohn, ya'll be safe hyar fo' 'wile," an elder said.

"Well, we're going to take advantage of the situation and get some rest tonight. We'll get some grub for tonight and tomorrow, and after that, we'll take it one step at a time," he said to the group, and then asked, "Crandall, are you going to start the watch tonight?"

"Nope, Pappy Carver's gonna start thin's ohff. Then, Timmah an'… Mika, don' wurry 'bout it. We'ins bin doin' dis afore you's an itch in yo daddy's ovahalls. Take Leza, git sum grub an' skedaddle," Crandall ordered.

"Cranda, t' chillurn is gittin' uppity now-adays," Pappy observed.

"Alright Crandall, we're outta here. Just let us know if anything jumps off," Mike said.

"Don' wurry, Mika. You'ins be t' furst t' kno'," he acknowledged. On their way out, Mike picked up eggs, bacon, a loaf of bread and a can of coffee. As they left the store, the day's last rays were pouring over the mountains.

"It's been a long day," Lisa was saying as they walked back to Barnes' cabin.

"We're taking survival one day at a time. We're not worried about tomorrow until it gets here, and when it does arrive, we'll deal with it as it happens. Why worry about what you can't change," he was saying.

"Holler philosophy?" she asked.

"No, personal philosophy. What you can change, change. What you can't change, why worry about it. That's got to be the easiest thing to say and yet, one of the hardest to put into actual practice," he was saying as the sun had disappeared behind the hills, leaving the day's glory fading to the west.

"You don't plan on cooking anything tonight, do you?" Lisa asked.

"If you're hungry, I will," he said.

"I'm more tired than anything else," she answered.

"Let's just hit the sack when we get back," he suggested.

"Good," she said and wrapped her arm around his waist and leaned her head on his shoulder.

JUNE 15

MIKE AND LISA

Awaking pre-dawn from the noise of crowing roosters, Lisa drank in the early morning holler sounds while lying motionless and partially under Mike. Felling the warmth of his skin on hers, Lisa longed for this moment to last forever. She wanted to lose herself in him. She wanted the simple life of running barefoot in the holler, swimming under the warm sun and living in obscurity. She wanted the safety that holler life promised. But in the back of her mind, she knew she couldn't hide here for long. Sooner or later, the agency would find them.

Deep down, she feared for Mike. Inexperience with the agency's treachery would eventually get him killed. Leaving him wouldn't protect him. They'd find him and kill him. If she hadn't been so mixed up in the beginning, she would have ordered the men out of the way and then, drove off. But fate ordered the course of events, she convinced herself. Fate had constructed the stage, orchestrated the characters, manipulated the players and all she need do, is play her part. Who's to question what their destiny is or who's to decide their future course of events, she asked herself while Mike's breathing caressed her shoulder. Does not destiny chose its own lead characters? She asked herself. Then, turning her head slightly, in the subdued light, she saw that Mike's eyes were open.

"Been awake long?" he whispered.

"No, not long," she whispered back.

"I guess you're still hungry," he guessed.

"Famished," she answered.

"Guess I'd better feed you before you get sarcastic with me," he stated and she knew he was smiling.

"If you don't feed me soon, I'll turn into a hundred percent bitch," she warned.

"Sorry, no bitches are allowed in the Barnes house, especially early in the morning," he quietly stated.

"Better hurry and feed me before I change," she said while exploring his warm skin with her hands. Mike responded to her caresses with soft, gentle kisses. With Mike spreading kisses on her, Lisa forgot about being hungry.

After satisfying their desires, Mike cooked breakfast. While he was busy at the old stove, Lisa made coffee.

"After breakfast, we need to go to the general store and find out what's happening," Lisa suggested.

"My thoughts exactly. And for the rest of the morning, I plan on giving you a proper tour of the holler," he said.

"Given that we have time and... and, I just remembered that you didn't pay for the food we got from the store last night," she recalled.

"Honey, when hollerfolk work for the farmer, the hours are credited to their account at the store. When they buy food stuffs, it's debited from that account," he explained.

"The barter system!"

"Yes, money is generally not used here because the community learned long ago to function without it. Instead of paying wages, the farmer has running tallied accounts of who works in the fields and that family has credit at the store. Everyone has credit at the store, even I do," he said and his last statement surprised her.

"Then, you lived here?" she guessed as they sat down to eat.

"No, I grew up down the road some distance from here. I discovered the holler one day when I was out exploring the cliffs. Bam! Walked right into it! What a surprise that was!" he said, smiling at the memory, and he went on, "after the hollerfolk knew who I was and who my parents were, I was accepted as one of their own. Came and went as I pleased, worked in the fields, spent summers with friends and spent days at the hill holler. Now, It's your turn. How'd you get away from the CIA in New Orleans?" he asked, and while she talked, he ate.

"It, basically, was simple. I went into the French quarter and boarded the Natchez. An industrialist rented the Natchez for a day to take a drunken party to his home near Baton Rouge. Obviously, law enforcement never considered the paddle-wheeler as a means of escape," she related.

"Someone *rented* the Natchez?" Mike asked in disbelief.

"Dear heart, if you have enough money, you can rent anything you want. And now that you're finished, let's go for a walk," she suggested.

"Yeah, let's leave the van in the shed for now. There's cars around if we should need one in a hurry," he stated.

"Like the one we saw upon entering the holler?" she questioned with a grin.

"Yeah," he said defensively as they cleared the table.

"Let's go," she said softly, beaming as she took Mike's hand and led him outside.

"It's already a beautiful day," he said admiring the morning light from the porch.

"I wish this beautiful day would last forever," she dreamily envisioned as they walked hand-in-hand onto the road and headed for the store.

"Every morning is fresh here, different but fresh. It's hard to explain. You're living in the woods, away from the mundane activities of routines in the big cities and you're eating healthy food," he was saying as a small knot of nine-year-olds ran up behind them.

"Mo'nin' Mika. Mo'nin' Leza. Ya'll hahv'a nice nite?" a freckled-face red-headed little girl asked as eyebrows worked up and down, insinuating more than she said.

"Good morning, Teddie. How's your day going?" Mike asked as he gently laid his left hand on her left shoulder and with his right, he gave her a swat on her butt. The child squealed and turned redder. Then, the knot of kids giggled, laughed and ran off. Mike took Lisa's hand and continued walking as if nothing happened.

"If you mentioned the holler to most folk in the cities, they'd probably image a bunch of people sitting on front porches rockin' back and forth. Or layin' under a tree or fishin'. At times those things happen, but by and large, there's a lot of activity going on here," Mike was saying as they walked around a corner and were in sight of the store when a stout lady hurried by, and Mike said, "morning Lizzy. Running kind of late today".

"Yah, Mika. Mah chillurn is 'bout t' run me raggit. Shud'da bin hyar 'are ago," Lizzy said as she rushed up to the market door and quickly entered. Walking cross the street, Mike and Lisa just stepped onto the boardwalk when a holler car slowly rolled next to the boardwalk where they were and stopped.

"Mika, der's sum'mun in t' sto' ta see ya," the driver said.

"Thanks, Billy," he answered and the car pulled away.

"He didn't say who," Lisa observed.

"That's because he doesn't know who it is. If it was someone from here or the neighboring holler, he would have used their name. Well, let's go find out," he said, and as he held the door open for Lisa, she saw who Billy was referring to and a large smile crept cross her face.

"Dion?" Mike exclaimed, and he moved toward his buddy. In the rear of the store, they clasped hands, hugged and slapped each other's back.

"Good to see you, Mike!" Dion said and he was all smiles.

"Same here. Let me introduce you to everyone," Mike said

and he began, "this is Pappy Carver, Tater Howard, Crandall Jenkins and his sons, Timmy and Ronny and this is Jess Hawkins. And, of course, you know Lisa. Everyone, this is Dion Marshall."

"We kno', Mika. He'ins bin hyar twenny minites. Bein' a gennelmin, he innerduced hisself," Pappy said.

"Hi everyone," he said to the men, and to Lisa, he said, "Lisa".

"Ah's got a fellin' we'ins gonna be hyar a'wile, so evahbody sit ohn down," Crandall instructed. Mike, Lisa, Dion and Crandall sat at the table while the other elders sat on a bench, rockers and recliners against the back wall.

"We need to talk," Dion told Mike, and he continued, "how much TV have you seen or have you read any newspapers?" he asked.

"Dion, we haven't had time for either," Mike answered and his answer slightly shocked Dion.

"You have no idea what's going on other than what you're directly involved with?"

"Dion, we've been kinda busy trying to say alive. Reading newspapers and watching TV are frills that of late, we haven't had time for," Lisa answered.

"Ok, in a nutshell. Your actions are driving the CIA to act crazy, which in turn caused the House and Senate members to take vacations. Two CIA agents killed each other in the White House which now resembles an armed camp. Most of Washington is an armed ghost town," Dion outlined.

"H'ain't nuttin'. Yestiddy Mika kilt the C-Ah-A Direktur afta day blo'd up t' Henervull bridge," Crandall said, and Dion's mouth dropped open.

"Mike, you two are absolutely rocking the power boat! I didn't know about the director – it hasn't been reported on any of the news yet," Dion said and Mike and Lisa just looked at each other in amazement.

"I wonder why that hasn't been reported?" Mike asked, looking at Lisa.

"In the project, the director is expendable. The goal has top priority. In this case, secure the serum back under wraps. If they can still capture us and the serum, the death of the director can be explained away. Mike and I will become the scapegoat and the project moves forward," Lisa outlined.

"So, the agency won't report his death until you're both caught or killed. They'll have to step up the effort because they can't hide his death for any length of time. He would be missed," Dion evaluated.

"What's the brigadier saying or doing?" Mike asked.

"He's hungry for information from you. He's got you at the head of the problem and he's hoping to solve it. If he can, it'll look good on him because I believe he's in touch with someone in the White House. See, that's the odd part. The news is reporting your actions, but there's nothing about the connection between you and the CIA. No statements from the agency nor from the White House," Dion related.

"The agency is maintaining a news black-out. They haven't done anything, so there's nothing to report to the news about," Lisa injected.

"But the death of the director is big news," Mike argued.

"If it isn't reported, then he isn't dead," Lisa rebutted.

"Then, we have to go public with what we have and know," Mike concluded.

"Not from here and not from a station with a transmitter broadcasting less than 50,000 watts of power," Lisa determined and everyone looked at her.

"A station with a broadcast power of 50kv," Mike repeated.

"What stations in this area would have that power output?" Dion asked.

"None I'm afraid. We'll have to go to a major city like Memphis or Nashville, but we can't use I-40 because it'll be saturated with agents," she stated.

"We can continue traveling north on the holler road. It's negotiable to central Kentucky," Mike said.

"Let's start thinking about Louisville. There's several stations with a wide broadcast area," Lisa commented.

"That's where we'll head, Dion. If Stranton asks, pass it along.

I have a feeling we'll need help before this is over," Mike guessed.

"Now thet yo' chillurln figgerd dis oht, ho's 'bout sum grub, Deone," Crandall asked, as he stood up and the others sitting at the table also stood.

"Sounds good to me. What 'cha got?" Dion asked as they started walking to the store front.

"We'ins got bobakew chickins, taters, beens and sta'berre 'shine delite," Pappy offered.

"Afta ettin' hyar a-spell, ya ki'na feel like movin'in, settlin'down an' havin' chillurn," Jess said.

"Children?!" Lisa said. When Jess said 'havin' chillurn', she suddenly realized she could have children and it hit her like a ton of bricks, and Mike leaned close to say something.

"Miniature versions of adults, honey," he said quietly but loud for everyone to hear.

"Damn you, Tanner, I know what children are – I was thinking of something else!!" she shouted while trying to hit him in the chest but he held his hands up loosely for protection, and everyone was laughing.

"Git 'eem, chile! Ever'un kno'd Mika needs a good wompin' okshunally," Jess egged her on.

"Dey's in luv," Pappy was saying to Dion.

"Oh, is this how love begins? What's the next step?" Dion dryly asked Pappy while Lisa was still beating Mike.

"Dey gots t' admit to deyself dey's in luv wit' e'chather, den dey settle down an' start takin' care o e'chather," Pappy patiently explained.

"This is one heck of a time to fall in love," Dion admitted.

"Luv an' babees gots deys own time ta enta t' worlt," the old timer said.

"Think we ought'a help Mike?" Dion asked.

"Naa, Mika kin' take care 'a heself. Bin' doin' it fo' y'ars," Jess answered proudly.

"Smart-ass!" Lisa emotionally stated after she stopped beating him and she was reddened in the face from embarrassment and exertion.

"Now ya' kno'd whut we'ins haid ta put up wit' all dee's y'ars," Pappy told Lisa.

"Your problem is that you didn't straighten him out," she boldly stated.

"We'ins tri'd, chile," Pappy said in his defense.

"Ok Michael, let's take the grand tour while Dion gets something to eat and he can catch up with us later," she firmly said, and Mike was still laughing.

"Yes dear," he barely got out, and then, Lisa grabbed Mike's hand and left the store.

"You bastard!" she said to him outside the door and she had to laugh too.

"Remember what Pappy said they were going to feed Dion? The strawberry 'shine delight? He said it so fast that Dion didn't realize he meant 'strawberry moonshine delight'. They're going to light his world up after they feed him," Mike clarified.

"Oh good!" she said, smiling at the thought, and just then, she saw Mary Beth walking their way,"oh greaaat," she added sarcastically.

"Hidee Mika," Mary Beth sang as she neared the couple. Lisa noticed she was wearing radically-short shorts and a light tan tight tanktop, and her nipples were obviously straining against the fabric.

"Hi Mary Beth. You remember Lisa," he said.

"Unfer'chanitly," she said, giving Lisa the cold shoulder. Listening to Mary Beth talk to Mike, Lisa could almost smell the blooming fragrant spring flowers in her voice as she conversed with the Green Beret and when Mary Beth had to say anything to Lisa, the blonde outlaw felt the bitter cold wind of winter blowing her way. She decided to let Mike do all the talking.

"I'm showing Lisa around while we have the time. I don't know when we'll have to leave, so while I have opportunity to show her around, I'm doing it. If you'd like to invite me to your place, you're also asking Lisa along because I have to know where she is every second of the day and night. When we have to leave, I've got to know precisely where she is, and the only way to do that is to have her next to me. We are not separating for a minute. Both our lives is riding on each decision we make, both here an after we leave. You might as well accept the fact and stop giving her the cold shoulder routine," Mike stated unemotionally.

"Aw'rite Mika, yo' win. We'ins'll tock 'notha time," she answered gracefully, and then, Mary Beth went to the store. Mike breathed a sigh of relief.

"She's in love with you, Mike. That's something that won't change. Now wouldn't be the proper time to deal with it, but sooner or later, it will have to be dealt with," Lisa gently admitted as she stood facing him on the boardwalk, and with misty eyes, she was trying to find the answer in his eyes.

"It's something that's been a long time in coming," he said as he ran an open hand over his short hair, "and I knew I'd have to do something one way or the other. But that's something from my past for me to deal with and it shouldn't have spilt over on you," he stated.

"You'd still have to make a decision, even if I wasn't here, but my being here amplifies it. Let it go for now and let's get on with the grand tour," she suggested with an earnest smile.

"Yeah, it'll keep for now. Let's just walk for awhile. It's been so long since I've been here and yet, nothing really has changed. Oh, the kids have gotten bigger, everyone gets a little older and the darn grass needs to be ate again, but the structural part of the holler doesn't change all that much. The town is still the same. The boardwalk has a few new boards and there's a new house for a new married couple. But compared to outside cities, there's hardly any change at all," Mike observed as they turned off the main street and walked along the boardwalk.

"Even in a backward society, change will happen. Subtle changes will occur over long periods of time, but they will happen. That's not what's bothering you, is it?" she asked when then stepped off the wooden walkway and into the dirt street. And then, they stopped and Mike faced her, wrapping his arms around her waist.

"No, changes or the lack thereof isn't bothering me. I should be overjoyed that Dion is here and that we're still alive, but... well...

what I really want to say is… ah," he tried when Lisa softly interrupted him.

"What you're really trying to say is that you're falling in love with me, it's only been a week, you're afraid to tell me 'cause you don't know how I'll take it and you don't want to scare me. Does that about sum it up?" she quietly whispered while slowly encircling his neck with both her hands.

"Yeah, That covers everything I wanted to say. How could you guess?" he whispered back.

"Because the same feelings are sweeping over me too. Everything that's happened to me this past week, shouldn't have happened, but they have and are continuing to happen. I keep telling myself, no, this isn't supposed to happen that way, but regardless of what I tell myself, it's happening," she said just before she kissed him. A car had rolled around the corner and slowly drove by the young lovers.

"H'ain't s'pose ta be kissin' in t' middle of t' stri't, Mika. Da's whut we'ins b'ilt houses fer. Dad-bern chillurn! Ahs hates it whin dey egnurs dey's elters. Jessa, ra-min' meh later ta scold Mika," Pappy directed.

"Yo' t'ink dat do eny good? Pappa, chillurn gots dey own mine. Dey do whut dey wants," Jess stated as they continued driving.

"Let's go back to the cabin," Lisa whispered.

"Ok," he answered and they slowly walked back to the cabin, warms wrapped around each other, each looking into the other's eyes and smiling, and Mike would occasionally catch her swinging hand and tenderly kiss it. They reentered the Barnes' place late in the morning and weren't seen again until late afternoon. They were in no rush. Lisa slowly undressed Mike, and then, it was Mike's turn. Time stood still as they savored tender stolen moments, and Lisa wanted the moments to stretch into eternity.

"Let's see if we can find Dion," Mike was saying as they stepped off the cabin porch, heading for the road.

"I hope he's not too drunk. How strong is that 'shine? 180 proof?" Lisa asked as they entered the road and walked toward town.

"220 proof and it will definitely change your attitude," Mike corrected and just then, as they looked across an open area, a block away on another road, they saw a car rolling along loaded with young men and women with Dion in the middle of the back seat laughing and holding a jar of clear liquid.

"Three sheets to the wind so early in the afternoon," Lisa said dryly.

"When it's time to party, Dion is the party animal," Mike explained as they stopped and watched the car as the driver gave Dion a rolling tour of the holler.

"Well, let's go to the store and find out what's happening," Lisa suggested.

"Good idea. They'll take care of Dion for the moment and we'll talk to Crandall about getting him outta here later. Since the revenuers were here in the thirties, we know the holler isn't completely hidden from all aspects of society. Some sections of the government are aware that Cliffty Creek exists but they've left us alone all these years. I'd give anything to know which government departments know of us," Mike was saying as they walked toward the store.

"I'm not able to confirm if the CIA knows. Once you've worked for the CIA, you become aware of the multitude of secrets permeating throughout the agency. To them, secrecy is a way of life. You could work on a project for twenty years and never know the full scope of that project. It's actually amazing in a way," she lied and was trying to sound convincing as they continued walking.

"I understand, honey. I hope I never ask you for more than you're able to give," he offered.

"Well, if you ever do, just don't be rude in the asking," she advised as they entered the boardwalk.

"Agreed," he answered with a big grin, and went on, "well, let's find out what's happening over at Henryville," he said as they were entering the general store. At the rear of the store, Mike saw

Crandall sitting at the table with Jess and Pappy and the phone was in the center of the table. Tater was in the recliner sound asleep. Enroute to the back of the store, Mike saw concern etched on the elders' faces.

"What's happening, Crandall?" Mike asked as he pulled a chair for Lisa and both sat down.

"Nuttin', an' dat's whot's bothern' us. Nuttin's hap'nin'," Crandall said.

"Explain what you mean, 'nothing is happening'," Mike stated.

"T' palice havh closed 240 b'yon' Henervull. Dey's alsa pi'kin' up t' helecopta ya shot down an' dey's ser'chin nort' o' Henervull. T'C-Ah-A is ovah in t' fed'ral buildin' talking', t' 'hole bunch un' 'em. Sum'thin' don' seem rite," Crandall estimated.

"It's part of regrouping. The search goes forward, the mess is being cleaned up, notes are being compared and they're in touch with Langley for instruction and information," Lisa lied again trying to sound as if she knew their tactics.

"Wud dey kno' uv' dis place?" Crandall asked.

"Hard to answer. The information may be on file somewhere or it might be on a database. I don't know. I, personally, couldn't conceive of any agency spending the monies to convert old records to a database, but they might have. But the records we're talking about now belong to the A.T.F., Alcohol, Tobacco, and Firearms. I seriously doubt the ATF would bother translating old records to databases and then share those records with the CIA. That sounds too farfetched," Lisa said.

"It's a fifty-fifty chance they know, Crandall. We'll rest up one more day here, pack some food in the van and tomorrow sometime, head north. We should plan on getting Dion out of here later today, so if anything unforeseen jumps off, he'll be out of harm's way," Mike outlined.

"Dat probably be a gud ahdea. We'ins monaturin' Pin' Bluff an' Henervull fer eny typ' uv massin' by eny palice or C-Ah-A. If in dey starts gatherin' tugetter, we kno'd dey be cumin' dis way. Don' wurry, Mika, bin doin' dis a-long time," Crandall said.

"Crandall, I do worry. This is something I can't change and it's directly going to affect not only us but the holler as well," Mike admitted.

"Mika, it don' matta'. We'ins bin hyar so long, if t' worlt fin's out 'bout us now, h'ain't gonna chn' us. O', we'ins'll make alotta monch from da tuk'rist, but it h'ain't gonna chan' us. T' elters kno'd dis day wus comin' – we'ins got contingincy plans whin it do happun. T' elters kno'd we'ins cain't stay hid furevah. So, don' wurry 'bout it, Mika. Whut's gonna happun, is gonna happun," Crandall explained.

"Like it's destiny," Lisa chipped in.

"Dat's rite, chilie. Et's 'are destina. We'ins tri'd t' explain et t' Mika afore, but he didn' wont no part uv t' intalek'ual 'rgument," Pappy revealed, and Mike rolled his eyes.

"I tried to explain the relationship of accidental events to the final outcome. Or that the altering of events would still have the same end, but he didn't want to discuss it," Lisa admitted.

"Not the destiny thing again," Mike moaned.

"Et wuddn't hurt ya', Mika t' expan' yure hurizuns a l'il. Lis'sun ta chilie. She'ins kno'd whut she'ins 'a talkin' 'bout," Jess tried to encourage Mike.

"Think I'll get some food stuffs ready and store it in the van," Mike stated as he got up and headed for the store front.

"Der he goes agin. Runnin' frum a gud 'rgumrent. Hos's dat boh gonna lern enathin' if'in he keeps runnin' 'way?" Pappy asked.

"Think I'd better go help him," Lisa said smiling.

"Mika mite be too olt an' set in hes ways fo' change," Jess reasoned.

"Mebba," Crandall added.

"And we'd probably better take some jerky and juice," Mike was saying to the storeowner, Berta, at the counter when Lisa approached with an award-winning smile. Mike took one look at her and knew what was coming, "don't say a word about it. I won't argue a non-definitive and subjective topic. It's an endless debate," he firmly said.

"I just came up to get some ice. The serum is probably floating in icy water," she said innocently and Mike knew he was suddenly out-flanked.

"Yeah! Right!" he said, but he was waiting for the surprise counter-move.

"Mika," Pappy Carver said while walking toward the front, "we'ins gonna havh a car sittin' in frunt uv t' store fer eny emurgincy. If we'ins get wurd dey's a-cumin', t' car'll cum' in rite handa".

"Pappy, we won't slip off to someplace secret. Well be very visible today and tomorrow, but I think tomorrow we should leave," Mike said.

"Gud ahdea," Pappy agreed.

"But for right now, let's also take something to fix for lunch. It's 2:30 and I haven't eaten since early o'clock this morning," she said with a devilish grin.

"I'd better feed this one Jess. If I don't, she becomes sarcastically dangerous. Either quality is bad enough alone but combined, it's more than any man can stand," Mike informed Jess.

"Heh, heh, heh," Jess laughed as he walked to the back of the store.

"Jessa," Pappy quietly said after Jess sat down at the table, "we'ins need t' tolk ta 'Nita at t' nus'paper in Pin' Bluff. Havh hur roun' up all t' artikals ohn Mika an' Leza".

"Ya kno'd wur gonna end up wit' a scrapbuk," Jess warned.

"Pur-cisely," Pappy said and the reason suddenly dawned on Jess, and both gave the other a knowing smile.

"We'll probably see Dion being chauffeured around," Mike was saying as he bundled up the foodstuffs and Lisa grabbed a bag of ice from the nearby freezer. Thanking Berta, the outlaws had just exited the store when the loaded car carrying Dion rolled up to the store and stopped. The fugitives could easily deduce from the wet trail behind the car and that some of the passengers were wet – that they had been in the creek for awhile.

"Mike!" Dion said loudly and most of the passengers started laughing. The 'shine delight' had been passed around until it was gone and then, they got more. Everyone was in various states of inebriation except the driver and judging from his displayed driving abilities, questions arose in Mike's mind about the driver's sobriety. "Come on, Mike. If you's two is going back to cabin, we'll give ya ride," Dion said and everyone laughed at him.

"You, dear," Mike said pointing at one of the girls, "sit on his lap and I'll have Lisa sit on mine".

"Obey the squad leader, dear and sit on my lap," Dion instructed.

"Everyone needs to stop drinking the 'shine because the revenuers might show up later today or tomorrow, and tonight, we need to get Dion outta here and on his way back to Jackson, Mississippi," Mike stated and he knew the key word was 'revenuers'. As the car pulled away from the store, Mike saw everyone's eyes lit up over hearing that word. He also knew the half-century old stories about the rev'noors coming to the holler and he knew how to spur the young men.

"Rite, Mika. We'ins'll put Deone ta bed an' git sum' rest 'arselfs," the driver said.

"Just don't put him to bed with her," Mike said pointing at the girl sitting on Dion's lap.

"Mike, ya killin' me," Dion said and everyone laughed.

"We're serious about the revenuers. There's a good possibility they'll show up, we just don't know when, so, everyone needs to be ready at a moment's notice," Mike was saying as the car approached the cabin.

"Hyar ya go, Mika, an' afta we'ins drop y'll of, Deone hits da rack," the driver said.

"Da torture rack, hunny," the girl on Dion's lap said and everyone laughed until tears fell. Lisa rolled her eyes.

"Thanks for the lift and go get some sleep," Mike directed.

"Rite, Mika," they all answered, laughed and drove off.

"I hope they follow my advice or their aim will be off," he said to Lisa as they entered the cabin, and then he asked, "how's spaghetti and meatballs sound?"

"Fine. I'll spice and roll the meatballs after I pack my bag with the ice," she said, and she emptied the water into the shrubs just off the front porch. After repacking her bag, she tore open the ground meat, added spices and began rolling the chuck into bit-size balls. While rolling the meat, she asked, "you think they'll show up today?"

"No, maybe tomorrow but not today. They're still searching north and when they have no sightings of us, they figure we're dug in somewhere. Then, they'll begin researching my background and they'll learn that I'm from this area. They'll quietly start searching Pine Bluff first if… if they don't know about the holler. If they find the ATF records, then they'll shoot right out here first, figuring we're here instead of being in town," Mike explained.

"Well, no sense in worrying over the future. It'll just have to happen as it happens," Lisa surmised.

"You're not going to start that destiny thing again, are you?" Mike asked wearily.

"No, I'm not!" she said emphatically.

"There's places I've wanted to take you here in the holler, but we'll have to stay where we can be found easily. Maybe after we eat we can borrow a car and drive around. You've only seen the main part of town. We'll stop at the store before going anywhere, let them know we'll be driving about, find out what there is to know and check back in with them before returning here. How's that sound?" he asked.

"I'd love to see more of the holler," she said beaming, and after a late lunch, they borrowed a neighbor's car and stopped at the store.

"Pappy, we're going to drive around for a little while," Mike said upon walking past the counter and seeing only Pappy Carver in the back, and he went on, "I'm going to show Lisa the holler, so we'll be on the roads. Before heading home, we'll check in with whoever is here. Ah… where is everybody?" Mike asked.

"Ever'un' is gittin' sum'thin' ta eat, Mika. Thar wus a strange davelupment. No fone calls wint frum t' fed'ral buildin' ta Langla. T' direktor made one call afore hes death, an' nun' wur made by eny wun. Kin'na strange, don' ya think?" Pappy stated, trying to figure it out.

"How do you know that no calls were made?" Mike asked.

"Ya kno's Billa Preston. Wull, he's wurkin' at t' fone cumpany an' he's racordin' all calls frum t' fed'ral buildin' an' no calls frum t' C-Ah-A wen' t' Langla. We'ins don' kno' whut ta make uv it," he confessed.

"I don't know what to make of it either. Tell you what, we'll drive around and put our heads together and see if we can make sense of it," Mike said.

"An' probubly, put ya lips tagether too," Pappy guessed.

"Pappy!" Lisa loudly stated and the old timer just laughed. The fugitives left the store confused, hopped in the car and sat there.

"No calls." Lisa said bewildered.

"I expected a flurry of calls back and forth," Mike said, stunned.

"Who's Billy Preston?" she asked, mainly to keep the conversation going.

"He's from the holler and he's been trying to work in the mainframe of the phone company for a long time. Guess he finally got the job he wanted. Another person from the holler planted in a strategic position. This one paid off in big dividends. It's not making any sense that they didn't report the director's death, not to me anyway," he admitted.

"The only reasonable explanation I can see is that they are trying to wing this one on their own, for reasons I can't... can't. I don't know. They way they're doing it defies logic. By all protocols, they should have called in," she said, trying to reach for answers as they sat in the car in front of the store.

"This is one possibility I never considered as being possible. How would they reason? If they captured us, would the recovery of the serum pacify the honchos in Langley concerning the director's death? Could that be their reason for not calling Langley?" Mike asked as Crandall, Timmy and Jess walked up. Just as the trio came even with the driver, Pappy came out the store door.

"Mika, if in yo' gonna sho' chillie 'round', ya furst havh ta' start t' enjun'," Pappy pointed out.

"Oh yeah, that's what we were going to do," Mike said looking at Lisa seriously.

"See if the engine will start, Mike," she directed, and when he tried, it started.

"Ok, I'll show her the holler now," he told the three elders.

"Dat's gud, Mika. Don' drive too fas' now," Pappy instructed.

"Here we go honey," Mike said, and they eased on down Main St.

"Whus is wit' dat boh?" Crandall asked as Mike and Lisa pulled away.

"Ah gist tol' 'em 'bout t' lack uv calls frum t' fed'ral buildin' ta Langla. Ah g'ess it shuk 'em up," Pappy estimated.

"Dat's all wein's need, havin' ta wa'ch tu gro'n chillurn. T' way t'ings ar' happunin', it's turnin' inta a mizzurble day," Crandall stated.

"Sum'mun otta keep a' eye ohn dem tu," Pappy said.

"Tima, call Tater an' tell 'em ta foller Mika an' Leza an' tell 'em why he 'ins is follerin' 'em. Cum' ohn bohs, let's set a-spell an' try ta figger oht whut's happunin' at t' fed'ral buildin'," Crandall said as he motioned everyone to follow him into the store.

"Ah figger dey's invessigatin' Mika's past. Dey'd fine oht he wus razed 'roud' hyar. Dem ol' rev'noors records w'uldn't be in Was'in'ton, deyk'd be in t' fed'ral buildin' whur t' rev'noors haid deys office. But 't quession is, w'uld t' C-Ah-A kno'd it?" Jess asked.

"T' C-Ah-A h'aiin't follern natcherl pracedjurs. By not callin' haid-kwarters, dey's steppin' oht ohn deys own. Dey's inventin' deys own methuds. We'ins can espect enythin'. Let's tell ever'un' along t' way t' keep alurt t'nite," Crandall instructed.

"It'd be a gud ahdea t' ra-min' t' holler 'bout t' slow' ringin' bell. Everyk'un'll kno' t' rev'noors is a'comin' whin dey heerd t' bell. H'ain't hurd thet bell in ovah fifty yars," Pappy recalled.

"Cranda, ahs don' ritely ba-lev' we'ins gonna figger oht whut t' C-Ah-A is fixin' ohn doin'. Ah t'ink ever'un' shud be reddy fo' enythin'," Pappy admitted.

"Ahs agree wit' Pappa," Tater said as he walked to the back of the store, "t' holler shud git reda fo' a reac'shun. Thet'd be t' smartest thin' ta do."

"Tater, you'ins sa'posed ta be wa'chin' Mika an' Leza!" Crandall stated.

"Dey's sittin' in t' car in frunt of t' cabin wit' t' moder off.

Dey's jist sittin' thar. Cain't foller sum'mun whin dey's sittin' still," Tater said.

"Wull, go see whut dey's doin' an' if'in dey take off, foller 'em," Crandall instructed.

"Tater's rite," Pappy said, "ever'un' shud git reda fo' a reac'shun".

"Aw-rite, hyar's whut we do, pass 'roud' whut we'ins jist tolk'd 'bout an' thet ever'un shud espect a reac'shun. If'in t' rev'noors makes a muv', we'ins start t' slo' ringin' bell. Whin t' bell stops, ever'un kno'd whut ta do," Crandall outlined.

"Now, dey's sittin' on t' porch swing," Tater announced upon returning to the table.

"Tater, if'in eny trubba happuns t'nite, git yaself ovah ta t' cabin an' alurt dem chillurn, den, open t' shed doors wide so's Mika don' run 'em down. An' make shore you's oht'a way so's Mika don' run's ya down ohn hes way oht. Ok ever'boda, let's start makin' sum calls," Crandall said.

⊕

Without saying a word to each other, Mike and Lisa were locked in their separate worlds as Mike drove back to the cabin and stopped out front. After turning the motor off, both sat in the car, shocked by the new development. Each attempted to assess future actions by the CIA independent office. Frustrated because of the oddness of the situation, they left the car to sit on the porch.

"It doesn't make any sense," Mike said.

"To them, it does. The only thing I can think of is, they're trying to redeem themselves because the director was killed in their sector. That's the best I can do," she admitted, and just then, Tater rolled up in a car.

"Mika, Cranda's gonna call 'round' ta tell ever'un ta be ohn t' alurt tanite. Don' nun' uv us kno'd whut ta espect. Pappy sed fo' ya'll ta git all t' rest ya can. We'ins woke Deone an' tuk 'em ta t' bus station. T' gurlz'll put 'em ohn a bus fo' Ja'ksun. He'll 'rive tamarra mo'nin'," Tater informed.

"Thanks, Tater. That's not a bad idea bout the rest. Since the sun'll be setting in an hour, we should turn in early," Mike said.

"Don' wurry, Mika, we'll be wa'chin' tanite," Tater assured.

"Thanks again, Tater," Mike said, and as he started off, Mike waved goodbye.

"Let's get something to eat and try to sleep," Mike suggested.

"No doubt this'll be a strange night. For the first time, I can't imagine what the agency'll do," Lisa admitted.

"If we keep trying to come up with answers, we'll end up second guessing ourselves. I'll fix a light meal, check the van and then, let's hit the sack," he said.

"I'm glad Dion is out of the way, whatever happens," Lisa answered.

"Me too. I was concerned with him being here. Let's stop thinking about the CIA and the possible reasons why they didn't call in or we won't get any sleep," he said.

"Agreed," she simply said. Mike fixed a light meal while Lisa set the table. Both were wrapped in their own thoughts and neither hardly spoke. After the meal, Mike checked the van while Lisa did the dishes. It seemed like the time for talking was over and they were just waiting for something to happen. It was the calm before the storm. Everyone knew it was coming, but the question was when. After checking and cleaning, they wandered to the front porch and sat on the swing.

"Night sounds of the holler are normal," Mike observed.

"I feel like I'm in a vacuum and have nothing to grab onto," she said.

"The sun's down. We might as well try to sleep," he said.

"'Try' is the key word. It's nerve-wracking when nothing is going on. When they were chasing us, I felt a lot better. I knew where they were, what they were doing and why. This not knowing is upsetting," she confided.

"I know. Come on, let's go," he said, standing up to encourage her to try.

"Ok, but if I hit you in the middle of the night, I'm sorry," she warned.

JUNE 16

MIKE AND LISA

She fell into a fitful slumber. She entered a world containing answers which were hidden in a pitch black void. Movement was non-existent. The future and past folded together into the present. Only the present existed in the empty void. Her present reality evolved into a dark search for answers. Descending into a black vortex that slowly spiraled downward, the solid substance of answers seemed just beyond her grasp. The empty dark void refused to yield the solid substance thus denying her direction for search. The solitary emotion of frustration filled her weightless being in the spiraling vortex. Her being ached for the answers hidden in the night-black spiral. Still and noiseless as death, the vortex towered around and above her and yet, she remained motionless in the center. No wind, no noise, no time, no motion disturbed her frustration that formed from the inability of untangling the mysteries wherein lay the answers. The growing vortex towered out-of-sight over her head as the spiral continued moving past, with her in the center.

Blackness surrounded her and slowly rotated, giving the slightest indication of movement. In her yearning for answers, a white dot far in the distance appeared. Looking again at the swirling blackness, she sensed nearby monstrously dark reasons that caused her dilemma. She tired attempting to grasp the answers from the black spiral, and then she noticed that the white dot tripled in size. The dark vortex retreated before the consuming white dot, and suddenly, she was thrust into the light.

"Good morning," Mike said softly as her eyes popped open, and Lisa was breathing heavily.

"I hope it is because I had a terrible night," she stated.

"You didn't move a muscle since you laid down which allowed me to get some sleep," he informed.

"I feel like I've been working all night trying to find answers," she said.

"Honey, it was just dreams. Let 'em go and let's get up and get the day rolling," he suggested.

"And speaking of rolling, let's leave this morning. I'm feeling weird about today," she said.

"You're feeling weird because of the dream. Would you like to tell about the dream?" he asked.

"It was strange enough the first time, I don't want to relive it a second time," she stated.

"Ok, let's have breakfast and then, head over to the store. Since no one came to the cabin last night, I'm assuming the CIA has made no move anywhere," he said.

"Ok, breakfast and then, the store and according to what we learn from the elders, we'll go from there," she agreed. While Mike cooked bacon and eggs, Lisa made coffee and toast. She shoved the dream aside and enjoyed helping Mike cook breakfast. On two pieces of toast she put grape jam and on two others, she put only butter. She finished buttering the last when Mike broke the eggs into the hot bacon grease.

"When we go to the store, let's take the van so we can leave immediately afterward," Mike suggested.

"Ok. Ya know, I feel a lot better when we're moving. This sitting in one place really grates on the nerves," she admitted.

"I know what you mean, but sometimes it's prudent to stop, hide and wait," he said as he scooped the eggs onto the plates from the pan.

"Is that philosophy from Green Beret training?" she asked as they sat down to eat.

"No, I just made it up," he confessed.

"I love salty bacon," she said licking her lips.

"I cooked the portion we didn't use yesterday, so there's a lot for the meal. Don't be shy and help yourself," he stated.

"When have you known me to be shy?" she questioned while grinning.

"Not lately! Now, finish your meal, tidy up in here while I check the van and get it ready," he directed.

"Yes sir!" she saluted.

"Oh, so early in the morning. Well, at least I know you're feeling better," he said as he left the table and walked to the shed.

As Lisa washed the dishes, she heard Mike checking under the hood, checked the weapons in the side door and finally, start the van. She had finished the dishes, wiped the table and stove, straightened the bed covers and was walking to the shed when Mike told her the van had warmed up.

"First thing I'm going to do at the store is get a bag of ice," she said as she climbed into the passenger seat.

"I'll check with whoever is near the phone in the back and learn what's happening," Mike told her as he was pulling out of the shed.

"If nothing has or appears to be happening, we're still leaving?" she asked.

"Yeah, I think it a wise move to leave this morning. We've pushed our luck staying this long," he stated, turning toward the main street.

"Or we had a lucky break," she added.

"Yeah, or that. And don't throw that destiny thing at me today!" he pointedly stated as he made a U-turn in front of the store, parked and faced the van toward the hills. Walking into the store,

Mike saw the original group of elders at the rear plus seven other older men he recognized.

"What's happening, Crandall?" he asked upon nearing the gathered men.

"Sum'thin's happunin', but we'ins h'ain't fo' shur' ezac'ly whut it is," Crandall said while stroking his chin, and he went on, "'bout tin agunts wint ta t' fed'ral buildin' an' we h'aian't seen 'em since, an' no lites lit up thar offices. Sum'thin' mighty pee-koolyar is goin' ohn, Mika."

"Well, we brought the van and I think it's a good time to leave before anything *does* happen. Lisa is refreshing the ice in her waterproof bag and then…" Mike was saying when the phone interrupted him and the sudden ringing caused everyone to start.

"Reallah, ok," Crandall said in the receiver, and after placing the phone on its cradle, he said, "five cars uv rev'noors is headin' dis way. Dey jist shot past t' wa'ch houses ohn t' gravel road. Dey'll be in sic' minutes. Yo' chillurn bes' git a-movin," he firmly instructed Mike. "Pappy," he said as Mike hurriedly turned to leave, "call t' bell t'ar".

"What's going on?" Lisa asked as she had just reentered the store when she saw Mike running toward her.

"They're coming!! Let's go!!!" he shouted at her and like bullets, they both shot out the door. As Mike exited the store, the first peal of a slow bell resounded throughout the holler. The moment Lisa shut her door, the holler exploded into activity. Men of all ages suddenly appeared carrying guns, cars rolled out of the woodwork to pick up women and children, and young boys with guns were running toward side streets with barking dogs following. As Mike eased away from the store, cautious not to hit anyone, Lisa saw Mary Beth standing stock-still with arms folded under her breasts on the corner of the block outside the market. The frozen Goddess of Hate was staring death at Lisa. As pedestrian traffic cleared, Mike increased his speed, but not before Mary Beth saw Lisa smile.

"Toorky shoot, toorky shoot," was the last thing Lisa heard as Mike sped down the main street, heading for the hills.

Speeding down the wide dirt road lined with massive trees, Lisa asked, "what's a turkey shoot?"

"The last law enforcement agency to enter the holler was the revenuers back in the '30s and '40s. They were looking for moonshine stills. The only still, that I know of, is at Homer Barnes' farm. They went racing down this road to a location where they thought a still existed and young men were perched atop an embankment, waiting for them. When the revenuers rolled by, tires and windows were shot out without hitting the driver or passengers. Some of those old men you saw in town were the young men back then that did the shooting, and to this day, they are excellent marksmen still. There hasn't been a turkey shoot in half a century and everybody's excited because the stories of old have been told and retold down through the decades," he explained.

"I guess they'll have new stories to tell after today, and all because Mike Tanner came home for a visit," Lisa said, beaming.

"Mike Tanner and his girl friend, Lisa Youngblood. Don't cut yourself short, honey. They'll gather all the news reports, all the available info on you and the stories will flow," Mike said.

"They won't kill the CIA?" Lisa asked, pointing behind her with a thumb.

"No, because then, there'd be an investigation, which means, the CIA or FBI would send teams into the holler asking a bunch of questions and taking names. To avoid that, the fathers and old timers will take the sons to the high embankment, that we'll pass in five minutes, and the youngest will shoot the tires and flatten the spare. The older kids will shoot the windows, because they've had more shooting experience. The trunk area is designated as a free fire target because of the location of the spare and the radio equipment. With all tires flattened, no one hurt, no radio equipment and no spares remaining, the agents will have to hoof it back to town to call to be picked up. After the agents are well on their way to town, Jess, Crandall, Buford and several other old timers will organize the young men and they'll strip the cars, separating the bodies from the frames, saving all usable parts. New tires will be brought to the site and presto! More vehicles! The engine area is off-limits as a target, so they don't have to unnecessarily replace those parts. The car bodies will be stacked and burnt, like those were," he said, pointing to a rusting stack of car bodies set in a niche off to one side of the road. Lisa recognized the early model Ford's and Chevy's which were meticulously stacked to remain a trophy for following decades. The mute trophy displayed windows shot out, bodies riddled with bullet holes, burnt-out interiors, and rust claimed two-thirds of the base vehicles which supported the stack. She tried to imagine the scene decades before.

"Right now," Mike was saying, "the unarmed women are hurriedly in the process of camouflaging the stacked cars. When the CIA rolls by, they won't see it. If they had, they'd stop immediately because the stack indicates what's ahead. After they have passed, the womenfolk will remove the camouflage. When the agents are forced to walk back to town, they'll see the stack and their thoughts will revisit the time the revenuers came to the holler. They'll know the holler got them just as they did the revenuers earlier in the century. The CIA won't start an investigation over shot up vehicles. If they did, they'd better set a watch on their vehicles," Mike said smiling.

"But when they get back to town, won't they be tempted to vent their frustrations on the people they meet?" she asked.

"You probably didn't hear or notice that slow bell ringing when we left. Everyone knows to disappear when that bell stops ringing. When the agents return, no one'll be around," he answered.

"But even still, if everyone's gone, the agents could easily burn the town to the ground," she ventured.

"No, they won't do that either. Just because they see no one, they'll know the town is being watched. Rows of cans will be lined up in different areas of the main road and on some of the side streets. When the agents walk into town, the younger marksmen will intentionally shoot a can. The agents will know they are being watched and if they try anything stupid, they'll be shot. Local agents won't risk their necks because their careers don't hinge on capturing us. They'll use the phone set out for 'em, and they'll leave," Mike outlined.

"The townspeople have it pretty well together," Lisa said. "Yes, from the retelling of the stories, everyone knew what was expected of them. The key word is 'together'. The holler exists singularly through the cooperation of unity. They want to live life their way because they're not interested in becoming modernized. They know of the advanced culture that the modernized, mechanized, industrialized world has evolved into along with the high-pressure drawbacks associated with a modern society. They see the spectrum of advanced diseases the modern culture develops as society seeks release from pressure jobs, stressful lives and fearful futures. People work hard to make enough money so they can enjoy life. Too much emphasis is placed on money. The barter system is a functional reality; it can replace money, but most people can't live without their money. It depends on what you want.

"You'd be surprised how few ever leave the holler to live in, we call it, the outside. Most get married, settle down, raise kids and live in this holler or move to another. To them, the quality of life seems much fuller here," he said.

"What about you? You've been in both places... where do you plan or see yourself as living?" she posed.

"If we survive our present ordeal... I don't know. Both societies have their positives and negatives. I really can't answer that question at this time," he stated, and before he could throw the same question at her, Lisa asked.

"Not to change the subject too fast or anything, but how far will we travel on this road before it ends?"

"The style of the road will change again and again. On this particular dirt style, we'll travel another five miles up the valley and then, after cresting the mountaintop, the type will change. Oh, here's where the turkey shoot will happen," he said and her mercenary memories analyzed how easily the revenuers were taken out. The road appeared to have been carved through a minor hill. Steep angled sides rose fifty feet, embankment length was about two hundred and seventy yards, trees and low bushes hid the crest, it was the dream ambush site against which, there was no defense. She could easily visualize the ambush; a lightening strike followed by everyone melting into the countryside. With the womenfolk camouflaging the trophy, the CIA wouldn't realize the trap until they were into it, and then, it was too late. And Mike went on.

"There'll be other hollers in various places along the way, but you won't be able to see them from the road because the locations were secreted by design. The general public enjoys following back roads, some out of curiosity, others for the novelty of following a back road. Along the way, the road crosses a creek and continues. Most people wouldn't think to turn in a creek and follow it. They simply follow the road. As the road intersects with others, their interest wanes and the novelty of following a back road dissipates. In the process, the holler remains secreted," he was saying and just then, both heard a popping sound behind them in the distance that rose to a crescendo and then, died down.

The two fugitives looked at each other with the knowing smile and then, settled back to enjoy the ride.

"Lisa, let me see the serum," Mike gently asked.

"No!" she defiantly stated.

"Why not?" he asked in disbelief.

"Because I don't trust you," she belligerently answered, and then, she laughed at him as she unzipped her waterproof bag. Pulling the vial and holding it at eye level, she shook the glass tube to show him its thickness.

"Ooh, it looks hideous," he said after seeing the orange serum's sluggish movement.

"The cream of an insane project," she said unemotionally, and she replaced the vial back into the ice. And when Mike looked at her after checking the road forward, she saw respect in his eyes without a word spoken.

"It must have cost you a lot personally to have stolen the serum, notes and having to escape from the agency," he seriously stated, and the gentleness in his voice slammed her emotions back to the Rose Motel.

"More than you can imagine and that I'll never tell you about," she said softly and Mike saw the tears forming. He decided to never bring it up again and to change the subject as fast as he could.

"If you could see through the trees, you'd see numerous homes over on those mountains," he said, pointing to the neighboring rocky finger, and he went one, "there's mountainfolk to this day, but modern society is completely unaware that hollers exists. There's a commercial holler over at Bentonville, Arkansas where the tourists can visit and buy various handmade items. They see that holler, have their pictures taken next to a holler car, buy what they want and go home. No one has ever asked if other hollers exist," he was saying.

"Then, the hollers communicate with each other?" she asked.

"To some extent, yes. If someone were to enter the holler in Bentonville and starts asking a lot of questions, as if he were going to write a book on the subject, great pains would be taken to satisfy his curiosity without disclosing the fact that other hollers exist. His picture would be taken and passed around the different towns with hollers nearby. They would know who he was before he ever arrived in a holler town," he explained.

"A holler town like… Pine Bluff?" she asked.

"Yes, some hollerfolk have moved into areas visible to anyone driving by. In time, the population grew into towns, but the ties to the holler remain firm. The town citizens jealously guard the existence of their roots by never talking to strangers about the nearby holler, thus shielding it from world view. The town is modern in all aspects and no one would suspect a secreted town is nearby. Driving down rural roads sightseeing, tourists only question what they see. They take pictures, buy fruit at roadside stands and look at farms as they pass by. No physical sign of a holler is evident from a public road. People see deliveries made to farms and think nothing more of it. Later, the deliveries are moved into the holler. At harvest time, harvested crops are transported into town by the tons," he said when Lisa commented.

"So, people see trucks moving from the farm to the town and think nothing of it. The holler families in town know what's going on and never talk about it. How much land does the farmer own?" she asked.

"Approximately fifteen miles in all directions from the town. See, he owns the pastureland and mountains and the land was paid off long ago. You have to remember that the purchasing of the land started almost two hundred years ago. Down through modern years, businesses and corporations have tried to purchase section of the farm, and while the farmer refuses to sell, he's always ready to buy bordering properties. Some of the homes, on that county road we used to arrive at the farmers' land, are owned by the farmer and occupied by holler families. They raise crops, pigs, sell craft items, maintain the property, but most importantly, they notify the farmer or the police concerning hunters," Mike was explaining.

"I was wondering about hunters. You said only kids probably would find the holler. How are hunters handled?" Lisa asked.

"All of the farmers land is posted against hunting. When hunting licenses are issued, warnings of posted lands are handed out with strict fines listed on the warnings. Usually, no one hunts on farmland, and access to the farmland is discouraged. Along the interstate, the sides of the roadbed drop away at sharp angles. Naturally, if a vehicle breaks down, there's ample shoulder to pull off on, but beyond the shoulder, it's a sharp drop-off. In the mountains, all accessible roads have been blockaded by huge boulders that appear to have been part of a rockslide. People, seeing evidence of a rockslide, are skittish about venturing into the area with their vehicles. You might be surprised how few people have ventured onto the farmers' land, and no one has discovered the holler nor the roads leading into it.

If you were to drive by the farm during harvest time, you'd see hundreds of people working the fields, automatically, you'd think nothing of it. People working in fields are so normal a sight, which is forgotten quickly because it's commonplace. Holler families work the fields, and no one on the interstate notices where the workers come from. It's easy to leave the holler and begin harvesting because the crops block the view, but as the fields are being cleared, the last acres harvested are near the roads or paths leading into the holler. As harvesting winds down, people slip back into the holler unnoticed, so, when the last acre is cut, no one is left in the field. The farmer rolls back to his house, all the folk are at home in the holler, and passerbys are none the wiser," he was explaining.

"They've proven life's so simple," Lisa analyzed, "without the complexities and transparent concerns, our modern society could learn an entirely new way of life, if only they'd slow down and listen. In relation, it's odd having so many people working together for one common goal. It's like they're relatives."

"It's not really a new way of life – they're still at the fundamental origins of society. All societies have had their basic origins from communal roots, only these people have omitted the one ingredient which destroys the community: progress. Progress cultivates the evolution of inventions on a multitude of levels, with new ideas replacing old concepts. Once old concepts are compared to new ideas, aggressive people embrace the new, quickly pointing to the advantages of new compared to old. Naturally, the base element of greed flourishes with progress because of the opportunity to capitalize on those uneducated to deal with the variety of new products being mass produced. That one subject, greed, could be debated, discussed, dissected, rehashed and re-analyzed, but in the holler, greed is non-existent. Look at everything that proceeds from progress as compared to life in the holler. In your own opinion, what are your thoughts?" he asked and he could see her reflecting on her visit. The question, basically, was unfair because it was her first exposure to holler life.

"Are you trying to convince me to live in the holler after we conclude this... ordeal, if we survive?" she wanted to know.

"Isn't that what you were really asking me a few minutes ago, where I planned on living or what I intended to do once this thing is over?" he challenged.

"Now, that was a legitimate question based on the premise that you grew up near and had intimate knowledge of the holler and presently, you're a Green Beret with advanced technological abilities serving in the elite forces of the military. You've experienced both types of worlds, and that was a legitimate question," she aggressively said.

"So, that's how you're going to qualify it – as a 'legitimate question'," he pointedly stated.

"Yes," she sheepishly answered smiling.

"Well, to repeat myself, I sincerely don't know what I'll do once this is over – assuming we survive. And I love it when you're caught in one of your little head trips, and the way you try to intellectualize your way out – is so cute," he said, beaming broadly.

"Smartass, if you…" she started

"If I wasn't, you'd have dumped me long ago," he said, finishing her sentence.

"I just hate it when you're right, you bastard!" she pouted.

"I know, and I just love it!!" he said, still broadly grinning as they began descending on the mountaintop road in the warmth of the early afternoon sun. From the top, Lisa viewed the green rolling expanse of nature spread to the horizon as if the world originated from the stony fingers. Calming down, she periodically caught glimpses of traffic, through the trees, moving on the interstate. Amazed, she considered the proximity of two societies to each other, and yet, only one knew of the other. The holler folk were totally aware of modern society with all its aspects, and modern society, with all its sophistication, remained thoroughly ignorant that a subculture existed so close to their own.

"Does the sheriff of the county visit the holler?" she asked.

"Yes, he's visited on numerous occasions, talked with the old timers, been in the general store, has seen all the holler vehicles and generally cruises around, checking things out. He's proud of the holler, plans to retire to one of them. He's openly admitted we have a better way of life, much healthier in peace of mind than he's known on the outside. I'd like to know how the CIA found out about the holler. Not knowing for sure, I could surmise that the revenuers left directions in an old report which the CIA, somehow, got a hold of. Any enlightenment from one who has had CIA ties?" he asked.

"I wasn't in that section of the agency, so I'd have no knowledge as to how they knew," she said, being careful how she answered.

"Ok, we'll let that drop. When I was a kid, friends and I would visit the mountainfolk, spending the day or two before returning. Leaving the holler, it was a half-day's walk to the hill homes, getting there was half the fun. We'd follow paths across fallen logs over flowing creeks, and naturally, someone always fell in. Wildlife was abundant. Often, a mature buck would chase us, scattering us in all directions. None of us were ever injured. I guess, the larger animals viewed kids as fair game, and chased us until we regrouped and, as a group, charged screaming at the attacking animal. Then, the animal would be gone in a moment. It's pretty scary when suddenly, a huge deer with a large rack of antlers, charges out of the bushes. Later in years, I learned that some of the animals were toying with us, because they weren't afraid of kids. They avoided the adults, but the kids, it's like, they were having fun with us or playing with us, in their way. I couldn't then and still can't precisely explain the feeling associated with that situation, but it wasn't a dangerous one.

"Then, the walk around the stony finger was awesome. Inside the woods near one of the fingers is a swimming hole and, of course, everyone knew its location. We'd strip off our clothes and swim for awhile. Next, we'd lay out in the sun by the base of a finger and dry off before the climb up. Standing at the base and looking up would blow your mind. There's a path on the inside valley of one of the fingers that winds from the bottom to the top. Of course, there's boulders on the path and we had to worm our way up," he concluded.

"Your childhood sounds wonderfully exciting," she said with a loving smile.

"Yes, it was, but it wasn't until many years later that I realized how deeply I appreciated having had the privilege of having grown up in and around unique people," he said, trying to convey the experience.

"Don't try to explain it. You'll end up losing something in the attempt," she warned.

"Ok, when we near the base of this mountain, the trees will again provide cover from patrolling aircraft. By now, the CIA would have pulled most of their people off the main roads to focus their search on the backroads, leaving minimum personnel patrolling main thoroughfares. We need to keep moving until we're well north of this area. It'll be late tonight when we get off the holler road in central Kentucky," he outlined.

THE WHITE HOUSE

Following the afternoon press conference, the President was visibly agitated because the nature of the questioning insinuated White House involvement.

"Why is the press corp. still questioning me concerning the Tanner/Youngblood problem? Why are they asking *me* if the CIA is involved? Why is the Senate And House members on a sudden vacation? They've all left town like a bunch of spineless cockroaches! And where is the CIA Director? I want to talk to him!!" the President angrily shouted at no one in particular.

"Mr. President," Marsha said, hesitatingly stepping forward to deliver bad news, "the Senate and House members voted for a vacation because of the recent instability of the CIA".

"The *What?*" he asked, not believing what he was hearing, and then, he said, "what the Hell is going on around here?"

"Mr. President," General Hansen started.

"Mr. President," an aide cut in instantly, "there's trouble in the

Middle East that looks like war. The War Room has urgently requested for your immediate attention and your chopper will be landing in one minute."

"Mr. President," General Hansen tried again, "request permission to go to Louisville, Kentucky to end the Tanner/Youngblood problem".

"Alright," the Chief said to the aide, and then, he asked the general, "how would you know to say Louisville, Kentucky?" and when he saw the general hesitate, he added, "General, things are starting to jump off kind of quick here. I need some straight up answers."

"Because we have a man on top of the problem."

"Would that man be Mike Tanner?" the Chief asked.

"Yes sir."

"How deeply involved is the CIA?"

"Mr. President, I don't have solid proof that I can lay on your desk at this time, but from what I'm hearing – up to their necks," the general said, and the Chief winced.

"Ok General, you've got the green light on what you need to do, but," he advised, "when I get everyone together, everybody is going to have a lot of explaining to do," the Chief said, and the noise from a landing chopper announced his departure.

MIKE AND LISA

Three hours after leaving the holler, they were passing under Interstate 40 through a viaduct. As promised, the road changed from dirt to gravel, gravel back to dirt, dirt to hunters' trails, trails to creeks, creeks back to dirt, the style changing with each passing hour. Along the way, they discussed explosives, ammunition, weapons, hunting, vehicles, techniques and tactics. Mike has learned Lisa not only tracked with his conversation, but related and questioned intelligently which challenged the depths of his knowledge and ultimately, his emotional disposition concerning some subjects. Some men cower before those women who possess towering confidence in their abilities to not only maintain pace with men in verbal sparing, but who also intimately scrutinize the emotions supporting their established convictions. Mike was comfortable with Lisa's verbal barrage as he allowed her the space to speak her mind on any topic.

Analyzing her discussions concerning the CIA, Mike realized

her conversation covered possibilities of reactions, the agency's anticipation of their destination and of monies spent in the attempt to capture the fleeing pair. But the subject of Lisa's involvement, other than her work in the research lab, was never discussed in depth. When the CIA was mentioned, Lisa skillfully steered the conversation away from her. And Mike wisely decided to let that point rest.

At times, while enroute through the countryside on back roads, they listened to the news on the radio. Throughout the day, nothing new was revealed, just the usual; the two dangerous criminals were still at large after blowing up the Henryville Bridge and downing a helicopter. On gravel roads, they passed by Bowling Green and Mammoth Caves on the eastside and were two hours south of Elizabethtown, Kentucky when Mike informed Lisa that the holler road was ending. The sun had set as Lisa pulled out of a creek and onto a dirt road, the road would lead to a paved artery whose on-ramp placed them on Interstate 65 north. Driving on the moonless night, the pitch-black darkness worked to their advantage. Vehicles passing in the opposite direction were indistinguishable. Both knew the Kentucky State Police needed to approach from the rear before recognition was possible. Every vehicle overtaking them was suspected of being hostile. Nerves were frayed. On the back roads, there was no traffic. As the holler road wound through the hills between many overhanging trees, they were, for the large part, hidden under the trees' cover. Although they maintained a watchful eye on the road and in the air, no traffic of any type materialized. Their fears had been temporarily suspended, but now, they were forced to travel a main thoroughfare.

"I know we talked about it before and couldn't come up with a game plan, but we need one. I keep mulling it over in my mind of how to go public with the serum and the notes, and I can't... there's..." she said, trying to verbally formulate a plan.

"Did you have a game plan when you stole the project?" Mike calmly asked.

"That was different. It was simpler. You just steal and run," she stated, and deep down she knew the reason for Mike's calmness.

He realizes there's no control on the action we're about to take, she thought. When I took the serum and notes and fled, that was merely a course of action, not a game plan. I didn't have to control any events other than the direction on my flight. And the direction of flight was to avoid the CIA. In facing unknown events, a levelheaded approach instills confidence that natural abilities coupled with analytical reasoning will solve what appears to be an impossible situation. He doesn't give place to fears unnecessarily. Why fear what you can't predict? He's going to wing it once there because we can't plan the action now. Ok Lisa, calm down. Take a few deep breaths, and in the dark van, Mike heard the deep breaths and he knew what she was doing.

"Feeling better now?" he again calmly asked.

"Yes, and do you know how irritating you can be sometimes?" she calmly asked, and Mike laughed.

"Yes," he simply answered.

Moving with traffic, the fugitives arrived at the outskirts of Louisville after an uneventful trip. Too well known to check into a motel, both decided to park the van on a used car lot for the night. Lisa located a lot just south of the city and backed the van into a vacant slot next to several other vans with one at the rear. She then moved to the rear to make the bed while Mike cleared the dash, bonnet and area between the seats to give the appearance of the van being for sale, should someone look in. After locking the doors, he closed the curtains behind the front seats and joined Lisa. While she was straightening the covers, Mike watched movement outside the van until he was sure their addition to the car lot went unnoticed.

"Let's get a good nights sleep before we take off in the morning," Lisa suggested.

"We need an early start in the morning," he stated, and they removed their shoes and went to bed fully clothed.

✦

Listening to her breathing as it slowed and deepened, Mike knew once Lisa laid down, it wouldn't be long until she was sound asleep. Quietly and gently, he slipped off the custom bed and moved to the front of the van. He plugged in the bullet and set the transceiver on its interior base on the dash and backed behind the curtain to watch while he talked.

"Dion, you got your ears on?" he quietly questioned.

"Yeah, man, right here," Dion stated in a normal voice.

"Ok, here's what happened after they loaded you on the bus…" and again, Mike replayed the events as they occurred, and he whispered saying, "and we're just south of Louisville now, parked for the night."

"After I left, the first stop we made, I called Stranton and informed him. When I arrived, we were loaded onto a C-130 transport and flown to Fort Knox. We're there now, and do you what kind of hangover I had from that 'strawberry shine delite'?" Dion questioned.

"Yeah, 'cause I've had 'em before too. Tomorrow at eightish we're going to air what we know. Haven't any idea at this time *how* we're going to do it, but we need to get this thing out into the open. That'll get the CIA off our backs," he softly related.

"You going on TV?" Dion asked.

"Yeah," Mike whispered.

"Whatever you do, don't walk in the front doors! You know who will be minutes behind both of you," Dion warned.

"Dion, pressure has been building and forcing the CIA to act and tomorrow, we're going to go public with the whole mess," Mike quietly said.

"You can count on us to be flying around about that time," Dion assured.

"I hope so! Well, I'd better get some sleep. Tomorrow promises to be interesting," Mike said.

"We'll be there, buddy," Dion affirmed and they both clicked off.

JUNE 17

MIKE AND LISA

6:30 AM

Waking up just before dawn, Mike looked through the van curtains, checking the car lot for activity. Seeing none, he kissed Lisa awake.

"Time to rise and shine," he softly said, not wanting to startle her awake.

"Oh, it's times like this that I wish I were someone else. What time is it?" she asked.

"It's time to roll before salesmen start showing up. We devoured the food packed in the holler and I think we should have breakfast before finding a TV station," Mike suggested.

"Oh great, Mister Growing Army Man is hungry," she said sarcastically.

"Yep, you're hungry too. I hate it when you're sarcastic and dangerous. Dangerous I can handle but the combination is too much for any man," Mike said while pulling the covers off her.

"When I'm fully awake, I'm going to get you Tanner," she threatened as she sat up on the bed rubbing her eyes and face.

"That's what I like first thing in the morning, attitude. I'll warm up the van sweetheart while you sit there and look pretty," he said.

"If I wasn't so tired, the second thing you'd have is an earnest wrestling match. But I'll spare you that since we don't have a padded mat," she said while shrugging each shoulder, loosening up.

"Now that's definitely something to look forward to each morning; Ms. Jekyll turns into Ms. Hyde at first light. That's an interesting twist in horror concepts," he was saying when Lisa moved to the front of the van and grabbed him.

"You're really pushing it this morning buster," she stated, grabbing his chin and turning his face toward her.

"What I'm doing sweetheart, is provoking your attitude to prepare you for the day," he enlightened.

"Your attempts are working better than you think," she said sternly.

"Dear, we both need to be mentally focussed for the day's events. Our imaginations have to be wide open to seize a moment of opportunity. You know how opportunity only knocks once and after that, Murphy's Law takes over," Mike instructed.

"Ok, enough of the lecture. Let's get something quick through McDonald's drive-by window and eat while we're moving downtown. We could go to WHAS on West Chestnut Street, that's channel 11 and they're the biggest TV station in Louisville," she suggested.

"Ok, sounds like the beginning of a plan. We'll drive by and check out the possibilities of getting in. I'm ruling out any ideas of walking in the front door. We'll need maybe five minutes of uninterrupted time. We wouldn't get that if we went in the front door," he pointed out.

"Fine, let's get going," she said and Mike pulled out of the car lot and located an on-ramp onto I-65 north after traveling a short distance on the frontage road. Blending in with the morning traffic, the fugitives moved into the downtown area and exited from I-65. Lisa directed Mike to WHAS on Chestnut and upon arrival, Mike drove past the main entrance and circled the block. Upon turning back toward Chestnut, Mike started passing the station's loading dock. Five single-axle box trucks were backed up to the dock. Pulling into a parking place opposite the station, both fugitives analyzed the scene.

"This looks like our best avenue of approach," Mike stated.

"Yeah, but there's cameras at opposite ends of the dock scanning the entire area," Lisa observed.

"True, but look at this truck on the left. See how close it is to the ramp leading into the building. The passenger side is in the camera's blind spot. That's why they have two, so the far camera covers the blind spot. That's the way in and all we need is some kind of diversion, just for a minute or two," Mike was saying and just then, a panel truck from Dunkin Donuts pulled in and parked between the ramp and the single-axle box truck.

"Opportunity's knocking! Make sure you weapon is concealed and grab your bag!" Mike excitedly instructed as he left the driver's seat and walked briskly across the street, heading for the Dunkin Donuts truck. Rounding the passenger side, Mike stepped inside.

"Hi! Is this the delivery for Todd Williams in the control room?" Mike asked, licking his lips.

"Ah, no sir. This is for Mr. Wells in programming," the driver said after looking at the delivery ticket. Then, the driver stuck the ticket in his mouth and reached for a large pink box with the name *Wells* printed on one side. Mike instantly hit the driver in the ribs and when he leaned toward Mike, the Green Beret knocked him out with a blow to the side of the jaw. Just then, Lisa stepped into the passenger door. Retrieving a company jacket from a nearby hook, Mike donned the official-looking apparel.

"Delivery," Mike said to Lisa with a smile, and added, "you're my girlfriend who's going to do the route starting next week and you want to see where you might be delivering donuts. I'll act like I've done it a thousand times, you act like it's your first," Mike instructed. As they stepped from the van, Lisa *was* excited that they had found a way in and with only minor trouble. Walking to the main service door, both saw a security guard watching the dock and guarding the entrance.

"Delivery for Mr. Wells in programming," Mike said, acting like this was a typical business delivery, and he added, "this is Beth Anderson. Next week she'll be delivering in this area. So, any orders after this weekend, you'll be seeing her."

"Oh, I love bringing donuts to people! This is my first time here! Where would we find the programming room? Are you always on guard here?" she jumbled together, and when the guard looked at Mike, Mike just rolled his eyes.

"Yes dear," he said patiently, and went on, "walk straight down this hall until you come to the stairway. Go up one flight and when you exit, turn left. You'll see cameras, lighting equipment and technicians. You'll be walking next to a wall with the equipment on your right. Be quiet in that area because in one minute, channel 11 will be broadcasting its live morning program. When you come to soundproof doors, turn right. Straight in front of you will be stairs. Go up the stairs and double back. Then, you'll be walking into the control room. The programming room is just beyond," the guard outlined.

"Thank you, I got it, and be quiet – I know! Thanks again!" Lisa said excitedly, and both outlaws moved to the stairway. As they climbed the stairs, Mike took off the company jacket and wrapped it around the box. Upon exiting on the first flight up, both saw Doug Proffitt on the morning news set. Make-up was being applied, wardrobe was brushing his suit and technicians were using light meters to ensure for proper lighting. The outlaws turned right and quietly moved behind the prop that would be seen on television behind Proffitt.

"Let them get started, then, we'll make our move. You walk around that side of the prop and I'll go this way to come up behind the newscaster," Mike whispered.

"Ok people, on the air in seven," the camera director was saying.

"Just say what you've got to and then, we need to get lost fast," Mike said.

"In five," the director said.

"Ok. Nervous?" she asked and Mike shook his head no.

"In three."

"Get ready," Mike said.

"Good morning Kentuckiana," Doug Proffitt was saying, "in the news today, more on why legislatures in the Nation's capitol have stopped debates on bills and have taken vacations. War seems imminent in the Middle East, and the hunt continues for Mike Tanner and Lisa Youngblood. The weather from Kentuckiana's Storm Team follows headline news…" he was reporting when interrupted. Mike and Lisa walked around the prop and Lisa sat down in the vacant chair next to Proffitt.

"Ladies and gentlemen, I'm Lisa Youngblood and this is Mike Tanner," she began and Proffitt was noticeably taken aback as he turned to face her. When she introduced Tanner, Proffitt then noticed the Green Beret behind and with a 9mm trained on him. Once again facing the cameras, Proffitt interlaced his fingers on the desktop as Lisa continued.

"I'm the one responsible for the break-in at the Jackson National Guard Armory. Mike and I are responsible for the subsequent actions of destroying numerous police cars, the downing of helicopters, the destruction of the Henryville Bridge and the death of the CIA Director. Nazi Dr. Hans Schuler developed a serum for the CIA which alters the physical appearance of an individual," she said as she unzipped her bag, showed the cameras the full vial and the doctor's ID badge. After replacing both in the bag, she continued, "the CIA has plans in place to take over a third world nation using the serum. It would be a CIA Nation complete with military governed by its own constitution and thoroughly independent from America. The CIA instigated the manhunt for Mike and myself in the attempt to secure the serum back under wraps for later usage. We'll take the doctor's notes and serum with us as we are still fugitives and now, we have to leave," she concluded. As abruptly as they arrived, they left. As they hurriedly departed, Doug Proffitt ordered the control room.

"Break in on national news now for a special news bulletin and rewind this morning's tape," he was ordering as the fugitives disappeared through the door. With guns at the ready, no one stopped Mike or Lisa as they exited the building and dashed for the van. In the distance, they heard sirens.

"You said 'Nazi Dr.' we don't know he was a Nazi Dr.," Mike chided as they jumped into the van.

"That was for shock effect. If there's anything the public hates more than the CIA, it's a Nazi doctor working *for* the CIA. Head for the river and turn left of Main St. Further down on West Main, we'll find an on-ramp for the Sherman Minton Bridge. After we cross the Ohio River into Indiana, we should think about giving ourselves up. We haven't wrecked anything in Indiana, so they shouldn't be too upset with us," Lisa answered with a smile.

LAWRENCEBURG POLICE DEPARTMENT

7:45 AM

"Ladies and gentlemen of the press, Police Captain Buford Randolph," the deputy announced, addressing the assembled media representative and they came to order as the burly captain walked to the podium with papers in hand.

"Ladies and gentlemen," He began, "on June 14th, at approximately 10:45am, the fugitives Lisa Youngblood and Mike Tanner were sighted in Lawrence County, and at the same time, the Lawrenceburg Police Department pursued the pair supporting the CIA's efforts to capture. At approximately 11:05am, the suspects effectively halted the ground pursuit by destroying the Henryville Bridge. At this point, no officers were injured nor wounded. The pursuit continued through the CIA's two fully armed Cobra helicopters. At approximately 11:20am, the fugitives shot down one Cobra and haven't been seen since. Onboard the downed chopper was the Central Intelligence Agency's Director Will Summers. The pilot and director were killed by weapons stolen by Lisa Youngblood from the Jackson National Guard Armory. We have recovered the remains and have positive identification. Questions?" he asked.

"Captain, why are we hearing this report three days late and from you instead of Langley or Washington?" a female CNN reporter shouted.

"Madam, I cannot answer for the CIA nor the White House. I am relating our findings and known facts to the press."

"Why has it taken three days to report what you know to be factual about the director's death?" a veteran newspaper reporter asked, shouting the question.

"While we confirmed his death, I allowed the CIA time to make the announcement. When it appeared they had no intention of releasing that information, I then decided it was in the national interest that his death be made public," Buford said.

"What happened to the second chopper?" a FOX 8 reporter asked.

"The second chopper attempted to establish contact with the fugitives, but his efforts failed and the pair apparently escaped," the captain responded.

"Captain, why didn't you have other police units in front of the suspects as well as behind?" another reporter asked.

"Sir, we did have units converging from both directions. The forward units were fifteen minutes away when the suspects destroyed the chopper. It was estimated that both airborne units could have delayed the fugitives long enough for the forward ground elements to move into a capturing position. Upon arrival at the destroyed bridge, the units doubled back, but were unable to determine which secondary road had been used by the fugitives and therefore, unable to reestablish contact," Buford explained.

"Captain, how many officers were involved in the search?" a local reporter asked.

"All police officers were involved in the patrolling efforts to locate the fleeing pair, establish and maintain contact while reinforcements converged on the area. Once we received an APB of the suspects' possible flight through our county, we immediately organized an overlapping, doubling-back search pattern covering the entire county. Off-duty officers elected to participate in the search, as the suspects were described as lethally dangerous and ordered to be killed on sight. Never having received such an order, all officers felt that it was in the county's best interest to absolutely ascertain the validity of the suspects' whereabouts, if in the county. I'm proud of my officers' involvement in the search, and their conduct reflects their esteem toward safety in the county," he answered.

"Then, why is it the suspects escaped?" the FOX 8 reporter asked.

"The CIA Director brought in a number of his people who preceded the police pursuit. I feel the CIA hindered police efforts to capture the fugitives because of their lack of knowledge of the county. Had the CIA left the capture to the police department, the suspects would be behind bars as we speak," the captain said.

"Was this a CIA operation?" another reporter shouted.

"In part, yes. When the CIA assumed authority over the police and aggressively pursued the fleeing pair, yes, it was then their operation and we backed them up. But from the beginning, it was our plan to initiate the crisscrossing and backtracking search patterns. Because of his position, he had the authority to take over the search and conduct it as he saw proper." Buford admitted.

"Is the entire Tanner/Youngblood affair a CIA operation?" the CNN reporter asked.

"I can't answer that question. I've told you what I know of the incident. The 'why's' concerning the fugitives' actions – I don't know at this time, and that'll be all for today," he said, and he left the podium under a hail of questions. The captain decided since the CIA intentionally neglected to inform the nation of the director's death, he'd allow only a short span of time before he'd drop the proverbial bomb on the world. And he planned to announce the results of the attack so the 8:00 am news reports would deliver the news with everyone's morning coffee.

LANGLEY, CIA HEADQUARTERS

8:00 AM

The assistant director had arrived earlier in the morning, entering into his office through secret passages, affording him the luxury of being at work without anyone's knowledge of actually seeing him arrive, hoping to communicate with the director on the Youngblood problem concerning the next course of action he should take to expedite their capture.

After ponderously downing a pot of coffee, he was sitting at his desk with a U.S. map spread before him. Putting his index finger on the map, her merely allowed his finger to wander north from their last known position. No sightings were reported on Interstate 40, nothing from Nashville or Memphis, and dismissing the idea of I-40, he let his finger continue on its northbound wanderings until it stopped on Louisville, Kentucky.

"Louisville! That's where she's going!" he said excitedly to himself out loud. Quickly dialing the Louisville office from the number off the Rolodex, he only heard two rings before the call was answered.

"Hello," was the unemotional response from the party answering.

"Yes, this in Johnathan Walker in Langley," John said, identifying himself.

"Oh, yes sir, so good to hear from you! How can we help you sir?" the voice said perking up.

"Lisa Youngblood and Mike Tanner are reported to be in Louisville. They are lethally dangerous and are to be killed on sight. Their descriptions have been faxed to all offices. Youngblood is carrying a serum stolen from a doctor that she killed. The serum must be recovered, kept refrigerated and returned to headquarters. Put everyone on the streets looking for her and Tanner, and don't take any chances. Kill on sight! The serum has top priority. If you get all three, put all three on a private jet and ship immediately, even if Tanner and Youngblood are dead. Any questions?" Johnathan asked.

"No sir. Everything is clear as crystal," the agent answered.

"Good! Roll on it and give me progress reports," John instructed.

"Yes sir," he enthusiastically responded and hung up. Still at his desk, John clicked the TV on to catch the morning news while sipping coffee. At three minutes past eight, a special news bulletin interrupted all regular programming and Johnathan leaned back to watch.

FORT KNOX, KENTUCKY

7:30 AM

"Load Up People," the Green Beret gunnery sergeant shouted. Two reinforced squads, numbering twenty-five soldiers, boarded three UH-1 Huey gunships. "You don't wanna miss the grand tour of beautiful downtown Louisville with its lovely ladies, shopping malls, state fairgrounds, and, as we pass... we will have... a standing ovation for the Belle of Louisville, the city's own paddle-wheeler. Move It People, the grand tour also includes a one-time pass over the elegant Churchill Downs, and, there will be no betting on the ponies, gentlemen." While the troopers were loading, Green Beret Brigadier General Tom Stranton, Army Joint Chief-of-Staff Bill Hansen and National Guard Major General Hammond boarded their observation chopper with their personal guard following in another chopper. Flight time to Louisville was almost thirty minutes.

Lifting off at 0735 hundred hours would place them above the northern Kentucky city at about 0800 hundred hours. The flight was uneventful, each trooper drank in the early morning spectacle from the cool lofty position. Each Green Beret soldier was fully briefed on the situation and each secretly thirsted for combat. But with Dion, the drive was different, the compelling was intense.

Dion had been there at the beginning. Mike had spoon-fed him information from afar. And in turn, the black intellectual informed Mike what info he could scrounge from news outlets or items he 'accidentally' overheard from the general's office. And now, with pressures, desperations and frustrations coming to a head, Dion yearned to be next to his buddy and squad leader. Everyone aware of the situation had been watching tension build within the agency and they waited for the pressured CIA to execute its desperation maneuver. The passing of each day had witnessed tensions build within the agency, and everyone privy to the affair – knew the breaking point was fast approaching.

In the chopper, Dion had two headsets on; one for internal chopper communications and the other tuned to Mike's mini-satellite dish – the dish having top priority. The general had ordered the pilots to follow Dion's instructions and the officer informed the pilots that the instructions originated from Tanner.

At 0800 hundred hours, the formation of five choppers flew over the outskirts of Louisville. Minutes later, they were flying above and following the Ohio River. Watching the early morning dawn of an innocent day, they knew the city inhabitants were unaware of the catastrophic events unfolding on their streets.

At 0805 hundred hours, the pilot turned his head and specking into the com headset, he addressed Dion.

"Dion, shit just hit the fan," he shouted above the din of the chopper engine.

"Mike and Lisa aired their announcement?" Dion shouted back.

"There were two announcements aired," the pilot said, holding up two fingers.

"Two?" Dion said surprised.

"Yeah, theirs and one from down south. Onboard a chopper Mike shot down was the CIA Director. Mike killed the CIA Director!" the pilot shouted, and Dion smiled, nodded an affirmative and mouthed the words, 'I know.' One corner of the pilot's mouth curled into a knowing smile. He was proud of Mike. Mike was rattling the CIA to their bones. Unaware that the magnitude of implications from his actions had just began impacting on the nation's capitol, Mike was merely reacting to combat and attempting to stay alive. It was combat, regardless of the face of the enemy. It was kill or be killed, and Mike had the point position, baring the brunt of assault from a skilled American agency, and he was holding his own. The pilot felt honored and proud to be ferrying Mike's squad to his aid. Turning forward, he determined that wherever was necessary to land in the city to assist Mike, regardless of the obstacle, he was going to land.

Fort Knox has viewed the special bulletins, flashed the contents to the Joint Chief and Hansen passed the communique onto the troopers. Deep down, everyone knew the situation had just turned ugly. Being the foremost combat element, Dion determined to lead all others, if combat erupted. More than ever, he wanted to be next to Mike. And all he could do, all they could do, was wait.

LANGLEY, CIA HEADQUARTERS

Johnathan stared, mouth agape, at the TV set as the news reports from Lawrenceburg and Louisville followed each other. The nightmarish situation stunned him motionless. The serum was announced to the world, the director was dead and he only would answer for the Tanner/Youngblood problem. Dreams of a CIA nation died with the director – a golden Phoenix would not rise from the ruin to save his day. Shocked, he switched off the set. Sweeping his hand down to straighten his tie, he slowly walked to his desk. Sitting down, he realized he'd be held accountable for all events. The humiliation of imprisonment was a foregone conclusion.

Pressure from public outcry concerning an ex-Nazi, especially one who participated at the roots of the Holocaust, being on CIA payroll and who headed the project, forced a compromising solution on the assistant. With eternal incarceration pictured in his mind while infinite numbers of congressional hearings promised to wring damning secret details of the project, Johnathan calmly decided upon his only possible alternative.

"Mr. Walker," Will's secretary said over the intercom, "the President is demanding to know your whereabouts and to speak to you."

"Give me a minute, Marg," he serenely responded. Slowly sliding open the top, right drawer, he cast about in his mind the next logical course of events. Public opinion would condemn his participation with an ex-nazi in a mad scheme for absolute power. At the pinnacle of Washington power, his audacious behavior denied him any recourse. Explanations would be attempts to justify actions. Regardless of any defense, public condemnations were inevitable, too many people had died, and, he was responsible.

Finally admitting to himself, fate decided it wasn't meant to be. Reaching into the open drawer, his hand closed on a recently cleaned and loaded .357 magnum. Thoughtfully and intentionally, he lifted the answer to his problems, and while examining the manufactured beauty of the weapon, he cocked the hammer. Turning the business end on himself, relieved feelings washed over him knowing he would escape the humiliation of national disgrace, endless questioning, imprisonment. Sticking the barrel into his mouth, he saw himself withdrawing from the multitude of entwining, complex overlapping problems created by himself and the director, in their bid for unlimited power. A bid that proved successful for nearly five years, until Youngblood came along.

A beautiful pawn wrecked so may well laid plans, he thought. Hearing subordinates running to his office, Johnathan felt secure in his decision to remove himself from his personal dilemma, knowing they could do nothing to alter anything, and, as they burst into his office, Johnathan walker, assistant CIA Director, pulled the trigger – splattering brains, blood, bone fragments onto the wall behind. Stunned and shocked at being eyewitnesses to their boss' suicide, the subordinates slowly began to realize that one of them was now responsible for the agency's actions.

"After the assistant director, the senior agent is next in the chain of command," one agent said.

"Oh no, the finance administrator is third in the chain of command," another agent asserted.

"Oh no you don't, you're not throwing the blame for this mess onto my department," an angry agent retorted, and after word had spread of the suicide, gun battles broke out between core groups, power rivals and the privileged insiders. Upon hearing the gun battles escalating, Marg frantically called the White House for help.

THE WHITE HOUSE

8:09 AM

Prior to the usual morning meeting with the President, where the day's agenda was discussed, modified and rearranged, the While House staff always watched the morning news to keep abreast of world breaking events and to advise the Chief accordingly. Video taping news for later analysis aided the staffers' assistants to discover subtle implications which might affect U.S. operations or policies. Viewing this morning's news, the staff was shocked to learn of the CIA Director's death, the depth of involvement of the agency in the Tanner/Youngblood affair and the implications of the inevitable shock waves which would be produced by the revelations. Instantly pulling the videotape after the special bulletins aired, they played it for the President.

"Why is it that I have to hear of the director's death from the news media and not the CIA itself?" President Threadmiller shouted. "Get on the phone, get the assistant director and if they can't find him, he's fired! Why am I not surprised to learn that the Youngblood thing has deeper entanglements with the CIA than they let on?! Marsha, cancel the day's appointments because I have a feeling that it's going to take the better part of the day just to figure out what's really been going on and probably take months to straighten out."

"Mr. President," Marsha said after the switchboard operator linked her out-going call to an incoming call from CIA Headquarters, "the CIA Assistant Director Johnathan Walker just committed suicide in his office and a gun battle is now in progress in the headquarters building. The director's secretary is crying and requesting help."

Exasperated, the President said to the Marine Joint-Chief-of-Staff, "get the marines in there and stop the fighting! Have the FBI go in with or behind you and I want the CIA arrested, within the exemption of the overseas operation, that division is exempt. Arrest everyone else, secretaries included! Move!!" he loudly ordered and those involved jumped into action.

"Mr. President," Marsha asked softly, "wouldn't the act of arresting the CIA have serious international implication which would breed distrust or contempt toward the agency?"

"The situation is already past being serious, and before our concerns involve other nations, we are first concerned with our own national security. The instability of the CIA seriously threatens our security which now must be resolved, and the entire incident must be publicly scrutinized because if we attempt to cover up the slightest detail, this administration will suffer in the same fate as the CIA. I only fear the details we don't know as yet surrounding this incident. I hope Hansen secures Youngblood and Tanner alive because it seems that those two are the only ones still breathing who might have all the answers."

MIKE AND LISA

"I feel a lot better now that this thing's in the open. Maybe now the President will order the CIA to explain recent actions which will remove them off our backs. Let's wait a short while until we see a reaction from the White House," Mike suggested as they were rolling along Main St.

"Ok, I'll admit that's a better idea, but let's get out of Kentucky for the time... ah... ah, Mike! I think that's the CIA right there on that side street looking at us! And he's talking to somebody!" she urgently said while watching an agent talk into a wrist radio.

"Yeah, and there's his buddies on the next corner!" Mike pointed out.

"Pull over! How come these bastards aren't watching TV! Then, they'd know it's over for 'em," she excitedly said, and as the van was skidding to a stop, Mike's hand was on the 'bullet'. He plugged in the power source, the remote mike and as the pentad summit parted, he set it on the roof. Nine minutes past eight, Dion began to hear noises on the headset tuned to Mike's satellite dish.

"Dion – Dion, you got your ears on, man?" came the frantic call.

"Yeah, right here, buddy. What's going on?" Dion calmly asked.

"We're in trouble! We're downtown on Main Street, outside the Louisville Slugger Building and we're lookin' directly at the CIA! The building's real easy to spot from the air – it's got a hundred and twenty foot bat leaning against the exterior of the building! The shooting's gonna start in about ten seconds! You're most cordially invited to join the party at your earliest convenience! Gotta go!" Mike hastily stated.

"We'll be right there, buddy," Dion said, and then, gave the location to the pilots and advised the generals of the situation.

As Lisa was jumping out of the van, her right hand dropped to snatch a bandolier of 9mm ammo. The bandolier was intentionally placed on the floor between the seat and the door as a precaution against leaving empty-handed. She had learned that upon a hasty exit, one needed to grab what was available in the event the opportunity would be lost to retrieve anything more from the van. After exiting the van, she headed for the rear to grab the '16. Slinging the automatic over her right shoulder, she then noticed two new police cadets standing by the glass doors of the Slugger Building. The newly graduated cadets displayed their greenness by awkwardly trying to accustom themselves to their new service belts which contained a police radio on the left side and a service revolver on the right side. Trying to figure out where their arms should land, if the arms hung normally, then they rested on the gun and radio. And when walking, the swinging motion would cause the arms to hit both radio and gun. They laughed a little as they were unaccustomed to the new equipment and occasionally, they glanced around to see if anyone noticed their greenness. Lisa knew she had to get the cadets inside the building or they'd be killed the first day after graduation from the academy.

She flung the bandolier over her right shoulder and with her thumb, pushed the '16's barrel behind her hair so the cadets wouldn't see either and quickly walked to their location. While enroute, Lisa saw the agents motioning to their partners to join them and one agent was talking on a walkie-talkie.

"Ah, good morning cadets. Would you mind accompanying me into the Slugger Building here for just a minute. I want to show you something that'll take only a minute," she said while closing the gap between her and the cadets.

"Our police captain said we should wait outside to keep an eye on things while he met with several city council members on the eleventh floor," one cadet responded.

"It's ok. This'll just take a minute and then you can go back outside. There's something wrong inside the police captain should be made aware of. It'll be your duty to report it," Lisa calmly said as she herded the cadets inside and pointed to an area away from the huge plate glass windows. Just as they cleared the windows, Mike came running in.

"Here they come!!" he shouted while running.

"You dear, go with that handsome gentleman when he gets here and he'll tell you what 'cha need to do. And you dear, get you gun out because in about three seconds you'll be fighting the bad guys and you'll be fighting for your life," Lisa calmly instructed.

"Is this for real?" the cadet incredulously asked and just then, gunfire shattered two picture windows as the agents attempted to hit Mike on the run. Lisa and her cadet jumped behind a thoroughly decorated concrete upright support pillar as three agents jumped through the shattered windows, charged the fugitives' position and were quickly gunned down by the outlaws and one cadet.

"Good shooting, dear!" Lisa complimented.

"I was just on the rifle range yesterday. I haven't had time to forget anything yet," she responded, and then, the remaining plate glass windows were shattered by gunfire, indicating an onslaught was beginning. Small arms and shotgun rounds erupted from the agents, covering their movements as they dashed behind support pillars and opened fire on the separated fugitives and their acquired help. Mike and his cadet were located behind a circular concrete pillar across the moderately wide lobby from Lisa and her cadet. Their positioning hindered the agents' progress as the latter couldn't advance forward because of the devastating crossfire. Bullets were impacting on the concrete pillar protecting Mike and his cadet, blowing showers of fragmented concrete in all directions while still more projectiles were splintering the decorative carved wood concealing the concrete pillar Lisa and her cadet were behind. In an attempt to stem the flow of rounds slamming into Mike's pillar/position, Lisa put the 9mm at the small of her back, swung the '16 around and raked the agents' position with auto fire. She didn't aim, just held the '16 beyond the pillar and squeezed the trigger. The agents immediately ducked for cover while five others moved into a position to cross the lobby. Knowing she only had so many rounds, Lisa fired conservatively. As soon as she stopped firing, she moved into view from behind the pillar, just as the five agents dashed across the lobby. She was waiting for such a trick. It was then, she heard choppers coming in and assumed the agents' backup was enroute. Squeezing the trigger, she killed two instantly, wounded a third, but two made it across and disappeared behind the elevator bank. She knew of the flanking maneuver. Laying down the '16, she then slid four loaded clips of 9mm ammo to Mike. After Lisa first opened up with the '16, Mike knew what to do; provide cover fire after she stopped. The agents' attempt worked to favor the fugitives.

Lisa mentally counted the number of agents a chopper could carry, she estimated they'd be outnumbered, at least, four to one. She watched Mike scoop up the fresh clips. She didn't want this to happen to him, she told him it could happen, but, the actual reality of it occurring, she had shoved the thoughts from her mind. Rounds slammed into the pillar, rounds flew past, and it was then, Lisa heard automatic weapons firing as they approached. Surrealism gripped her. It was over. The CIA would win the final battle. They would win and lose at he same time. Hers was a desperate gamble, and at least, the serum was where it should have been. Picking up the '16 in her right hand, aiming it behind her to defend against the flanking agents, Lisa pulled the 9mm with her left hand. Rounds were impacting on the full pillar side opposite Mike, effectively pinning him and his cadet in place, and sometimes not allowing them opportunity to get a shot off. The auto fire was getting closer, the noise almost drowning out all other sounds. Lisa was so busy trying to kill agents to relieve pressure from Mike that she wasn't aware of his communicating with Dion, and then suddenly, the Army jumped into the lobby firing point-blank at the agents, and the agents turned on the Army. The roar of auto fire was deafening, Lisa saw the agents' last act; the dance of death. Over the din of auto fire, Mike caught Dion's attention and hand signaled where flanking agents would appear. Dion had just a moment's notice before the two agents slid on the polished floor and suddenly, were behind the fugitives in an excellent firing position. Instantly and simultaneously, Dion, Kelly and the squad opened fire on the agents across an unobstructed lobby. The excessive amount of auto-fired projectiles flung the two agents backward, bounding them off a concrete wall, but they were dead before hitting the wall. As the dead bodies landed on the floor, Dion and Kelly led the squad to secure the area.

"Why, there's the other two Musketeers," Lisa said, recognizing the troopers, tears blurring her vision, and inadvertently having her weapons trained on Dion.

"Howdy little lady! How's your day been going?" Dion asked in passing.

"Kinda crazy," she squeaked loudly, tears rolling down her face as troopers moved past.

"Secure," Dion shouted after establishing a line-of-sight with other troopers down the corridor, and both fugitives were watching Dion when they heard a booming command voice behind them.

"Green Beret Spec. Four Mike Tanner!" came the loud voice.

"Yes sir," Mike said respectfully said after turning.

"Lisa Youngblood!" came the same authoritarian voice.

"Yes sir," was her small respectful response.

"The President wants to talk to you both," he stated, and then, he raised a hand holding a mike and said, "the area has been secured and I have Mike Tanner and Lisa Youngblood standing before me unharmed. You are clear to move in sir."

And just then, it struck Lisa: it *was* over!

"Ding," came a sound indicating the arrival of an elevator car.

"Heads up!!" came the booming command order from the army major, "the occupants of the building are coming down – do not shoot them." As the car doors slid open, three soldiers took a provocative step toward the elevator with weapons at the intimidating ready.

"Gentlemen, I'm the Police Captain of Louisville," he offered.

"Yes sir, please do not touch your weapon at this time," a soldier requested and all three stepped aside allowing the captain room to depart the elevator. Upon exiting the car, the captain observed a medium size chopper and a heavy gunship land on Main St. in front of the Slugger Building and as the occupants disembarked from the medium size chopper, he instantly recognized the Army Joint Chief of Staff. Also unloading behind the Joint Chief were two commanders the captain had no knowledge of. The landing choppers had captured his attention and as the army brass began moving toward the building, the captain started to notice the lobby. To his right, the floor was littered with glass shards, empty shell casings, a potted tree was repeatedly hit and dirt scattered, dead bodies, blood and guns. The shock of the contrast from his earlier arrival momentarily held him motionless.

Upon his initial arrival, he met business men and women with whom he would meet on the eleventh floor for yet another planning session. Some he knew and several were unknown newcomers. All had entered an organized lobby that had recently been painted and the sun reflected off the polished floor through newly cleaned large plate glass windows. Everything was so normal on a sunny day that he felt secure in leaving his cadets outside the lobby to enjoy the average, warm business day. His cadets!

Looking instantly to his left, he immediately recognized Lisa Youngblood who was helping his Cadet Fergusson to her feet, and across the lobby, was Cadet Paulsen sharing humor with Mike Tanner!! As Lisa walked away from Cadet Fergusson to where Mike was standing, the captain noticed that bodies littered the length of the lobby floor. Bodies were immediately outside the building and they were on the sidewalk with the army standing guard.

"It's really over, isn't it?" she asked as Mike put his arms around her and she started to cry.

"Yes honey, it's really over," he said as he hugged and held her.

"I thought for sure they were going to kill you. I didn't want it to end that way," she cried.

"Everything's alright now, darling. Dion brought the squad with him this time," he answered, kissing her hair.

"Good to see you two again," Dion said after going back to Mike's position.

"Thanks, Dion," Lisa barely got out, and she laid her head on Mike's chest.

"I always love leading the cavalry to the rescue," Dion announced proudly.

"Saved our bacon," Mike observed.

Shocked at the scene before him, the police captain started toward his cadets and then stopped when he heard glass crunching under foot. Looking behind, he saw the Army Joint Chief walking in to the lobby with two grim-faced commanders following on either side behind him.

"Have you two been watching TV lately?" the Chief aggressively asked Mike and Lisa.

"We've been kinda busy lately," Lisa obstinately answered from between Mike's arms.

"Just to inform you two, the White House closely resembles an armed camp! Two CIA agents killed each other in the White House and the President ordered the marines to guard the House! The house and Senate members voted to take a vacation because of your actions which was driving the CIA to act crazy! The various representatives won't return until you two are captured! On one of the choppers you shot down was the CIA Director! And when you announced the serum was to be used to start a CIA Nation, the CIA Assistant Director committed suicide – in his office! After that, a gun battle broke out in CIA Headquarters that the President had to send the marines in to put down, and then, the Chief had the FBI arrest the CIA!! And the President wants to know, 'What the hell is going on??!!' You don't have to answer me because he's asking the question! We'd ask those directly involved but they all seem to be dead! The only ones who know what's actually happening are you two, and because of you two, Washington is an armed ghost town! Every federal building has been vacated and is under military armed guard! We're leaving right now to go to Washington and we'll sort everything out there," the Joint Chief said. While the Chief informed the fugitives of reactions associated to their actions, the Louisville police swarmed to the Slugger Building and sealed off the area.

"Chief, I'll need my waterproof bag from Mike's van. In it is the doctor's notes and the serum. Both should be handed over to the President," Lisa said and the Chief gave the Major the nod of approval.

"Chief," Mike addressed his superior as they began to leave, "the remainder of the stolen armory weapons are there in my van," he said, pointing to his vehicle. Mike them pulled his 9mm and handed it to the commanding officer and Lisa followed suit. The Joint Chief ordered the major to personally oversee the return of the weapons and van to the Jackson Armory. The army had blocked off Main St. for the brass to land their birds and as the ranking officers filed out of the Slugger Building, the police sealed the area. Walking hand-in-hand through the growing knot of police, the two most wanted fugitives followed the army commanders to board waiting choppers. They lifted off from Main St. and minutes later, landed at Standiford Field at the Army Guard Reserve Unit where a Leer Jet waited. The night black jet whisked the fugitives away from a successfully concluded battle to face an angry President.

"Don't tell anyone except the President about the holler," Mike whispered in Lisa's ear as they were enroute to Washington. Leaning her head to Mike's shoulder, Lisa let her thoughts wander.

There is no difference between the male and female, she was thinking as the jet gained altitude, *other than the inherent female function to bear children along with the support systems. But that function completes the male's role. Otherwise, there is no differ-*

ence. All that is female… is male. The sensitive natural emotions have been repressed in the male. Only of late has he accepted his sensitive side and no longer fears discussing his emotions. Fear restrained the male growth in sensitivity. Only by releasing his fear of peer ridicule can man achieve his full potential. Subtle fear suppresses the growth tendencies toward emotional tuning in to each other. So afraid to let go of the 'unemotional he-man' image, a lot of men unconsciously reject the possible potential of completing themselves with women merely to maintain the facade of manliness. True manliness contains the potential to become all that is female, and she smiled at the thought that some men would be offended at her conclusion.

The President had been informed of the incident in Louisville, that the fugitives had been captured, that fifteen agents were dead, four soldiers were wounded and all concerned parties were an hour away from the Capitol. The chief, in turn, ordered his press secretary to advise the gathered media of the event in Louisville. Not taking any chances, the Presidential chopper was waiting for the entourage from Kentucky to convey them directly to the White House. As soon as everyone disembarked at the White House, Mike and Lisa were escorted to the President who was patiently waiting for them.

"Mr. President, Mike Tanner and Lisa Youngblood," the Joint Chief announced.

"You two have turned the United States upside-down, and effectively destroyed the CIA – among other things. I'm going to talk to you together and then, separately and privately."

"Mr. President, I respectfully request to speak with you last because you're not going to like what I have to say," Lisa boldly said, and the request caught the Chief slightly off-guard.

"Granted, and now, let's go to the Oval Office where we can talk," he said leading them to the office. Half an hour later, Lisa emerged alone from the office, and she left her bag inside. She aimlessly wandered through the halls examining the furniture, looked at the portraits and finally, sat down on a chair near a window overlooking the driveway. She observed the marines still manning defensive positions in the drive area. Some were smoking and talking, some checking their weapon, trucks were moving into position to hook-up to trailers and tearing up the lawn in the process and a few were catnapping. So much had happened in two weeks, and it all started from an accident.

"Back to the destiny thing again," she softly said to herself, and she smiled at the irony of the events that occurred because of a simple accident. While she pondered the past, staff members came for her. It was her turn to speak privately with the President.

She didn't see Mike while she was enroute to the office nor was he in the Oval Office when she walked in. Letting the thought slide, she took care of business first; she turned over the doctor's notes, serum, and ID card, and then, she requested new identification. Next, she told him everything. The good along with the bad came out. She held nothing back. She didn't care how it sounded or what he thought of her, she unloaded the whole story.

The President listened patiently for thirty-five minutes as Lisa related the course of events. Sometimes he frowned, sometimes he was angry, but for the most part, he passively listened. After she was finished, he led her from the office to where a small group was waiting.

"Mike Tanner disappears right now," he pointedly told the Army Joint Chief. "You round up his squad and send them out of the country. No names on flight chits, no check-ins, no chow hall sign-ins, no name tags, no dog tags, nothing! You see to it personally."

"Yes sir," the Joint Chief crisply said.

"Lisa needs new identification," Threadmiller was saying to the FBI Director, "and don't tell anyone her new name, especially me, because she's going to disappear also."

"Yes sir, no problem. I'll get right on it," the director said.

"Well, let's break some bad news to the media – that ought to make them happy. Bad news sells papers and we're got nothing but bad news," the President said.

CLIFFTY CREEK

"Dem reporta's wus awful upset whin t' Presedent tol' 'em Mika an' Leza wus victums uv sercumstance an' thet t' chillurn wudn't be ans'erin' no kwesshuns," Pappy was saying to the assembled group of the holler folk. The elders had the chairs brought outside so they could sit on the boardwalk where women, young boys and girls and children had gathered when they heard that Mike and Lisa aired the classified secret. They also heard the news reports of the shoot-out in Louisville between the fugitives, the CIA and the army. News reports stated that the outlaws met in the Oval Office with the Chief and after that, they disappeared. Television cameras filmed reporters continuously pummeling the President with a barrage of demands to interview Mike Tanner and Lisa Youngblood. Reporters demanded to know why the two most dangerous and most wanted criminals disappeared from the White House and obviously with Presidential approval. The news media was furious after learning that the fugitives were released because they were 'victims of circumstance.' The focus then shifting to the CIA's involvement and eventual revamping. Angered reporters slanted stories, slinging verbal mud to display their vehemence against the administration. Bizarre headlines followed by wild stories of Presidential involvement filled the front page of major newspapers whose reporters were angered at the press conferences by questions sidestepped or not answered at all.

"Ah sincurly hopes t' Presedent keeps aul them sol'ja bohs 'roun' 'em. Thur's sum' angra raporta's up in Was'in'tun," Crandall said.

"Oohh, ah sa'pose dem raporta's'll settle down afta w'ile. Dey cun be angra fo' onla so long," Lizzy was saying.

"Pappa, is Nita collektin' all t' stor'es 'bout Mika an' Leza?" Tater asked.

"Yessur, she is, an' be glad you' don' hav'ta tote thet stack 'roun'. It w'ays 'bout much as yo' do afta yo' et," Pappy answered.

"Jessa, yo 't'ink t' Presedent sint Mika an' Leza o't t' cun'try?" Berta asked.

"Don' kno', chilie. T' Presedent wunts 'em o'tta site an' not ans'ern' no kwessions. Dem tu cou'd be enywhar," Jess answered.

"In t'ree 'ars it'll be gittin' da'k. Ah wush t'chillurn wud sind a mess'uge o' kall us t' let us kno' ever'thin's ok," Timmy said and just then, everyone heard horses fast approaching from the creek.

"Heeyyaa," Mike shouted at the horse as both former fugitives thundered around a building and headed down Main St. One length behind Mike, Lisa laughed as both flew past the shocked gathering and the various parked cars.

"It's dem! Day's ba'k!" the children squealed, and Mike turned right to head for the cabin, but Lisa rode straight down the street heading for the new trophy.

"Afta 'um!" Tater shouted and people started flying toward the cars, but the elder folk smiled and watched the excitement.

"Ahs glad dey's ba'k," Crandall said as he saw Mike heading back toward the main road and not far behind Lisa. Cars were kicking up rooster tails from spinning wheels, kids were shouting, and everyone was in everyone else's way going down the road.

"Mite as wull git extra 'shine o't. Dis is gonna be wun joyful nite," Pappy said.

"Not fo' Mara Beth, it won'," Tater noted.

"She git ovah it," Berta said with a grin.

The End

PRESIDENTIAL EPILOG
The Youngblood Project

    I, President Threadmiller, have
prepared this report, which I have named
'The Youngblood Project', to warn future
Presidents to the dangers various agencies
pose while they're in existence. It's
inconceivable that we should dismantle the
CIA and eradicate its existence because of
one mistake, and yet, if the full extent
of The Youngblood Project were known, the
public would rise up and destroy more than
just the CIA. To prevent civil unrest,
this file will be locked in the Oval
Office forever. I am personally infuriated
at the reckless disregard of human life by
the late Dr. Hans Schuler, the late CIA
Director Will Summers and the late CIA
Assistant Director Johnathan Walker. The
exact number of Americans, who lost their
lives at the hands of the mad doctor, will
never by known. Why and how the doctor
came to be on the CIA payroll is still
under investigation. Knowing the CIA, we
more than likely won't appreciate what we
will find.
    The outlaw agency is currently under
arrest by the FBI, within the exception of
the overseas operations. The marines used
a tank to blast their way into CIA
Headquarters to stop the fighting. Twelve
agents lost their lives in the battle,

five marines were wounded, and totally,
over sixty known people have died since
the Youngblood Project began. A terrible
price for a mad scheme. The Nazi ideology,
the use of humans for experiments, must be
unquestionably destroyed. Such ideology
has no place in this or any other country.
I had thought that such practices died
with the end of the Second World War, but
this latest atrocity proves me wrong. In a
way, we were very fortunate that the CIA
just grabbed and used the individuals and
never bothered to check backgrounds. Had
they checked out Russel Travers, they
never would have selected him as a
subject. His dossier required extensive
reading, which portrays a very intelligent
man with vast and varied experiences and
abilities. The CIA simply picked the wrong
person to experiment on.

As of this writing, the FBI is
presently sifting through CIA files,
searching for evidence concerning the
project — and no doubt they are savoring
the moment. All findings will be forwarded
to the Justice Department for evaluation.

Special praise goes to Mike Tanner for
his participation throughout the ordeal. I
am especially proud of his achievements in
bringing the serum and Lisa through the
affair, alive and intact. Naturally, Green
Berets Dion Marshall and Kelly Harry will
be promoted and honored for their roles in
the episode.

Lisa Youngblood. The one who has
suffered the most is the one person who

page 3

has said the least. How many wrongs has this person suffered and yet, she's not lost her sanity?!? An amazing quality of person.

Finally I write this for all future Presidents, that they may read and… beware.

President Averrill Threadmiller

The Youngblood Project

Printed in the United States
By Bookmasters